WHEREABOUTS
UNKNOWN

What Reviewers Say About Meredith Doench's Work

Advance Praise for *Whereabouts Unknown*

"A terrifying story of grit and courage, *Whereabouts Unknown* is a novel about women saving themselves."—Chelsea Cain, *New York Times* best-selling author

"Theo Madsen is everything I love in a detective—fierce, vulnerable, smart, and determined to solve the cases of two Ohio girls who disappear in mysteriously similar circumstances. *Whereabouts Unknown* is the perfect cross between police procedural and outstanding, page-turning thriller. Trust me, you won't want to put it down."—Mindy Mejia, author of *Leave No Trace* and *Strike Me Down*

Deadeye

"This is a good solid murder mystery that I'm very glad I read. …If you love great mystery books, get all three novels in this series and read them in order."—*Rainbow Reflections*

"Doench has created a compelling series that balances character and plot. Her writing is top notch—you become completely immersed in the settings, the action and the character."—*C-Spot Reviews*

"I must tip my coffee cup to Meredith Doench because she started off this captivating story with a big bang and I was reluctant to put my kindle down to be a responsible adult and go to work on time. There's nothing that I love more than getting sucked into a thriller with a psychological twist!"—*Lesbian Review*

Crossed

"*Crossed* is an eyeblinkingly good first novel with unique and original takes on old subjects."—*The Art of the Lesbian Mystery Novel*

"A very well written serial murder investigation that is made different by the emotional state of Luce Hansen, and her personal story. The layered approach works really well and ensures the reader is often off-balance, just what you need in a murder mystery."—*Lesbian Review*

"I highly recommend *Crossed*, which turned out to be a great freshman thriller from Doench. While there was not a lot of romance, prepare yourself for an emotional ride filled with disturbing scenes that show a lack of human decency; a ride that also makes multiple explorations into the human psyche."—*Queercentric*

Forsaken Trust

"What's not to love? This is a proper police procedural with lesbian characters that is not propped up by a romance. I'm ecstatic that this kind of book is being created, it shows how much the lesbian fiction market has grown in the last few years. This book gives lesbians (and others) a really good story that you would probably see on *Law & Order*, *CSI* or *Rizzoli and Isles* without the hetro-normative characters or the need to 'ship' characters."—*Lesbian Review*

"If you love crime fiction or television shows you will love this book, but do not go in expecting a romance. Readers of James Patterson, Sue Grafton and the like will enjoy this book."—*The Lesbian Talk Show Podcast*

"Definitely Recommended: Doench's writing is top notch—there's an authenticity and realness in her depictions of the seedier side of the town and inhabitants and she inserts a grittiness to the the crimes that involve women who have been victims for far longer than just the moment that they were murdered."—*C-Spot Reviews*

Visit us at www.boldstrokesbooks.com

By the Author

The Luce Hansen Thriller Series

Crossed

Forsaken Trust

Deadeye

Whereabouts Unknown

WHEREABOUTS UNKNOWN

by

Meredith Doench

2022

ISBN 13: 978-1-63555-647-6

This Trade Paperback Original Is Published By
Bold Strokes Books, Inc.
P.O. Box 249
Valley Falls, NY 12185

First Edition: March 2022

CREDITS
EDITOR: RUTH STERNGLANTZ
PRODUCTION DESIGN: SUSAN RAMUNDO
COVER DESIGN BY INK SPIRAL DESIGN

Acknowledgments

This novel would not exist if it weren't for the support and kindness of other writers. The pandemic was hard on my writing, but writer's block found me long before Covid hit. It took a solid three years for me to write this novel. Most of that time was spent not writing. Instead, I obsessed about why I wasn't writing. The pandemic taught me the value and strength of the collected energy of writers, whether in person or in a zoom room. The following writers inspired me to write and, at times, carried me on their backs toward a word count:

Chelsea Cain, Jen Sammons, E.F. Schraeder, Katrina Kittle, Erin Flanagan, Masha Kisel, Shazia Rahman, Kristen Lepionka, Mindy Mejia, Geoff Herbach, Kristen Gibson, Sharon Michalove, Rebecca Brittenham, Margaret Dwyer, MB Austin, Elle E. Ire, Riley Scott, Stefani Deoul, Gale Massey, John Copenhaver, Laura McHugh, Cheryl Head, Ann Aptaker, Andrew Welsh-Huggins, Tonja Reynolds, Brad Shreve, Gabriel Valjan, David Swatling, Jamie Lyn Smith, and so many more. See a name here you don't recognize? Take a few minutes to find and read the work from these amazing humans.

Many thanks to my family, immediate and extended, for their support and encouragement. I'm particularly indebted to my mom (who listened to a lot of that obsessing about not writing) and my cousin, Sarah Maynard, who slogged through early drafts of this book.

A humongous thank you to the mental health professionals who have been the backbone for so many throughout the pandemic. This novel would not have made it into your hands without their guidance, particularly in these last three years.

My continued thanks to the University of Dayton's English department and the University of Dayton community at large for all their support.

A big thank you to Len Barot and the Bold Strokes Books team for publishing my work. A special shout out to Sandy and Ruth Sternglantz for all the tireless work to help writers like me.

Last but never least, a huge thank you to all the readers of my past books and short stories. Your words of encouragement, reviews, and social media posts have kept me going on my worst writing days.

Dedication

In loving memory of Lawrence V. Davis
Rest in peace, Cousin

PROLOGUE

Annabelle's panic built, crashed, and receded like waves of the ocean.

If only this was the beach.

She felt an enormous wave begin to wane, and it gave her the needed strength to slam her fist against the wall one more time. Annabelle's knees gave out, and her exhausted body crumpled into the corner. The hot steel seams burned Annabelle's bare legs. She'd been screaming for hours, slamming her fists and feet against the four metal walls.

Time was running out. She had to make more noise.

Annabelle didn't know how long she'd been locked inside the container. It felt like the earth had fallen out beneath her feet. She'd been sucked into a vacuum, an endless well that stole everything, including the sound of her own scream. Cartwheeling through space, she fell arm over leg, hand over foot into the abyss.

Annabelle slowly crawled toward him. She reached until her fingertips found what could have been his leg wrapped inside torn jeans. It helped to know he was close, that she wasn't alone, and she settled into a fetal position. Her hands and feet thrummed with injury, the bloody bruises building from the inside out. Metal scraped against metal. The chained clamp around her ankle had rubbed away her skin, the steel biting harder and deeper against her bones.

Minutes passed. Possibly hours.

Annabelle hummed a song that reminded her of her mother. She focused on the two small openings above, catty-corner. Rectangles no bigger than a children's shoebox. A piss-poor attempt at ventilation that allowed the flies an entrance to swarm on him.

That god-awful smell.

Once, her mother had accidentally left a pound of hamburger in the back seat of their car on a hot summer weekend. They couldn't drive that car for a week afterward and then only with all the windows rolled down. That smell paled in comparison.

"Don't think of it now," she whispered in the darkness, startling herself with the sound of her own voice.

Annabelle's raw and swollen tongue had glued itself against the hard-ridged roof of her mouth. Her cracked lips fell open, begging for fresh air. With open hands against her stomach, Annabelle tried to push her hunger down, to silence it. Her palms stuck to the fabric of her T-shirt when she pulled her hand away.

Annabelle sat up. So…sticky. She opened and closed her fists, feeling the pasty substance.

The waves inside her were stewing, another large one building, building, building.

Annabelle reached for him again, and this time her fingers grazed over his bare skin. She yanked her hand away from his arm. Swollen and gelatinous. His insides leaked through his skin, leaving Annabelle's hand and the area around him wet.

She had a sudden vision of herself from above. Dirty. Sweaty. Half-naked with blood-clotted hair. Face streaked with the last of the life beside her.

Falling.

Screaming.

Careening into that inky-black void—arm over leg over hand over foot.

CHAPTER ONE

Detective Theodora Madsen stepped harder on the gas pedal while the car radio crackled with updates. Edwin C. Moses Boulevard snaked along the Little Miami River where water churned beside them in choppy swirls. She'd been sent to follow up on one of the department's high-profile cold cases—Grace Summers, a missing teen.

Theo's partner, Detective Hannah Bishop, was out for the day, and the chief sent the team's newest member, Cody Michaels, to ride with Theo. Cody's knee occasionally bounced up and down against the passenger door while he picked his nails. He was wound tighter than the average soul; he always had been. Theo tapped her fingers against the steering wheel and pressed down harder on the gas. She'd just spent the last week walking Cody through their active cases and orienting him with the team. Mentoring this newbie to the murder squad made her anxious.

It wasn't really that Cody bothered her, but his father had been her colleague for years. Now Dayton's police's chief, Alcott Michaels was better known as The Bull around the station for his outrageous temper. Theo had found herself on the receiving end of that temper more times than she cared to admit, but she knew underneath it all was a person who gave his whole heart to the job. Because of their history, Theo was surprised to find she'd be training his son.

"Take it for what it is, Theo—a sign of respect," Bishop had told her when Theo lamented her worries. "The chief knows you're our best. He wouldn't put his child with someone who could get him killed."

"Rule number one," Theo now said to the new detective beside her. "Anxiety plagues us all, Cody. Try welcoming that beast. It keeps us awake and aware. Just don't let it show so much on the outside."

The car shivered with December wind, and Theo reached for the thermostat. She cranked the heat as Cody took a deep breath and slowly exhaled. She understood that so much of Cody's nerves had to do with how hard he was pushing himself to please his father, job performance anxiety times a hundred. She wondered whether Cody would have gone into law enforcement if his father hadn't been Bull Michaels or the chief of DPD. As a kid, he'd shown interest in law enforcement, but he'd also been interested in mechanics and basketball and the environment—whatever caught Cody's attention in the moment. Theo and so many of her colleagues believed a person was born with a calling to law enforcement, a lineage of blood passed down from generation to generation. Theo wasn't sure yet how much of that law enforcement heritage had made it into Cody Michaels's blood count.

Theo rolled her shoulders to ease the ache in her tired arms. That morning, on her daily row along the Little Miami River, she'd fought the rushing current. This ache was a good thing—at least, that's what Theo told herself. It meant she was getting stronger, and she was soon going to need as much strength as possible, both physical and emotional. Bree, her lover, was almost nine weeks pregnant.

A *baby*.

Theo had to say that word a few times to herself to understand, as if she'd never heard that word before.

Another word that confounded her: *parent*. Soon—too soon—Theo would be exactly that.

"Detective Madsen." Cody broke her thoughts. "You said alibi checks are usually a matter of formality. We could call the employer for reverification on Henry Nerra's whereabouts, correct?"

"Cody!" Theo gripped the steering wheel and shook it with exaggerated frustration. "For the millionth time—it's Theo."

"Sorry. *Theo*." He chuckled and clasped his hands between his knees. His thick dark curls fell over his eyes.

Theo took a deep breath and gave Cody the side-eye. After his lifetime of calling her Theo, he now insisted on formalities, and it drove her crazy. He'd even called her ma'am a few times and Miss Theodora. Only once. She almost took his head off. No one called her Theodora except her mother and grandmother, both long deceased.

"Rule number two. Face-to-face contact reveals more information than a call or email," Theo said. "And anything that even remotely relates to the Grace Summers case is not typical. The anonymous tip makes the face-to-face even more important."

Three months ago, Grace Summers disappeared from Carillon Park, a popular and historic green space along the Little Miami River. She left behind her phone, ID, and a partial bloody handprint on the sidewalk. The large park had a few security cameras in place, but the cameras were offline that week for a systems upgrade. The security company posted guards on-site all night as a stop-gap measure, but Grace had gone missing before dark. Even after an exhaustive interview with the park employee who found Grace's items and a separate interview with the child's mother, Theo still didn't have enough evidence to call the teen endangered.

On the surface, the disappearance appeared to be a runaway case, although Grace's mother reported she had no history of running away. And unlike most teen runners, Grace didn't leave a trail. No debit or credit charges on her card, which she'd left behind in her bedroom. No withdrawals on the small amount of cash left in her bank account. Other than her phone, ID, and bloody handprint, there was very little to suggest anything had happened to Grace. Sure, her silence on social media platforms and with friends was unnerving, particularly given the high rates of texts and posts before she went missing. Unnerving, though, wasn't proof of a crime. There wasn't much Theo could do without evidence, but she reported the teen missing to the national database and encouraged the media and her family to keep Grace's story active.

From the start, Grace's strange disappearance needled Theo awake in the early morning hours and left her puzzling over what was left behind. She had a feeling things wouldn't end well.

There were no new developments for weeks. The case lost steam. Chief Michaels wasn't happy with any lingering open cases on the docket. At the time of Grace's disappearance, Dayton struggled with an increase in its crime rate and a reduction of its police force. DPD didn't have the resources to devote to a case that went cold so fast. Theo managed to make the case for an active anonymous tip line through their department, though it had been a battle.

That very tip line had remained silent until an hour ago.

An anonymous caller claimed Henry Nerra, a Dayton resident, had been seen with Grace the day before her disappearance. An officer ran Nerra's record and found he'd been picked up during a sting to catch online predators with underage teens a few years ago. He showed up at a home in Toledo hoping to find a thirteen-year-old girl alone and curious about older men. Instead, he found police with an arrest warrant. Nerra was tried and sentenced for the felony and served his time. He'd kept himself clean ever since.

The call to the hotline surprised everyone. They hadn't had anything other than a few hang-ups on the line for almost four weeks. Most anonymous callers began with the phrase *I'm probably overthinking this, but...* This caller, a young female, sounded angry, and Theo considered it could be a prank. Tragedies brought out the worst in people. Was she an ex-lover hell-bent on revenge? A relative angry over a family inheritance? A daughter angry at her father?

While officers tracked down the caller, Theo was dispatched to question Nerra's employer for an alibi. And Cody, her new shadow, was going with her for the experience.

"Here we go," Theo said, rolling into the Castleton Motors lot.

The building sat against the river, a tired structure that had weathered the surrounding neighborhood's decline. The rutted lot was a minefield of potholes from the past few winters. Theo bounced her department sedan into a spot while coffee from the console spilled into Cody's lap.

"Sorry!" Cody grabbed his freshly laundered pants leg and pulled the cloth from his thigh. The hot coffee spread across the fabric.

Theo gripped the steering wheel reminding herself to be gentle. Cody's anxiousness left him with a terrible habit of apologizing for everything.

"Don't apologize." She shut the engine off and pulled the rearview mirror toward her. Theo ran her fingers through her carefully gelled dark hair and realized it was almost time for a cut. She'd need to get an appointment with Lyle soon. Everything about her hair— including her amazing stylist—was an attempt to look as though she didn't care. Truth be told, Theo gave quite a bit of thought to her style, butch and professional all rolled into one.

"Tissues in the glove box."

Cody unlatched the glove box, and its entire contents emptied on the floor. He reached between his legs and sifted for the crushed box of tissues. "I know, I know. Don't apologize."

"Ah, you're finally getting it."

Theo had been a rookie once, a long time ago. She'd recently celebrated her twenty-five-year anniversary with the Dayton PD. In the metropolitan heartland city, she mostly worked alone or with the members of the small homicide team. Over the years, she'd risen to a senior detective position alongside Hannah Bishop, one of her best friends and current partner. Climbing those ranks had been a long road. She wanted to help Cody Michaels find his own path, preferably outside the Dayton PD. Bull Michaels was a hard man to please, and that was when you weren't related to him. It must be impossible if you shared his last name and his workplace, full of cops you'd grown up with.

CHAPTER TWO

Inside the lobby of Castleton Motors, it looked like the Santa's elves had vomited Christmas spirit. Tinsel covered the welcome desk where an employee popped up wearing a Santa hat. A glitter script along the headband read *Brittany*.

"Happy holidays!" Brittany chirped. "How can we help?"

Theo unhooked the badge from her thick belt. "Detective Theodora Madsen. Mr. Castleton, please."

"Is he expecting you?"

"I just have a few questions."

Brittany pointed them toward a small waiting area where a blinking tabletop tree sang "The Twelve Days of Christmas" in an annoying nasally whine, then slipped away from the desk to alert her boss.

Dick Castleton looked exactly like he did in his television commercials. He had a long comb-over dyed an unnatural black, a ghoulish look next to his winter-pale skin. His worn button-up shirt stretched across his belly. He shook Theo's hand and then Cody's as she explained they needed some information on Henry Nerra for a case.

"There must be some kind of misunderstanding," Castleton said. "He only took some candy. We've handled it internally. Henry will be back from suspension next week."

Theo shot a glance at Cody. "Henry Nerra's been suspended?"

"Yes, for vandalism of the vending machines. Stealing candy and snacks," Castleton said. "I had to take that company violation seriously—those machines cost a fortune to fix."

"Is this the first time Nerra's been in trouble on the job?"

Castleton put his hands on his hips and considered her. "If you aren't here for the vandalism, why are you here?"

"A different circumstance entirely. We need to verify employment and Henry's whereabouts," Theo said, handing him a paper with the dates on it. "Your records could really help us out."

"I hope it's nothing serious. He's had trouble, you know, in his past," Castleton said. "I hired him as a favor to a good friend. He works in the garage, so he has no contact with kids. We've had no issues with him."

"Until now," Theo said. "Stealing candy."

Castleton nodded. "So many of my employees do that, though. I'm just trying to put a stop to it."

Castleton checked his phone for the third time, a nervous response, and then turned for his desk. "Some of the guys, you know, they talk. I've heard rumblings that Henry and that missing girl knew each other. But Henry doesn't have enough game to keep up with a teenager. He's guilty of stealing Baby Ruths and Kit Kats, not people."

"We just need official verification to clear the call, and we'll be on our way," Theo said, handing him the date in question on a notecard.

As Castleton stepped behind his desk and began a search, Theo took in the office. It was a large open space with a few chairs scattered throughout. Dark wood paneling lined the walls, and she felt like she'd stepped onto a movie set from the seventies.

"We have another location in downtown Cleveland," Castleton said. "Henry's a real asset because he's willing to work wherever we need him most. He's usually here at the Dayton site."

Theo said, "It must be difficult to work both locations. Does Nerra have a spouse? A family?"

"Henry? No, he keeps to himself. I haven't heard him say more than a handful of words about his life outside work." Castleton waved her over with a thick hand. "Here, take a look."

Theo leaned over the computer, standing behind Castleton's desk next to Cody, his notebook out, scribbling notes. She sandwiched Cody in behind the desk with Castleton.

Castleton pointed at the document on the screen. "Henry was logged in to the system that day."

Bam!

Someone kicked the office door open with such force that it lodged the doorknob into the drywall behind it. A hulking barrel-chested figure filled the doorway, an automatic rifle at his side. The man gulped air as if he couldn't get enough, his chest heaving.

Theo pivoted into a defensive stance while turning her back to a wall. She angled into a nearby corner where she could get a view of everyone in the room. Withdrawing her gun, she had the man in her sights before Cody reached his weapon.

"Drop the weapon," Theo called out, angling for a better shot. "Now!"

The man grunted but didn't comply.

Cody steadied his aim on the man and moved closer to her side, a wall of enforcement they hoped this gunman wouldn't try to penetrate.

"Henry!" Castleton yelped with genuine surprise. "What are you doing? Put that thing down!"

Nerra's eyes darted from Theo to Cody to Castleton and back again as if he couldn't determine where to settle his focus.

Theo took advantage of Nerra's confusion. She signaled to Cody to move back against the wall. Nerra was nearing a breaking point, and she needed control of the situation fast.

"Take some breaths, Henry." Theo dropped the urgency in her voice a few notches. "Whatever you want, we can work this out. Just drop the weapon."

Nerra continued to cycle the aim of the rifle from one to the other of them.

"What I want?" Nerra's laugh came out more like a bark. "What I *want*? I want to come back to work and be with my family."

"We want that, too," Castleton said. "Please. Henry!"

Nerra's face flushed red, and his glassy eyes raged. "You called the police? For this?" he screamed at Castleton. "Everybody steals from the vending machine." The rifle shook in his clenched hands. "Why are you getting rid of me?"

"Whoa, Henry," Theo said, watching the rifle's muzzle quiver. "We aren't here about the vending machines."

Nerra didn't appear to hear Theo or anyone else in that room. "No!" he hollered. "Ever since that girl. That *stupid* girl!"

Nerra's escalation left Theo cold. "Henry…"

"I don't even use the vending machines!" he spat at her.

"Last chance." Theo steadied her aim on the shoulder of Nerra's shooting arm. "Drop the weapon or I *will* shoot."

Theo's vision tunneled in on Nerra. A buzz rang in her ears.

Nerra screamed for everyone to listen to him, to *just fucking listen.*

Nerra pulled the trigger. A bullet nicked Theo's bicep as she fired. The shot knocked off her aim, and the bullet missed Nerra. He turned his rifle on Castleton who went down.

Gunfire filled the room. Theo returned shots, and she saw it all like a slow-motion film moving frame by frame. Cody was next in Nerra's sights. Theo aimed for Nerra's chest, pulled the trigger, then launched herself toward Cody, knocking him to the floor.

Silence filled the large office save for the ringing in the air and the smell of gunpowder. Theo rolled over, her body screaming with pain, and caught sight of Nerra. He was down with a gaping hole in his chest. Castleton lay beside Theo and Cody with half his head blown apart. Thick splatters of his blood covered her shirt.

"Cody!" Theo tried to stand, to make her way to Cody to be sure he was okay, when a white-hot pain exploded in her lower right side. She covered her hip with her hands. Blood seeped between her fingers. She crumpled into a fetal position using the floor to put pressure against the wound.

"Madsen?"

Cody had been calling out her name from what seemed like miles away. She was no longer inside her body, floating somewhere above, watching the scene unfold. Theo heard Cody yell into his radio for backup and paramedics and anyone else available. The ringing in her ears pitched into a full scream. The smell of gunfire bit her nostrils.

Someone shook her by the shoulders.

"Madsen?" Cody was beside her. He lifted her head and balanced it on his thigh to help open her airway. "Take some deep breaths. Help is on the way."

Theo tried to speak, but nothing came out. She wasn't even sure if her mouth was following the signal from her brain to move. Cody gently moved his leg from under her head so he could clear the scene. He'd already secured Nerra's weapon, and she tried to ask him if he'd been hit. Nothing came out except gasps.

Everything below her belt felt warm. Wet. She thought she might have peed herself until she saw her own blood drenching her right pants leg and pooling around her. Theo's eyelids grew heavy—way too heavy to hold them open. She'd lived through enough of these crime scenes to know this was serious.

Finally, sirens.

Bree, Theo thought with a grip of panic. *She can't see me like this.*

Screams erupted from the open doorway. Soon they were replaced by the clamor of work boots, the sounds of gear. A paramedic checked Nerra and Castleton for signs of life while another kneeled at her side. Someone helped Cody to his feet and escorted him out of the room.

Medics slipped tubes up her nose with a sudden blast of oxygen, and she felt the cold pressure of a needle in the bend of her arm. Theo realized she was no longer gripping her hip. She distantly heard paramedics mumbling instructions. It felt like the medics were in an entirely different realm.

Then, warm hands. They cradled the sides of her head while the others worked to secure her to a backboard.

"Theo? Can you hear me? We're transferring you now to the gurney."

Theo tried to nod.

"You'll be okay. Keep those deep breaths going."

Theo recognized the touch against her face. She knew that voice.

Medics lifted her onto the gurney, secured her, and readied her for transport to the ambulance. All the while, warm hands cradled Theo's head. "I've got you, Theo," she said. "I'm right by your side."

Theo willed her eyes to open. Finally, the edge of her left eye responded. Her eye felt like it cracked wide open. Her own heartbeat blasted inside her ears. Her vision focused as the gurney began to roll. Theo found Bree's tear-filled eyes, hazel flecked with starbursts of gold, staring right back at her.

CHAPTER THREE

J ust hold on."
It had been Annabelle's mother's refrain through most of her life. *Hold on, Annabelle. Just hold on.*

Annabelle tried to focus on the sound of her mother's lilting voice instead of what was happening beside her. Things weren't just crawling on him anymore. She felt those tiny legs scurrying up her bare arms. And the smell. It had become mind-numbing.

Just hold on.

Her mother hummed a few bars of a tune Annabelle knew well. When she was a kid, she'd begged her mother to sing the rainbow song. It was a rare evening to have her mother home to tuck her into bed, but when she was, the request never failed.

"Sing *our* song, Mommy," Annabelle whined.

Her mother. The thought of Rose Jackson used to bring on a strong mixture of anger and eye rolls from Annabelle. Now, though, encased in darkness, she wanted her mom. That same mom who worked sixty hours a week waiting tables at a high-end bistro in Cleveland and waged war with the gray filtering through her long ginger hair. That same mom who loaded the pantry with Cheerios, Frosted Flakes, peanut butter, and bread before leaving her alone for days.

"Sing to me, please," Annabelle whispered in the dark to her mom. "You remember the words, don't you?"

Annabelle hummed the melody, feeling her mother's fingertips brush through her filthy, dried-bloody hair.

Annabelle leaned in closer to the body beside her. "Mom," she mouthed into the darkness. "I want to come home."

"Oh, A-Bird." The pet name her mom always called her. Tears ran from Annabelle's eyes.

Her mother hummed the song until Annabelle joined in. She curled her body and ignored the fact that the chest beneath her head sounded with an occasional gurgle of decomposition.

She'd needed him to be okay.

She'd needed him to help her out of here.

Now that was all over.

But her mother's voice was here. It had come from the depths of the sweltering darkness. A surprise, really. Maybe, just maybe, her mother had heard her cries for help. True, her mother had made a ton of mistakes. There was no denying that. Alone in the darkness, though, Annabelle saw that her mom had sung her the rainbow song often enough that they called it their own. Maybe that had been enough.

Just hold on.

Annabelle knew this feeling, this painful waiting. She'd been here before, too many times.

Her mom had always enrolled her in after-school day care, and she remembered walking home one evening to an empty apartment. It had been over a week since she'd seen her mom. Gran was gone by then, safe and happy in heaven. Otherwise, she would've insisted Annabelle stay with her after school instead of taking care of herself. Annabelle dropped her bag at the front door and turned on the television. The noise of it made her feel as though she wasn't alone. Eventually the phone rang. It always did.

"A-Birdie?" her mother said. *You're as small and delicate as a bird, my Annabelle.* "I'm stuck here at work. You can make yourself a PB and J sandwich, right?"

Annabelle didn't have to open the cupboard to know her mother had stocked an extra jar of peanut butter a few days before. "I'm fine, Momma."

"Have a good sleep, Birdie. I'll be there when you wake up in the morning."

When Annabelle woke the next day, she warned herself not to expect her mother to be there. But it happened. Every single time.

"You'll be there this time," Annabelle whispered into the strange darkness. "Won't you?"

CHAPTER FOUR

Four days after the shooting, Theo woke in a hospital bed drenched in a cold sweat. Monitor wires tied her to beeping machines. She listened to the sounds of medical staff talking in the hallway outside her room. In her mind's eye, she could only see the partial bloody handprint. Fresh and blindingly red, swollen droplets ran from the bottom of Grace's palm. Since the shooting, that sinister image mocked her, clinging to the edges of her vision, begging for some kind of answer.

Theo moaned. She wanted to sleep for days, weeks, months. Anything that would take her outside her body the same way she had been after the shooting. Since the surgery, she'd been stuck inside her flesh. She'd broken her pelvis and femur. The bullet wreaked havoc in her hip and surgeons had replaced the joint with a shinier plastic version. But the nerves—they were a whole other animal.

Theo reached for Bree. The chair beside her bed was empty save for a butterflied book across the seat. Theo's breath caught in her throat—she couldn't remember the last time Bree had left her side in the last four days. Did Bree's absence mean she was stable and her body had begun the slow work of healing?

"Hello?" A knock at the hospital room door. "Detective Madsen?" The door inched open, and Cody Michaels slipped in. He did a double take when he saw Theo in the bed, her right leg in a soft cast from knee to midthigh. He quickly turned away as if the injuries were some kind of secret. An unmentionable.

"Hi," Cody said, barely above a whisper. He offered a fistful of grocery store cut lilies, the slight tremor of his hand making the thin pale petals shiver.

"Thanks." Theo's voice croaked with so little use in the past few days. She held the thick stems of the flowers, unsure what to do with them.

She had wondered if Cody would come to the hospital at some point, but she honestly hadn't expected it. She figured his nerves would get the best of him and that his father, Bull Michaels, would warn him to stay away until the shooting had officially been cleared.

The sight of Cody opened the floodgates of her memory. Images rushed back on Theo, sounds from the shooting. Theo heard Castleton scream beside her and felt the searing pain that tore through her hip. Gunpowder bit her nostrils as her heart leaped into her throat.

Theo looked away.

"Sorry." Cody took the handful of flowers out of Theo's hand. "I'll just put them in some water for you."

He stepped into the bathroom to fill a cup with fresh water, reemerging a few moments later with the vase.

Her eyes followed Cody as he moved across the room and arranged the flowers above the air vent. It wasn't often Theo found herself at a loss for words, but here she was. A furious shame storm had been looping in her mind for days since the very first bullet fired inside Dick Castleton's office: *I should have paid more attention. I should have prepared Cody better for the call. What was I thinking?*

It didn't matter how many times she went through this or how many different scenarios she imagined. Nothing would change the facts. Henry Nerra shot and killed Castleton. Theo shot and killed Nerra but not before he shot and injured her. Still, there were so many unanswered questions.

"I can go," Cody offered. "If you're tired."

"No, stay." Theo nodded at the chair beside her.

Cody picked up Bree's book and flipped it over. Two women walked down a path holding hands. He grinned and sat down.

Theo shrugged. "Bree loves books and movies where there's lots of drama and then the girl gets the other girl in the end."

"Ah. A rom-com fan," he said. "I know these types."

"Do you have someone, Cody?"

"Not anymore." He set the book on the floor, careful to keep Bree's spot and balanced his elbows on his knees. He wore freshly laundered jeans with a crisp white button-up. "Long story or not long enough. Depends how you look at it."

Theo chuckled. She'd been there.

"How are you feeling, Madsen?"

Theo wanted to tell him what it was like to wake up from surgery and feel stuck to her bed. She wanted to tell him about the dead weight of the lower right half of her body. The surgeon had wrapped both her legs in compression sleeves. The regulated squeezes that pulsed against Theo's legs were meant to help keep her blood from clotting. Theo wanted to tell Cody about the pure terror that tore through her when she realized she could hear those sleeves pumping up, pumping up, pumping up. But she couldn't *feel* anything but pressure on her right side.

"Cody, it's okay," she said. "*I'm* okay." When he didn't look convinced, she added "Detective rule number three—never assume something routine will only be routine."

He broke into a smile, showing off his years of orthodontic work, but tears brimmed along Cody's dark lashes. "I would have died in that office if it wasn't for you, Theo. You saved me."

"I did my job."

"You had my back," he said. "Thank you."

The heater kicked on in the hospital room, its buzz filling the space between them. Theo nodded, but the words caught in her throat.

Cody ran his hand through his curls, the way he did when he was in deep thought. "I keep thinking about other ways this could've gone down. I mean, what if I would have moved faster or confronted him sooner? There's a million other things I should have done so we could all walk out of that room."

"Same," Theo admitted, her own eyes threatening tears. "It comes with the territory, doesn't it? The constant revisions in our minds. I never saw this coming, Cody. I'm so sorry."

"Now it's my turn to say don't apologize. If I could take your place in that hospital bed, I would. In a heartbeat."

She believed him. It was why she'd jumped in front of Cody in the first place.

Cody was twenty-seven years old, tops. If something this intense had happened to her at the beginning of her years as a detective, she most likely would have quit the force altogether. Hard stuff, no matter how long you'd held the badge. She hoped there wouldn't be any charges of an officer-involved shooting that would follow Cody's career. The thought turned Theo's stomach. But Cody hadn't given up. Perhaps that blue blood ran thicker in him than she'd first thought.

"I cannot believe Nerra was there."

Theo had gone over this point a million times in her mind as well. "Nerra was suspended from work and barred from the Castleton Motors property. What was he doing there?"

Cody looked up at her. "Someone must have tipped him off."

"Only one outside person knew his name. The caller," Theo said.

"But she had no idea if we would actually show up at Castleton Motors for verification. Like you said, we could have called. We arrived in an unmarked vehicle wearing plain clothes. Nerra had to have been watching the building." Cody popped his knuckles. "He must have recognized *you*."

Theo had thought of that, too. She'd been on the local and network news a few times during the early part of the Summers investigation. Nerra most likely knew she was leading the investigation for Dayton PD.

"Have you seen the media coverage?" Cody asked. "They're reporting on Nerra's past crime and pairing that with the disappearance. People think he kidnapped her for sex and then killed her. It's all over social media. If he wasn't already dead, I'd be worried about his safety."

Theo shook her head. "It's a good story, but there's no evidence."

Cody stood up and paced at the foot of her bed, back and forth. "Reporters are spinning it with Nerra as the classic lone gunman in the workplace. They announced his suspension and said he felt slighted and picked on by his boss because of his sex offender status. He let his workplace rage loose on us, supposedly."

Theo shook her head. "If Nerra was so upset with his coworkers, why shoot up Castleton's office? Why not go directly to his coworkers on the floor? That theory doesn't hold water."

Theo felt life flowing back into her body. Shoptalk always ignited her, and it was a welcome feeling in comparison to the constant worry about the prognosis for her hip and leg. Cody clearly loved it, too. This was something they could both engage in rather than focus on what was really between them—her damaged body.

"Nerra had an alibi," Theo said. "Castleton's records completely cleared him. There was something he didn't want us to know."

The door opened. Bree arrived with a steaming cup of coffee in hand and a *Dayton Daily News* tucked under her arm. "There's a horrendous line for coffee," she complained and offered her hand to Cody.

"Bree, this is Cody Michaels, the officer who was with me at Castleton Motors."

"I remember," she said. "I'm glad to see you're doing okay."

"I can't thank you enough for your help that day."

"It was my pleasure."

Cody looked at the one empty seat in the small space. "I think I've taken your seat."

Bree insisted he stay. "I need a good walk, anyway," she said, leaning into Theo for a kiss. Her eyes searched Theo's for affirmation, with an unspoken *You okay?*

Theo gave her a slight nod and watched her turn to go. Bree's long hair was even curlier than usual. It was what she liked to call her horrid humid hair, so it must have been raining out. A mixture of gratitude and love swelled in Theo's chest as she watched Bree's curls bounce. Theo had always known Bree was a caretaker at heart, but their relationship had always had the opposite dynamic. Theo was the strong one, the older one, the person Bree relied on. Now, everything had instantly flipped.

"I've had some time on my hands lately." Cody interrupted her thought with a sad smile. "I've been reading the Grace Summers case file. I wanted to see it myself. I've heard so much about it from my father and the department."

Theo held back a groan. She could easily guess what Bull had told Cody about the case. She'd regularly butted heads with him over his theory that Grace had simply run away. Bull argued that she most likely had met someone online. It was true—Grace didn't get on well with her mother—but there was no evidence of any kind of online romance.

"Her friend," Bull repeated every time she raised the case. "She told her friend she wanted to go away and start a new life."

"Why would she need to do that?" Theo had asked him.

"If we can figure that out, we'll find her."

The chief had formally assigned the case to Theo as he slowly withdrew his full support. They all knew the stats. It had been too long—most likely Grace was dead or doing everything she could not to be found. Either way, the last thing the murder squad wanted was the unsolved disappearance of a teen girl who could be in danger.

"In all the chaos," Cody told Theo, "I don't think you heard the full message or the new info that came in, tracing the whereabouts of the anonymous caller."

Cody was currently on administrative leave until the Nerra case cleared, but he was around his father and had picked up the latest progress on the case.

She pushed herself up in the bed. "Tell me."

"By the time the shooting happened, they'd already traced the call to a public pay phone in the lobby of the YMCA. Probably the last public phone in this part of the state. The caller says Nerra had been meeting underage girls like Grace ever since he was released from prison. He called it his work."

"Interesting work."

"We've got all his computer equipment, and the team is on it. They've found messages with some kind of code. It looks like they were meeting in Woodland Cemetery."

"Woodland?" It was one of Dayton's oldest cemeteries and stretched over two hundred hilly acres that held Dayton's celebrities. Paul Laurence Dunbar. Erma Bombeck. The Wright Brothers. "They have a lot of security there. Cameras. Locked gates. If that's true, it shouldn't be hard to prove."

"The caller alleges Nerra disengaged some of the cameras in the cemetery. I stopped in and met with the groundskeeper. He's found three cameras tampered with so far."

The damaged cameras reminded Theo of the disengaged cameras in Carillon Park, the night Grace disappeared.

"Your case notes show that one of Grace's friends thought she might be pregnant," said Cody.

"It came up. There were questions about how well this person really knew Grace or if she was looking for her own attention. Either way, she claimed Grace refused a favorite breakfast smoothie right before the disappearance. Later, the friend wondered if it could've been morning sickness."

"This happened only once?"

"That's what the girl said. No one else reported any pregnancy concerns about Grace, including her mother. It might have been as simple as Grace didn't want the smoothie that morning."

"Could be," Cody said.

Silence settled between them. Theo's brain flipped through the case information like a Rolodex. "You're thinking the father could be Nerra."

Cody shrugged. "It's possible. There's another option." Cody leaned forward, settling his elbows on his knees. "I keep coming back to the mother's boyfriend. Sam Polanski was living in the home with Grace. Mary Summers reported her daughter didn't care for him."

"There were issues."

Theo had looked into Sam Polanski. He had a prior arrest for a bar fight and another for a DUI. He volunteered to do a lie detector test at the time of the disappearance and passed. He also had an alibi—Grace's mother, Mary Summers. "He's been cleared."

"I stopped by Mary's home earlier today," Cody said. "Sam's gone. He left her with no warning five days ago. Mary doesn't understand what happened. She thought their relationship was solid, and she's torn up about it."

Five days. One day before the shooting at Castleton Motors.

"Maybe the weight of Grace's absence was too much for the couple."

"Possibly, but there's something else. Sam Polanski and Henry Nerra served time together. Same prison block."

Finally, something that wasn't held together with someone's flimsy word against another's.

Theo closed her eyes. The media photo of Grace filled her mind. A rainbow of colored rubber bands over braces. Her thin long neck and pimpled chin. Dark-framed glasses that looked too big for her small face. "I see where you're going with this," she said, the thought turning her stomach.

"Parole clipped Nerra with sex offender restrictions. Polanski had free rein," Cody said. "One hand greases the other."

Theo took a breath before adding, "CSI hasn't found anything too damning or there'd be a warrant out for Polanski."

"There isn't much," Cody agreed. "Which is why you need to get back to work. We have a case to solve, Detective Madsen."

CHAPTER FIVE

One of DPD's old roller chairs groaned beneath Theo. She moved closer to Gertrude Miller trying to hear her. She'd forgotten how loud the department's bullpen could be with all the ringing phones, screaming alerts, and constant chatter.

"Okay, Mrs. Miller. You've got my attention."

It had been weeks since the shooting, and more than anything, Theo wanted to go back into the field. Her body, though, wouldn't allow it. She'd been working desk duty and would remain there until her injuries healed. Sitting behind a desk had always felt like punishment to Theo, and she'd spent most of her time worrying about what might happen if she didn't get her strength and stamina back to where she'd been before the shooting.

Gertrude Miller sat beside the steel desk with her pocketbook clenched against her lap. She refused to part with her walker, even for the few minutes she spoke to Theo. It leaned against the desk, clogging up one of the main paths into the squad room. Theo couldn't help but smile at the cloth bag attached to the walker that screamed—in the way only BeDazzling can scream—*I'm a diva!* The bag overflowed with tissues, hand sanitizer, and gossip magazines. Mrs. Miller was a regular at DPD, always demanding justice for her perceived personal slights.

"You've made a big deal about seeing a detective," Theo told her. "This isn't the usual protocol, you know."

Theo's words didn't register with the older woman. She'd been a pain in the department's side for years, and this wasn't Theo's first run-in with her. Chief Michaels asked Theo to calm Mrs. Miller down.

"Tell me again," Theo said. "What happened?"

"I am telling you! It's that missing girl. Running in the streets. Wild."

"Grace Summers."

"Yes, Grace! The girl who was all over the news. Her mother lives in my neighborhood. She's *not* missing."

Theo leaned back in the squeaky chair. "And what is it you think Grace did, exactly?"

"She lit up a pile of dog poop on my front stoop." Mrs. Miller scrunched up her nose. "Do you know what burning shit smells like?"

Through Mrs. Miller's rantings about the heathen teen in her neighborhood, Theo was able to extract enough of the story to draft the report. A young woman, who she believed to be the missing Grace Summers because she had light-colored hair just like the missing girl, had taken to walking a dog in Miller's yard.

"She lets that thing shit all over my lawn," Miller said. "Dog urine is killing my bushes and flowers. It's poisonous, you know."

When Miller screamed at the girl, she'd upped the ante. Bags of dog shit appeared on Miller's front stoop almost every morning.

"You think the bags are left in the middle of the night?" Theo asked. "How do you know it's Grace?"

"Because I know."

"Do you have any pictures of her doing this? A video?"

Gertrude Miller looked at Theo like she had four heads. And then she wanted to take all four of them off when Theo told her the police could do nothing without any sort of proof.

"You've been in here before about this," Theo said. "I'm sure other officers have checked into your case. Who have you worked with in the past?"

"I've been here many times for this problem, and your people do nothing." Gertrude Miller leaned into her conspiratorially. "Listen, I've narrowed it down to three possible houses. I've watched enough *CSI* to know you all can do a stakeout to catch her."

Theo leaned back in her chair and fought the urge to laugh and cry at the same time. *Welcome to my new world of work*, she thought. Months ago, Theo had been working one of the biggest cases of her career. Now, she was taking a report about dog shit on a front porch, grateful she could walk with a cane instead of her own BeDazzled walker.

And then there was the murder squad. At first it had been a relief to be back at the station and among her colleagues. That took a turn when everyone's cheers for a quick recovery grew as tired as Theo felt. Their compassion was real, but Theo didn't know what to do with it particularly since her body hadn't been responding as quickly to physical therapy as everyone hoped. Theo's colleagues now dropped their heads and mumbled a hello as they passed her desk. The only member of the team that didn't treat Theo as if she was on the edge of some kind of death was Hannah Bishop. Cody had been partnered with Bishop in Theo's absence, and he'd taken to leaving expensive K-Cups of different coffee flavors on Theo's desk as some sort of silent apology for her injuries.

Theo's new work life required her to review officer reports and to interview people like Gertrude Miller, who demanded the time of a detective. Theo had been told that some officers took to desk duty well. She was not that detective. Theo hated the paperwork and promised herself it would only be a matter of time until she returned to Homicide. It was the only thing that kept her coming to the station day after day.

Theo pushed the hair from her eyes. Her gaze settled on Gertrude Miller's walker, and Theo thought about her own, folded up and hidden from view inside her bedroom closet. She gave the older woman a smile. "Give me some time to look into this for you, okay?"

"You won't get rid of me that easily," Mrs. Miller said in a huff. "I know how you people work. If I don't hear from you in forty-eight hours, I'll be back."

CHAPTER SIX

Theo held a resistance band and looked out over her backyard. The sun had just come up, and Bree had taken on the day's physical therapy session with way too much enthusiasm. Theo had been doing tactical physical therapy through her workers' comp, but Bree developed a morning workout for Theo that supplemented those appointments. Every morning they yoga-ed together through a modified sun salutation and a stretching routine that left her muscles like Jell-O.

"Think about what it felt like to be in your body before the shooting," Bree said, her hands cradling the new swell of her baby belly. She'd tied her hair in a messy dark knot at the tip-top of her head, and Theo hoped the baby would be blessed with a head of hair like their mother's.

"I need a lot more coffee before we get into this woo-woo stuff," Theo said.

"Stop!" Bree chuckled. "It's not woo-woo or hocus-pocus. It's called Holistic Health Care, and it's proven to increase the likelihood of full recovery."

"You forgot mumbo jumbo."

Theo closed her eyes and tried to imagine what Bree asked. Her life had been cleaved into two sections, a clean sharp cut that segregated her body before the shooting from her body since the shooting. It had happened so fast, her life upended. Her eyes flew open.

Bree stared back at her. "Jokes aside, it works."

Bree believed that all bodies had memory, and one of the only ways back to health after an injury was to reclaim and activate those memories. Bree spread a few drops of oil from a glass bottle on the tablecloth and the scent of lavender mixed with something citrusy filled the space. Bree had been adamant that aromatherapy could help Theo, along with a hundred other methods that simply felt like shots in the dark. She couldn't really argue with Bree's method given her progress, but Theo bucked the notion that good happy thoughts and meditation could fully heal her hip.

Theo wrapped her hands around the warm mug of coffee and considered Bree still in the gray fleece pants she always wore to bed and an oversized *Give Blood!* T-shirt from her station's latest drive. She hadn't been asleep long—her shifts put her home around three a.m.

"Feeling okay today?" Theo asked.

So far, Bree had rocked her pregnancy. Theo worried about what the last trimester would bring, particularly because Bree insisted on maintaining regular shifts. Theo knew Dayton Rescue needed Bree—she was top-notch in her field.

Bree had worked for the Dayton Emergency Medical System for a good three years before she'd caught Theo's eye around the station. What initially impressed Theo most about Bree was her willingness to stay on as a paramedic when she had the qualifications—she was a licensed ER nurse—that would have allowed her to drop that gig for good. So many people burned out on the emergency squad schedule—the late-night runs, the high adrenaline, the drama of it all. But Bree was the opposite. She seemed to thrive on it.

Bree had been a topic of station gossip since she began working for the city of Dayton. The men on the force wanted to date her, but there was talk that she wasn't into guys.

"Duh," Theo had said when she heard the rumor.

The question was finally answered for everyone when Bree told a patrol officer she couldn't date him because he carried the wrong equipment. Or so he'd claimed.

Theo had marveled at her coworker's lack of gaydar, and the confirmation made Theo grin for days.

"I'm feeling okay." Bree yawned in the morning light. "I seriously miss my five cups of coffee a day."

Theo put her hand over her mug, feeling guilty about what was in it. "Go back to bed, babe. I got this."

"You can't get rid of me that easy," Bree said, pulling her knees into her chest for a stretch. She had the long lean frame of a dancer and practiced yoga at least three times a week. "Come on," Bree said. "Let's get your morning started right. It's just a few exercises, and I found a few new band exercises to try." Bree ignored Theo's groans. "Come on, Theo. Give it a chance."

Theo knew the shooting had scared Bree. She'd always seen Theo as her rock, and Bree needed Theo to be that again, particularly with the new baby on the way.

In the long days since the shooting, Bree had helped Theo navigate from a walker to a cane. Dr. Willis, her surgeon, couldn't believe the progress Theo had made or that she was walking so well, given the severity of her injury.

"It's remarkable, really," Dr. Willis had said, hitting her knee for a second time with a rubber hammer to verify the first reflexive kick. "You've made tremendous progress in such a short time."

Bree winked at her. She'd been working extra hard at all the exercises.

"When will the feeling in my leg return?" Theo had asked. "Sometimes it throws my balance off."

The nerve damage from the bullet and subsequent surgeries had left Theo with distorted feeling in her lower right leg and foot, which messed with her balance. The injury to her femoral nerve was still healing.

"Well, that's the answer we all want to know, right?" Dr. Willis said. "Keep doing the physical therapy. Keep up the positive attitude. You've done so well in your recovery so far, but I cannot say when the nerves will completely heal."

Theo ran her fingers through her hair and bit at her lip. That wasn't what she wanted to hear. "When can I get a medical release for duty?" she'd asked.

The doctor wheeled his stool away from Theo. He pressed a few keys on his laptop. Theo groaned. It was never a good thing when the orthopedic surgeon looked at the records and not her.

"Listen, you've proven me wrong every step of the way," Dr. Willis said. "But you're not ready for the field. You've got a ways to go before I can release you to active duty."

The surgeon continued to babble on, now speaking to Bree rather than Theo. Bree looked so professional in a button-down with her hipster glasses, particularly sitting next to Theo, who wore a worn T-shirt and basketball shorts.

"You're saying you'll continue to evaluate Theo as she heals, correct?" Bree asked.

Dr. Willis agreed and talked more about the physical therapy Theo needed. "Sit tight," he told them and left the room to talk to his physician's assistant.

Bree moved to Theo's side. "Scoot over," she said, pushing herself on the examination table beside Theo and taking her hand. Theo felt the warmth of Bree's hand in hers and noticed how all her limbs were cold in the sterile room, her skin bluish under the bright lights.

"Look at me," Bree insisted until Theo looked her in the eye. "He doesn't see you. I do. It's going to take time, but I *know* you will beat this."

Tears of frustration ran down Theo's cheek. "What if I can't this time?"

Bree laughed. "I've never heard you use the word *can't* in reference to yourself. Ever."

"This feels so big, Bree. I just feel so...tired."

"It is really big. But not so big you won't scale it. Just trust me, okay? Trust me and not that guy who doesn't know your heart the way I do."

"What if..."

"No what-ifs. We'll be okay as long as we stick together."

Theo nodded as Bree rubbed her thumb across her cheek to wipe away the tears.

"Together we're unbreakable," Bree said.

Theo had agreed, but when she'd maneuvered her walker out to the medical office entrance, she felt broken. Even with Bree by her side.

CHAPTER SEVEN

The afternoon sun beat down and heated the steel around Annabelle like a firepit. His body had gone from stiff to mushy beside her, but she refused to move away from him. The swell of her belly rested against his bony hip, and she wondered when she'd begin to feel contractions.

Daniel had come to save her—Annabelle realized that now. He'd come to pay some kind of atonement for what he'd done wrong. And there was so much to atone for.

Daniel's death was her fault. Annabelle had begged him to come. She'd understood the dangers but decided to gamble anyway. It was almost as if she'd slit Daniel's throat herself.

Annabelle closed her eyes against the darkness. Her corneas burned and teared. Her entire body hurt, and she felt the rash across her face pulsing with each heartbeat. How long had it been since she'd last taken her medicine? A week? A month?

Annabelle pictured Gran, imagining her soft touch and soothing voice. There was that distinct whisper in the darkness: *You are so strong, child.* Gran often said this to Annabelle, her granddaughter who carried the weight of the world on her shoulders and lived in a constant state of overwhelm. Now, Annabelle felt the gentle weight of Gran's hand on her shoulder, a touch that calmed her racing heart. Annabelle took a deep breath and let herself fall in and out of random memories.

When Annabelle wasn't fending for herself as a young kid, her mother left her with Gran. One evening, Annabelle sat on a stool in the corner of the kitchen and cried as Gran cooked dinner. Ruby, Annabelle's older cousin by five years, had brought her an offering, a chunk of carrot that hadn't made the roasting pan.

"Stop crying," Ruby told Annabelle. "You'll go home soon."

Annabelle turned the carrot over and over in her small hands. She knew Ruby was right, but her tears continued. Her face burned with anger, and she hated that she missed her mom so much. She had been through this long enough to know she was generally the last person on her mother's list. Annabelle was also old enough to know her mother wasn't really going to work that night but was out with the man who'd been hanging around their house for the last few weeks.

"Why did Mom even have me?" Annabelle asked. "She doesn't want me."

Gran set down her spatula and came to Annabelle's side. She was still relatively healthy then, her touch strong and confident. "Annabelle, you listen to me." She wrapped an arm around Annabelle. "I've always said that you're special, yes?"

Annabelle nodded, staring at the carrot in her hands.

"Do you believe me?"

When Annabelle didn't speak, Gran lifted her chin. Annabelle looked into her grandmother's wide green eyes.

"You have the mark. A butterfly on your face."

Annabelle's hands shot up to her cheeks, touching the rash that had been blooming there for the last two days. The skin along her cheeks and across her nose burned red. Sometimes the small bumps itched, and other times they were too tender for her to touch.

"Butterfly?" she asked.

Gran reached for her purse on the kitchen table and returned with a pocket mirror. She held it up for Annabelle. "Don't you see it, sweetheart? The wings of the butterfly spread across your cheeks." She traced the outline of Annabelle's rash without touching the skin, over her cheek, across her nose, and around her other cheek. When Gran pointed it out this way, Annabelle saw the shape of the wings, though it wasn't nearly as beautiful as the butterflies she liked to look at in her Life Science class.

"Mom says it's a nasty rash," Annabelle said. "She told me it's always there, but it only gets red when I'm sick."

"You've been feeling sick for the last few days, haven't you?"

Annabelle nodded and told Gran all about the way her tummy hurt and how she didn't want to eat because everything tasted funny and how her throat hurt and felt fat when she touched it.

Gran smoothed Annabelle's long hair and kissed her gently on the forehead. "It's time to see a doctor," she said. "You'll probably have to start taking medicine every day. No skips," she warned. "It will help everything feel better."

"Will it make the butterfly go away?" Annabelle asked.

"I'm afraid not." Gran's eyes filled with tears, but she didn't let them fall. "It fades sometimes, but lupus will be with you your entire life. You know who else has lupus?"

Annabelle smiled. She knew this answer. She pointed at her grandmother.

"It's something we share. I found out I had it when I was about your age. I've learned to embrace all the sensitivities that come with it," she said. "And someday you will, too."

"It makes us both special, Gran."

She nodded. "Never forget this, Annabelle—sometimes it will make things really hard for you in life—sometimes you won't be able to go the places you want to or eat the foods you like or be healthy enough to be around the people you love. Other times, you'll thrive. You've been given the gift of sensitivity. You'll feel things more than others, while noticing the colors and shifts in energy. No one can ever take that from you, Annabelle."

Tears seeped from the corners of her eyes as Annabelle heard her grandmother say it once again inside the darkness. *It's your superpower, child. Make use of it.*

Annabelle heard movement along the side of the container until it reached a chink in the seam no bigger than the size of a dollar bill. It was one of the only places that allowed air to circulate, and Annabelle heard a soft whimper. She pushed herself up and crawled to the corner. A dog's nose pushed in through the opening to greet Annabelle, sniffing as if the animal's life depended on it.

"Tillie!"

Annabelle held the dog's warm snout in her hands and told the dog through her tears how good it was to feel her again. "I thought they killed you, Tillie."

Tillie licked the dried blood from Annabelle's fingers. For the first time in days, Annabelle felt something other than despair.

CHAPTER EIGHT

Theo rarely entered DPD's evidence locker. The cavernous space always felt creepy to Theo, a quiet grave of sorts for humans who had been wronged. The evidence clerk was always there, though, a steadfast rule she could always count on. Theo's cane clicked along the tiled floor behind the clerk.

Computer records showed Gertrude Miller's numerous complaints of harassment, as well as property destruction to her home and automobile, dating back over eight years. Most of the reports were for minimal damage to her property or prank phone calls. The message was clear. Someone wanted Miller out of that neighborhood. She held on, refusing to move. Theo wondered what the woman's attachment was to the home or neighborhood. Most would have moved out long ago.

The evidence clerk pulled a small box from the shelf and carried it to a side table for Theo. As Theo lifted the lid, the evidence clerk went to meet another officer at the door. Theo unpacked the few items, including a rock the size of a baseball that had been thrown through her garage window. Miller had reported damage to her front door, porch, and yard on different occasions from objects like this rock. Photographs showed that her garage door had been vandalized with eggs at one point. What could this woman have done to upset her neighbors so much? She was cranky and difficult at best, but it was rare for a disgruntled neighbor to continue such antics for more than a few months.

Theo looked up and what caught her gaze stopped her cold. An evidence box with Grace Summers's name scribbled across the cardboard stared back at her. No matter how hard Theo tried, she couldn't get away from the Summers case. It met her around every corner, a constant reminder of everything that went wrong at Castleton Motors. At least the Nerra review was finally done, the investigative team concluding that Theo and everyone else on the scene had followed procedure that day at Castleton Motors. Cody was back on the job full-time in Homicide, riding with Bishop. He'd taken over her place.

Theo pulled Grace's box down from the shelf. Inside, there were only two items. Grace's phone had been bagged up and marked as evidence along with her high school ID. Theo held the packaged phone in her hand and ran her fingertips over the bloody markings on its casing.

That evening, Theo had been the homicide detective on duty. Dispatch called to say an employee reported blood in Dayton's Historical Carillon Park.

"He says he knows you," Dispatch said. "Clayton Brown."

"I'll check it out," Theo said, and Dispatch sent her a recording of the call.

Carillon Park was famous for its looming bell tower. Large open fields surrounded the bell, and a reproduction of a local historic village had been built on the property along with a restaurant and tavern. By the time Theo pulled into the parking lot, everything was closed. Clayton met her in the brightly lit lot, a flashlight in hand.

"If anyone can figure this out, it's you," he said when she climbed out of her car.

"Sounds like something really shook you up tonight."

Clayton rubbed his short gray hair and whistled. "I'm not sure what to make of it."

Theo walked beside Clayton down the winding stone sidewalk toward the bell tower. He explained that a group walking had found a phone near the base of the tower with a girl's student ID lodged inside the phone case. They picked it up, realized it was wet with blood, and immediately dropped the phone. They alerted Clayton who checked the scene out for himself.

"That's when I found this." Clayton shone the beam of his flashlight at a marking on the sidewalk. "At first I thought it was sidewalk chalk, but it's blood."

Theo knelt down. With a gloved hand, she touched its edge. The blood had already dried.

"How long ago did you find this?"

Clayton glanced at his phone. "About two hours? I called your station, but they told me there was not much they could do and to hold the phone in case someone returned for it. But there was blood, you know? That's when I started calling in for you." Clayton rocked back and forth on his feet as if to calm himself.

"You see it, right?" Clayton pointed to the edges of the bloody spot.

Theo moved to her right, and at that angle she did see something—a partial handprint. It looked as though someone had tried to use their thumb, forefinger, and middle finger to push themselves off the ground, leaving behind a bloody mark.

"Did you find blood anywhere else?"

"No, I walked all over this area, looking. There's nothing."

Clayton had left the phone on the ground. Theo picked it up with a bag and gloved hands. Inside the clear plastic phone casing was the ID for Grace Kelly Summers, a blonde with thick black-framed glasses who lived in Dayton.

"She just turned sixteen four months ago," Theo said. She used the department camera to snap off a few pictures of the bloodstain, two fingers splayed wide.

"Is there really nothing you can do?" Clayton asked her. "It's spooky, you know?"

"Yeah, it is." Theo took a few more images for good measure. "But we need evidence that someone is hurt or in danger before we put alerts out. It's possible this girl fell and cut her hand. She dropped her phone in the fall, got up, and went home. She may be back for the phone tomorrow."

Theo looked out over the field around the bell tower. Nothing but spotlighted darkness stared back at her.

"Do you recognize this young woman…Grace?"

He nodded. "I've seen her here a lot in the summer. Respectful, unlike some of the other kids that hang out at the park. She's usually on her own."

"And no one has come back to this area since you found it? Looking for the phone?"

Clayton shook his head.

The bell tower had an elevated base, and Theo climbed up on the ledge. Looking down on the scene gave her a different view, a fresh angle. It was all so out of place—blood in this location where families congregated, and people recreated. Her stomach clenched and her fingers tingled with what she and Bishop jokingly called their spidey sense, that overwhelming feeling of certainty that something was wrong.

She still felt that same certainty.

Theo dropped into a nearby chair and tears welled in her eyes. She wanted nothing more than to be in the field, working Grace's case. She never imagined that an injury might end her career at the age of fifty-three with a baby on the way. Honestly, it felt like she had her best years of work ahead of her.

The gunshot. It changed everything.

CHAPTER NINE

Annabelle leaned her back against the side of the container and sat near the tiny opening. Tillie's soft pink nose rested in her hand through the open slot as Annabelle's breath rattled in her chest. Soon she launched into another bout of coughing, the thick metallic taste of phlegm inside her mouth.

Annabelle's mind flipped through time and memories like a deck of cards. She landed on a memory of when she was nine years old and had her first go-around with pericarditis, a rare condition for children, and the full effects of the illness came on fast. When her mother left for a shift, it seemed like Annabelle had a bad cold. Two days later, the school sent Annabelle home with concerns she might have something much more severe. Annabelle's head had throbbed with the severe coughing, and her chest rumbled like a cat purring with every breath. She would learn that fluid had filled the area around her heart and lungs, making it difficult to take a full breath.

"Shh, baby." Gran had tried to soothe her. The butterfly rash felt like fire across her cheeks, and Annabelle shivered despite her sweating body. She'd later passed out walking from the bathroom to her bed.

Annabelle hardly remembered that first visit to the emergency room and the surgery that followed. There were memory snippets of the tubes placed inside her to drain the fluid, the weird sound of suctioning, and the bright lights of the operating room. She remembered the kind nurses and doctors gave her cherry suckers and

7Up for her belly when the steroids made it hard for her to eat. That's when she met Dr. Amy, a childhood rheumatologist, who became a constant in her life. Annabelle was formally diagnosed with childhood lupus, and the quest to find the correct medications began.

"You'll always need your medicine, Annabelle," the doctor told her. "It's just as important as brushing your teeth before bed." Dr. Amy explained that lupus was an autoimmune disease and affected everyone differently. The meds would be trial and error, and they would have to work together to treat Annabelle's body when the lupus flared.

When Annabelle finally returned to school, her classmates knew she'd been ill. She was the girl with heart trouble, and they teased her by gripping their chests and pretending to faint. Annabelle knew the truth, though. It wasn't really her heart. Her body was at war with itself. She had special proteins in her veins that battled Annabelle's healthy organs and tissues so intensely, it left her insides scarred and damaged.

Every year, when the weather changed from the cold of winter to the warmth of spring, Annabelle fought pericarditis. It lurked inside those seasonal changes, and she occasionally ended up in the hospital for the same draining procedure that left her weak and breathless but gave her body enough space for her heart to beat freely.

When Annabelle was fourteen, Gran died from kidney failure brought on by her own battle with lupus. Annabelle sat by her side as much as she could, holding Gran's frail hand.

"Remember what I told you, child."

Annabelle nodded. "Lupus makes me special."

Gran started to laugh, and it ended with a deep, guttural cough. "No, it's not the lupus, baby, it's the *sensitivity*."

"That makes it sound like I'm really a weak person."

"Not at all. Sensitivity doesn't make you frail—it makes you strong and ready for anything. You're attuned to all your surroundings and everyone around you. This gives you great wisdom. Learn to trust it."

The year Gran died was the same year Dr. Amy started Annabelle on a fixed regimen of antimalarial drugs and a cancer drug. At first, she felt no different than with any other cocktail of meds she'd tried. Then her hair began to fall out whenever she washed or brushed her hair, and her face swelled. Dr. Amy told her to hold on, to trust her, and she'd begin to feel better. Sure enough, after a few months her joints didn't hurt when she walked or ran, and her stomach didn't blow up when she ate gluten. Her hair loss slowed down.

"You're not in remission," Dr. Amy told Annabelle. "But we are getting closer to having a handle on it. Lupus is a sleeping beast. We cannot let our guard down. Always check in with your body. You know it better than anyone else on this planet."

In the shipping container, drenched in sweat, Annabelle heard her chest rumble when she tried to take a deep breath. She held the dog's warm wet snout in her hand.

"I don't think it's sleeping anymore," Annabelle told the dog.

She could feel the pressure of the fluid around her heart squeezing her chest. Her due date loomed. It could be any day now, and she worried incessantly about the baby. How would the lack of medication affect the baby? Would she even have the strength to give birth? She worried about whether her body would have the fluids and nutrients to breastfeed the baby. If not, well…that thought terrified her.

"Tillie, girl"—Annabelle leaned down and kissed Tillie's snout—"there has to be a way out of this place. Help me find it."

CHAPTER TEN

"Close your eyes, Theo," Bree said. "Think about what it felt like to be in your legs, running, rowing, walking. *Feel* your knees bend, the *roll* of your weight along the soles of your feet."

Theo sighed. Why did these morning sessions always feel like such a horrible rerun? "I can't do this anymore."

Bree raised an eyebrow over her water bottle. "What's going on?"

"I'm done trying to remember what my toes felt like before the shooting. I don't care how my knees felt against the fabric of my pants when I walked. I'm just done."

The porch windows were open, and the slight morning breeze brought with it the sounds of birds chirping. A dog barked somewhere in the distance.

Bree made her way over and sat down in Theo's lap. She wrapped her arm around Theo's shoulders, her touch warm and confident.

"Come on, you've been through a lot," Bree said, nestling her head against Theo's shoulder. "Everyone keeps telling you the neurological system is a finicky beast. Look how far you've come."

Theo sighed. "I still have dreams where I'm in the middle of a six-mile run or on the shooting range with my percentiles kicking everyone's ass. Did I ever tell you that I was in the ninety-eighth—"

"Ninety-eighth percentile for shooting. Yes, you have," Bree smiled. "About a hundred times."

"I miss my athletic self."

There were so many things Theo missed, including Bree's body beneath her, the feel of their legs entwined, and Bree's hot, wanting breath on Theo's shoulder.

"You'll get back to her." Bree leaned in, hugging Theo tight. "It's just going to take some time."

Bree didn't pull away. Theo smelled the edges of sleep still on her, a sweet scent of clean sheets, light sweat, and warmth. Theo brushed her lips slowly along the line of Bree's neck, pausing for a moment against the hardness of her jawline before continuing up to her ear. Theo's lips traced the outer coil of Bree's ear, circling before she nibbled on the swell of the earlobe. Bree turned to meet her mouth. They locked in a kiss.

"Detective!" Bree pulled away. "You cannot get out of your exercises that easily." She unraveled herself from Theo and stood up. She handed Theo a resistance band. "Get to it."

Theo leaned back against her chair with a groan before she half-heartedly complied.

"Don't let the band go slack," Bree instructed.

Theo groaned but tightened her grip. "Tell me about your shift."

"Here you go," Bree said in mock exasperation. "Another distraction technique. Working vicariously through me."

Since Theo had been on desk duty, she'd wanted to hear all of Bree's paramedic stories. She wanted details about the medical runs and how Bree nursed her patients through some of the worst moments of their lives. But Bree was only half right. She had an ulterior motive. She wanted to hear these accounts just in case something popped, possibly related to Grace Summers's case.

"Keep moving and I'll indulge you," Bree said. "Same old, same old. Heart attacks and heartburn. You know how it goes." She looked over at Theo carefully. "I saw Cody last night. He was on-site when we arrived to handle an injury in a restaurant. He asked about you."

Theo looked down at her hands and picked at an already torn fingernail.

"I know you miss your squad, Theo. And I know that you can't stop thinking about that missing girl," Bree said. "But you are so much more than a detective badge and a part-time athlete."

Bree's words caught Theo off guard, and the answer came before she had time to think it through. "Am I?"

"So much more. I wish you could see that." Bree reached out and ran her fingers through Theo's dark hair. "It's getting thicker."

Bree was right. The shooting and surgeries had thrown off Theo's immune system, and it had manifested in the form of hair loss. She'd always kept her hair short, but over the last few months she let it grow to hide the thinning patches. It fell below her ears now, uneven and long enough to be constantly in her eyes.

"I always wanted a coif," Theo told her.

Bree chuckled. "Rockabilly! I can see it. Lyle will fix you up. No more buzz cuts?"

"Something new." Theo wasn't exactly sure what she meant by that.

"You don't have to have all the answers right now," Bree said.

She ran her fingers through Theo's hair again, brushing it away from Theo's forehead, letting her warm palm rest against the side of her face. Theo closed her eyes to the touch and, for the first time in a long time, allowed herself a few moments to remember what things were like in the before.

Chapter Eleven

B ishop smiled at Theo from across the booth as she reached for the mustard squeeze bottle. "I can't pass up a Tanks Burger for the world."

"The best of the best. It's been too long since I had one." Theo dressed her own juicy burger, thinking about the last time she'd been to Tanks. It had been the day before the shooting.

It would be easy to miss Tanks Bar and Grill along Wayne Avenue if you weren't looking for it. Tanks had long been their favorite local place for meetings, celebrations, drinks, and its all-day breakfast and burger menu. She and Bishop found themselves there more often than just for team meetings, settling into one of the side booths where the friendly waitstaff left them alone.

Bishop swallowed her first bite and watched Theo mess around with her burger. "I'm glad we have this chance to catch up. I've missed you, partner."

Theo raised an eyebrow. "You're not having as much fun with Cody, I take it."

"No one can replace you, Theo. We need you back in the field."

Theo wiped her mouth with a napkin. "I'm doing everything to get back there. Desk duty is not my thing."

Bishop agreed. "That's why I wanted to talk with you today. I received this report two days ago."

"Does it have to do with dog shit and desecrated flower beds?"

Bishop laughed and pulled a case file from her bag. She set the olive-green folder on the table between them, still stiff and new. "I need your help, Theo."

"What's going on?"

"Another missing Ohio teen. I spoke to the lead detective this morning," Bishop said.

When Theo reached for the file, a photograph slipped out. A high school picture of a young woman that looked a lot like Grace Summers.

"This is Annabelle Jackson from Brecksville. Cleveland area," Bishop said. "She disappeared about three weeks ago without a word. She was seen leaving high school after the day's last bell in her own car. On the day she went missing, two hikers reported seeing her in the Brecksville Reserve, a large and popular local park, near dusk. She never arrived home. A few days later, someone in the park found her phone, high school ID, with some dried blood."

Theo picked up the photo to examine it more closely. It was uncanny how much Annabelle resembled Grace Summers. Just like Grace, Annabelle was slim, almost like a comma, and her long dark blond hair fell below her shoulders. Unlike Grace, Annabelle had recently had her braces removed, and her teeth were perfectly aligned.

"The Reserve has video in their parking areas. They have recordings of her arriving alone and leaving alone that day. She did not appear to be injured in any way." Bishop popped another fry in her mouth.

Theo bit her lower lip the way she always did when her mind flipped through the catalog of cases inside it. "A few years ago, you remember?" Theo asked. "Those three young women who were held captive for ten years in a home in Cleveland."

Bishop nodded. "That bastard, Ariel Castro. Those girls survived him, thank God."

Theo nodded, remembering the media coverage. "I considered that case when Grace first went missing. The way those girls vanished in Cleveland." Theo rubbed her brow. "Something about it just feels so familiar."

Bishop nodded her agreement. "I've thought of it, too. But Castro's house was in the Tremont neighborhood. Brecksville is a small suburb outside the city," Bishop said. "These two places are a world apart."

"Upscale community?"

Bishop nodded. "Annabelle comes from a single-parent household. Mom is a server at a popular high-end restaurant in downtown Cleveland. She works long hours. The detective on the case believes it's to give Annabelle everything she needs to succeed in that well-heeled world. Annabelle goes to a prestigious Catholic high school in the area, a full ride because of her grades and statements of the family's financial need. It sounds like Grandma did most of the mothering for Annabelle, particularly when she was young."

"Any other similarities?"

Bishop hesitated before adding, "There are rumors of pregnancy, but nothing confirmed."

Theo picked up a stack of photos and shuffled through them. It was a different girl and a different park, but déjà vu hit Theo in a way that made her dizzy.

"Does this girl have any siblings?"

"No, just like the Summers case."

Theo placed the pack of photographs inside the folder and closed it. "What aren't you telling me?"

Bishop gave her a quizzical look over the rim of her glass.

"Come on. This girl went missing three weeks ago. Why is Brecksville just now contacting Dayton?"

Bishop reached for the ketchup. "From the start, detectives thought it was a copycat thing. You know, some kind of prank or a way for the girl to get a lot of attention. They said it seemed too neat, too clean for a kidnapping. They thought she must have known our girl from Dayton and decided to try her own vanishing act from her own local park."

"It's possible."

"Sure," Bishop said. "Particularly since there are reported sightings of the girl around the Cleveland city proper. The mother has looked at the videos and admits that the person in them looks a lot like her daughter."

"Does she claim any of the images is her daughter?"

"She's not sure. The Brecksville PD has her working with a psychologist."

Theo shook her head. It was very clear why Bishop wasn't more concerned and headed to Cleveland herself. Everyone believed this kid was playing some kind of game. Given the circumstances, her mother could be in on it.

They both fell silent as the bartender called back an order and someone dumped a basket of clean silverware on a table to be rolled.

"Brecksville PD is relying on the narrative that the teen ran away of her own volition, even if it's only a handful of miles from her home." Bishop slid a business card across the table. "One of theirs wants to talk to the head detective on our case," Bishop said. "And that would be you."

Theo pushed the card back to Bishop. "Not anymore."

Bishop looked down at the business card and back up at Theo. She held her gaze. "Come on. This case was yours from the start."

"Ours," Theo corrected her. "We were—are—a team. Besides, I'm parked at the desk. I can't be in the field. You know that."

"What I know is you're the best detective Dayton has to offer. Desk duty or not, you're the authority on the Summers case."

Theo bit her bottom lip, chewing at its edges. "What about Cody? Have you talked to him about this yet?"

"I have."

The front door jangled with folks arriving for dinner. Soon the place would fill up.

"Cody agrees that you should be the one to contact Brecksville PD," Bishop said.

Theo leaned back against the booth and crossed her arms over her chest. Her entire burger had been pushed to the side of the table, and after the server offered them another beer, Theo settled in, watching her friend and colleague closely. She asked again, "What aren't you telling me?"

Bishop refused eye contact with Theo as she polished off the last of her fries. A plate of sizzling steak rolled past their table, and the smell of grilled meat was to die for. Theo didn't say another word. She needed to know everything, and she could wait Bishop out. It was one of her superpowers on the job. She could wait out just about any suspect under her interrogation.

"Spill it, Bishop."

"Okay," she said. "I didn't want to get into this, but if you insist." Theo insisted.

"Bull Michaels gave us the command to leave the case alone. He only wants us giving the Brecksville PD the information they request and nothing more."

In other words, the chief didn't want anyone from their team involved in the Brecksville investigation after the initial consult with their detective. Bull didn't want anyone going to Brecksville, joining forces with their detectives, or welcoming them into the DPD house.

"Why not send Cody?"

"I need my best on this one, Theo. Besides, you've always been the one who believed the Summers case was more than a runaway. This disappearance in Brecksville proves something. Best case scenario, we have a teen playing copycat. Worst case, it's another abduction by the same person or persons. No matter how we spin it, Theo, it's *something*."

Theo reached for her pickle and took a bite.

Bishop cracked a grin. "I *loooove* it. Those wheels are a-spinning."

"Any word on Sam Polanski?" Theo asked. She'd been curious about Grace's mother's boyfriend. He'd been living with Grace at the time of her disappearance, and word was the two didn't get along. He hadn't been heard from since his own disappearing act, five days before the shooting at Castleton Motors.

"Nothing. Wherever he landed, the guy's keeping clean." Bishop waved the server over and exchanged a few bills for the receipt. "My treat tonight. Take the amazing burger home to Bree."

While Theo packed the burger for carryout, Bishop slipped the file across the table. When they stood to leave, Bishop gave her a quick pat on the shoulder, which was the closest she came to a hug. "I miss you. It's so good to see you back on your feet." Bishop squeezed Theo's shoulder. "Thanks for looking into this for me."

"Of course." She understood why the chief wanted Dayton out of the Cleveland case. The last thing the department needed was another round with the media after the highly publicized shooting at Castleton Motors.

They made their way to the front door, Theo's cane clicking along the tile floor. Tanks sat below street level. The handicap ramp was steep and led her up and out of the hole. When Bishop pushed through the closed wooden door, the evening sky was aglow with the deep blues and purples of the settling night. She pushed the bangs from her eyes as she checked her phone. There was still time to drop in on Lyle before he closed up his barbershop for the day.

Gravel bit and spit under Theo's wheels in Mary Summers's driveway. The lights were still on, and Theo decided to stop on her way home.

Mary had tended bar at a popular South Dayton lounge for years, working a hectic schedule that would put most to shame. She was generally the one to open the bar and the one to close it in the early morning hours. Once Mary's daughter vanished, everything changed, which was why Mary was home on a Thursday night to open the door to Theo in pajamas and well-worn slippers.

"I only let detectives in on weeknights." She smiled, looking down at her pajamas, and welcomed Theo in. "Have you heard something about Grace?"

"I'm sorry," Theo said. This was the worst part about the investigation—letting Grace's mother down every time she saw her. Those same feelings of shame over the unanswered questions also drove Theo to continue with the case. It was the proverbial double-edged sword.

Mary and Grace's home was no bigger than what people used to call a shotgun home. It featured rooms arranged one behind the other, where a single shot could travel through all the rooms, from the front door to the back door. Theo followed Mary to the kitchen and was offered a seat at the table.

Mary pulled two cold sodas from the fridge and pushed one toward her. "Good to see you back on your feet, Theo." Mary sat down across from her. Her eyes were swollen with lack of sleep and what looked to Theo like a recent crying jag. "I've been thinking about you. Hoping you're healing okay."

"It's slow going. I need some of your Dayton-famous energy to really get back to my normal."

Mary's boss had claimed she had more stamina than three teenagers put together. She could hustle the crowd on any given night and light up the bar with her laugh. Mary managed the entire bar by herself in a pinch, and over the years she'd become something more to her customers than just a bartender. It seemed like everyone in Dayton knew or knew of Mary.

She took a few weeks off for the search when Grace first went missing. When Mary returned, she was a very different person. She'd slowed down and confused more than a few orders. Mary Summers was completely off her game.

Mary cracked a smile. "I miss all that energy, too," she said. "I didn't realize how fast things can change."

Theo trailed her thumb down the side of her cane and nodded. "Whiplash."

"Yes." Mary pulled her long hair behind her shoulders. After a moment she added, "I've been hearing all kinds of things at the bar about what might've happened to my girl. When I saw you in the drive, I hoped you had some news."

Theo couldn't imagine what it must have been like for Mary, returning to the bar after her daughter vanished. Everyone had a theory. Some believed Grace ran away and was looking for attention. Others loved to spout off half-baked ideas of where Grace might have gone and what dangerous encounters she might have faced. Unfortunately, Mary heard it all.

"Your place was on my way home," Theo explained. She thought about the take-out burger still fresh on her passenger seat and the warm evening. "I wanted to check in with you."

Mary's phone rang for a second time since Theo had arrived.

"Sorry, it's Sam's mom," she said. "She's been having some problems. Gotta take this."

Theo sipped her soda and scrolled through Cleveland dispatch reports on her phone for any updates on Annabelle's car. A nationwide BOLO had been issued for the gray 2000 Hyundai Accent registered in Annabelle's name, which went missing right along with her. Unfortunately, people rarely reported such a common car.

But Theo wondered if the silence in this case indicated the car wasn't in use. It could have been ditched somewhere along the way. It had been three weeks since Annabelle disappeared. Public parking areas, businesses, and apartment complexes regularly checked their lots for abandoned vehicles. Someone should have noticed an abandoned car by this point. Theo had to hand it to Annabelle. Just like Grace, she was smart with her movements. But how would two sixteen-year-old girls from Ohio's suburbs know how to evade police and navigate the world without help?

Mary returned, tossing the phone on the counter. "Sorry about that."

Theo shrugged. "How's Sam? Have you heard from him at all?"

Mary shook her head. "He's just…gone."

Gone. It was such an empty word, mysterious and cavernous like a gaping mouth.

"He's never done this before, Theo. His mother hasn't even heard from him. I guess he's not coming back."

"Do you think he left on his own?" Theo asked. "Or do you think something else has happened?"

Mary shook her head. "On his own, I guess." She held her head in her hands, pulling at the ends of her hair. "Everything's strange, you know? I miss Grace so much."

"I do." Theo reached out and squeezed her arm. "I'm so sorry, Mary."

After a few moments, Mary looked up at Theo and ran her fingers through her shoulder-length hair. She looked like she could sleep for a solid week. Mary wiped her eyes and reached for her soda can. "I've been thinking a lot about whether Sam had anything to do with Grace disappearing. They didn't get along, but he only wanted the best for her." She traced the edge of her fingernail over the markings on the can. "Sam and I did all those searches together, driving and walking for hours. He wore himself out, even more than I did. I can't believe he had anything to do with this."

Theo nodded. "I'm not saying he did."

"Everything with Grace was a lot of pressure, you know? And the media." Mary sat back in her chair. "Sometimes I think he just couldn't take it anymore."

"Take what?"

"The sadness," Mary said. "It's so heavy."

Theo nodded. She understood the weight of worry. "Did Sam take all his belongings with him?"

She nodded. "He must have really wanted to cut things off. His old number is out of service. One of our friends saw him at a bar up north, and he said he just needed some time."

"Up north?"

"Toledo, maybe?" She lit a cigarette. "He likes to fish on Lake Erie."

Theo made a mental note of how close that was to Brecksville.

Mary blew out a stream of smoke through her nostrils. "I know I'm better off without Sam," she said. "I've learned that these past few weeks, but I sure did love that man. His mother's a mess without him. The bastard."

Mary's phone rang again.

"Has anyone contacted you about Grace?"

Mary took another pull on her cigarette. "One of the counselors dropped off some of her schoolwork. Seems ridiculous, honestly. I mean, I'm terrified my girl's been killed, and they're worried about a missed biology test and English paper."

"Does Grace have any friends in the Brecksville area? It's a suburb of Cleveland."

"Never heard of it. I doubt she has, either."

"What about other kids at school. Did any of them move to that area? Or maybe a coworker at Wendy's?"

Mary shrugged. "I don't think so. Grace was a really quiet kid. Nothing like me." She chuckled. "She didn't really have any friends she saw outside of school and work." Mary blew out another stream of smoke. "What's going on, Theo? What's this about?"

Theo shifted her weight away from her damaged hip. "There's another sixteen-year-old in the Cleveland area who has gone missing. Her case is like Grace's."

"What?"

Theo could see the wheels turning in Mary's mind, the way she was putting her daughter together with this unknown girl from Brecksville. "Oh my God. The same person could have taken both girls."

"Hold on," Theo cautioned Mary. "There are a lot of unknowns here. All I can really tell you at this point is that the Brecksville PD thinks their girl ran away."

"Of course they do!" Mary threw her hands up in the air. "It's a whole lot easier if she just took off on her own, right?"

"Mary…" Theo cautioned again.

"What if they're together," she said. "Maybe there's a whole group of kids, you know? Grace was never the brave one in any group. She'd never run off on her own like this. But if there are others…well, it makes some kind of sense."

"Possibly," Theo said, "but we need evidence. We need something that shows where Grace might've gone."

"What if she's captive in a house? That happened in Cleveland. He had that houseful of girls. For years. And they *survived*."

Before Theo could say anything about the Castro case, Mary jumped up. "Theo, this means Grace might still be alive."

The phone rang again.

"Sam's mom." Mary slammed her open hand on the table in frustration.

"What's going on?" Theo asked.

The phone went quiet for only a few seconds before it rang again.

"Someone's damaging her property for the millionth time. I told her to call the police."

"Wait…is her last name Miller?" Theo asked.

Mary looked surprised. "Yeah, it's Sam's stepfather's last name."

Theo grabbed her phone and keys.

❖

Gertrude Miller met Theo on the doorstep, ready to rumble.

"You believe me now, Detective?" she barked, pointing down at the plastic bag of dog shit that had recently been burned.

"Mrs. Miller—" Theo started.

"Save it." Gertrude held up her hand. "Find the girl who keeps doing this."

"Where's Sam?" Theo asked. "It's important that I talk with him."

"Sam? He's not here. Can you blame him with all this neighborly love going around?" Her words dripped with spitting sarcasm. "I told you that girl wasn't missing." Gertrude held up an old flip-style phone. "I took some pictures of her this time."

Theo flipped it open and tried to make out the blurry images. A young person in a hoodie filled the small screen, but the darkness of the night made it hard to see any facial features.

"Mrs. Miller, I need to know when you last spoke with Sam."

"He's got nothing to do with this."

Theo reached for her own phone and scrolled through emails. She opened up an image and magnified it, holding the screen out to Gertrude Miller. "Have you seen this man, Henry Nerra, with your son?"

She leaned in closer and squinted to get a better look at the photo. "He's the one that died. The car store shooting, a while back."

Theo nodded. "Nerra knew your son. I'm wondering if that's the reason you've been targeted for the recent damage to your property."

"He stayed here for a while, when he first came out of prison. Sam said Henry had nowhere to go. He was only supposed to stay a few weeks."

"Where did Sam meet Henry? Prison?"

Theo had located Sam's records. He'd served time for drunken and disorderly conduct and a bar fight. By all accounts, Sam lost control. The target of his rage permanently lost his hearing and had to have multiple surgeries to rebuild his face.

Mrs. Miller looked away from Theo.

"I know about Sam's history, Mrs. Miller. I'm only trying to help, as you asked me to do."

Miller shook her head, then finally spoke. "Sam knew Henry before prison. They ran in the same circles, I guess. He spent a lot of time here."

"When did Henry start coming around?"

"I don't know. Two years ago? Maybe a little more."

This confirmed things for Theo, but the connection between Sam and Nerra ultimately called into question who the burning dog shit was really about.

"Sam is a good boy," Mrs. Miller said, more of a plea than a statement.

Mrs. Miller took a sharp breath. "There!" she yelled. "There she is."

Theo turned. The girl in the dark hoodie froze in a neighbor's yard about thirty feet from Theo. Their eyes met and held for a few solid seconds.

Then the girl took off.

CHAPTER TWELVE

Three different locks held down the accordion door of the storage container. When the first lock snapped open, the blood rushed inside Annabelle's ears so loudly, she thought her heart might explode.

In that wave of noise, she heard Gran's soft but persistent voice: *You are special, Annabelle.* She felt the weight of an invisible hand on her chest, and the touch that calmed her racing heart.

When the second lock opened, Annabelle backpedaled and wedged herself into the far corner of the container. Cowering. Shivering with fear.

The last lock clicked open.

Sensitivity. It's your superpower.

Slowly, the steel door rolled open. The brightness of the morning sun assaulted Annabelle with such force, her eyes teared. Annabelle threw up her hands for protection from the light and tried to turn away. Her belly was so swollen she couldn't pull her knees up to her chest, so they splayed out to the sides, butterfly style, with the soles of her feet planted together in front of her. Slowly, Annabelle moved her fingers, letting her eyes adjust to the sudden light. A rush of fresh air rolled through the container.

Annabelle sucked in a scream. In the morning light, the container looked like a full-on horror movie set. Daniel's skin had turned purple, and he was misshapen like an overinflated balloon. Fluid leaked and pooled beneath him. His lips pulled back from his teeth, and maggots crawled everywhere.

Pearle stood at the entrance, her figure blacked out against the burst of a new day behind her. She stepped in, a cutout of herself in the light, and the heels of her boots echoed against the steel bottom of the container.

Pearle dropped a full plastic jug of water on the floor and kicked it toward Annabelle. Then she flipped over an empty milk crate and sat down beside Daniel's body, not far from Annabelle's feet. She toed him once, and then again, harder. A gassy noise shot from Daniel's body, and Annabelle gagged at the odor.

Pearle pulled the bandana around her neck up over her mouth and nose. "He's ripe, your man." Turning back to Annabelle, Pearle hitched her chin toward the water. "You're worried I poisoned it?" She laughed, a laugh that froze Annabelle's heart. She turned away, remembering what Daniel had said the minute she told him about Pearle: *Something's definitely off with that woman.*

Annabelle choked back a laugh and a sob. Daniel was right. Something was definitely off with Pearle, but it was so much bigger than that. How could she have missed it? She'd given up *everything* for this woman.

"Drink!"

Annabelle reached for the gallon jug and popped off the plastic top. She couldn't contain her thirst any longer. The water poured into her mouth, filling her cheeks and throat. It felt like her entire esophagus had been scorched, and she couldn't get her body to follow her mind's directions to swallow. She retched.

"Look at you, wasting nourishment. Brains have never been your strong suit, have they, Annabelle? At least you could show some gratitude." Pearle leaned closer to Annabelle, the crate tipping at the backside. "Don't go thinking I care one iota for you. This is all for the baby. There's enough food and water here for a few days."

"Thank you," Annabelle managed to squeak out. She wasn't sure if she was thanking Pearle for the water and food or the fresh air that rolled into the unit like a tsunami. It swam up her skin, leaving goose bumps, and it was the first time she understood exactly how excruciating the heat had been the last few days. Annabelle took a deep breath, and the abundance of fresh air left her light-headed.

The baby rolled against her ribs, and more of the water came up. "Sitting in your own filth," Pearle chided. "You disgust me."

Annabelle's stomach lurched and seized until there was nothing left inside her. She used the back of her hand to wipe her mouth as tears sprang from the corners of her eyes. She wasn't in control of her life or her body any longer.

"You didn't have to kill him," Annabelle eventually choked out. "Daniel wouldn't tell anyone. The baby was always yours, Pearle."

Pearle's hazel eyes had a razor's edge to them, a darkness that Annabelle hadn't seen before. A hard glint against her sun-weathered face. "This was never about Daniel, dear heart. It's always been about you. And your lies."

Annabelle's breath caught in her throat. She heard the rumbling whine of an old boat motor.

"About time," Pearle said. "I give that boy everything." She shook her head and looked over at Annabelle. "Just like you."

"Please, Pearle. I didn't lie to you."

Pearle held up her open palm in a full-stop signal. "We're beyond that now, Annabelle. Eat up. Nourish the baby. It's the only thing keeping you alive."

The boat motor stopped. Soon another motor rumbled closer until she could make out Emmett driving the four-wheeler to the opening of the container. He climbed down and lumbered toward his mother, his large figure throwing Pearle into shade.

Pearle leaned down and set an object on the floor that looked like a doorbell. "We don't have much time, you know. This is the alert. If you begin to have contractions or cramps or your water breaks, ring me." Pearle nodded at the button. "Go ahead, try it."

Annabelle set the water jug down. "You'll help me? With the baby?"

Pearle nodded again. "Ring the bell."

Annabelle reached out, hesitating before pushing the button. Pearle took that moment to lunge for her, wrestling her to the floor.

"Emmett! Dammit, clamp her!"

Emmett grumbled under his breath, and soon Annabelle felt his paw of a hand grab hold of her calf. She screamed and kicked at him, her heel making contact with his chin. But the pressure of his grip was too much. In seconds, he closed the steel cuff around her ankle. Annabelle was too weak and overcome with nausea and terror to put up much more of a fight. Soon Emmett had attached the other end of the chain to a thick metal ring along the side of the container.

"I can't have you running off on me now, can I?" Pearle stood just beyond Annabelle's reach. "This heat! The baby needs fresh air. I'm going to leave the door open today." Pearle gave Annabelle a wicked grin. "Go ahead and scream all you want, love. There's only the trees and water to hear you."

Emmett swiped his forearm across his brow and glared at Annabelle. A heavy forehead shadowed his dark eyes. Annabelle realized she'd never heard him speak.

"Emmett! Get him out of here before he ruins the container," Pearle said.

Emmett obeyed, leaning over Daniel's body. He tried to grab Daniel under his armpits, but Daniel's skin peeled off in his hands. Emmett coughed as a new wave of odor from the body filled the container. He wiped the skin and ooze from his hands on the thighs of his jeans.

Emmett tried again, this time taking hold of Daniel's T-shirt, heaving his body toward the container's entrance. Emmett's pants drooped in the back. He grunted while pulling Daniel's disintegrating body across the container floor, leaving a mucous trail.

"Where are you taking him?" Annabelle felt a sudden pang of terror. She didn't want Daniel to go, even if it meant his body might completely liquify beside her in the container. "Leave him here."

Emmett ignored her, shoving Daniel's body off the lip of the container and hoisting him into the back carriage of the four-wheeler. Emmett's shoulders hunched against his thick neck in a way that reminded Annabelle of Shrek as he walked around the vehicle.

"I'll catch a ride with you, Emmett," Pearle called out to him. "This heat is wearing me out."

Emmett waited for his mother to get in before he reversed the machine, and then they slowly drove away. Once Pearle had her back to Annabelle, she spread her arm out above her head and gave Annabelle a giant wave.

Annabelle lunged for the entrance, the chain snapping and flinging her to the floor. "Bring him back!" she screamed. "Daniel!"

Annabelle crawled to the stain of him, the dried blood around the outline of his body. She screamed Daniel's name and her apologies over and over again until her throat bled. Annabelle fought against the chain until her knees gave out, and she collapsed with exhaustion on the steel floor.

Eventually Annabelle woke to a warm wet tongue across her cheek. Tillie licked Annabelle's tearstained face while gazing down at her with those wide honey-golden eyes. She circled her tail a few times before collapsing against Annabelle's belly. The dog's body heat warmed Annabelle all the way to her heart. She put an arm around Tillie, her hand burrowing into the dog's thick black and white fur, welcoming the creature's warmth against her skin.

"Thank you, Tillie," Annabelle whispered. She took a deep breath of the fresh air rolling through the container. "I'm going to get us out of this mess."

Annabelle closed her eyes, letting exhaustion overtake her. But all she could see was Emmett dragging Daniel's body into the four-wheeler, his legs and feet dead-thumping against the base of the container.

CHAPTER THIRTEEN

Theo made it to the end of Gertrude Miller's street before her hip gave out. Her knee collapsed under the pressure. Theo had fallen enough times since the shooting to know how to save herself. She rolled to her side and let the meat of her body hit the ground. The bite of the cement didn't hurt nearly as much as her damaged ego. Only a few months ago, Theo could have taken the runner down in minutes, had the suspect cuffed, and been back on her feet within seconds.

Theo smacked the cement with an open palm before she sat up. There was no one around on the quiet street. She crab-crawled to the side and gave herself a minute. The muscles in her legs burned as she sat on the curb. Thankfully she hadn't heard anything pop or snap. Theo ran her hands down the length of her legs and rolled her ankles. Nothing broken, nothing torn. Angling her knee under her, Theo tried to stand. This time her wrists gave out and she tumbled back to the cement.

Shit. She was going to have to call someone for help.

She reached for her phone. It literally pained her stomach to think of calling Bree or Bishop for help. Her face burned and her eyes pricked with tears.

"Are...are you okay?"

Theo looked for the location of the small voice. The girl. In the hoodie.

"I saw you fall," she said. "I'm sorry."

"Could you help me up? I think I'm okay," Theo told her. "My hip gives out sometimes."

The girl came closer, cautious and ready to bolt at any moment.

"Look, I only want to help," Theo said when the girl froze. "I'm not here to arrest you."

Under the streetlight Theo saw the resemblance to Grace. Gertrude Miller hadn't been totally wrong about the similarities, but this person was younger than Grace, no older than eleven or twelve. Her hair was tucked away inside the hoodie, much darker than Grace's. She had Grace's pale blue eyes and the soft features that seemed to all meld together.

Finally, the girl stepped forward. Theo talked her through how to help her up and how to balance Theo's weight away from her damaged hip.

"I have a cane," she told the girl. "It's closer to the driveway. Could you walk back with me? Until I find it?"

The girl was apprehensive but wound her elbow through Theo's as instructed. Theo understood the girl felt obligated at this point. She planned to milk it. Yes, Theo was slow-moving at this point, but she purposely slowed herself down to a near crawl. She needed to get the girl talking.

Thank God for eleven, Theo thought. Another year or so, and the kid would've been long gone.

"What's your name?"

"Mara."

"Mara, I'm Theo. I'm doing my best to find Grace Summers. From the messages you've been leaving at the Miller house, it seems like you are, too."

Theo's right foot scraped along the cement. All her muscles screamed with exhaustion.

"They know where she is," Mara said, slowing her gait to match Theo's.

"Who? Mrs. Miller?"

Mara shook her head. "Her son. He followed Grace for months before she went missing."

"How do you know?"

"Grace told me," Mara said. "And I saw it. Once, we went for a walk, and he followed us in his van. We ran through the neighborhood yards until we lost him."

"That must have been terrifying."

Mara took a deep breath and began to drop her shoulders away from her ears.

"Grace showed me his house when we rode bikes and told me he was doing this to other girls. She wanted me to stay away. Now she's gone. My mom told me she's not coming back. She says it's been too long for her to come home."

"How did you know Grace?" Theo asked. "It sounds like you're good friends."

"She's my best friend. I mean, Grace has been babysitting me since I was six. I don't need a babysitter anymore, but we still hang out."

Theo had been frustrated in the early parts of the investigation because Grace didn't have any friends. No one saw her outside of school, and teachers reported that she rarely spoke to other students in class. Her only real interactions were at her part-time job at Wendy's. But even her coworkers seemed to think of her as a stranger. But this girl had been around Grace for years. She was exactly the person Theo had been looking for to help understand Grace and her movements.

"Are you sure it was Mrs. Miller's son Sam? There was someone else staying with them for a time. Would you be willing to look at some photos for me?"

"I...I don't know."

"Please? It would be a big help to Grace."

As they neared Gertrude Miller's house, both saw the car in the driveway, a car Theo recognized. Miller stood with someone else on the front stoop. Bishop had already arrived. Mara pulled back, panicking.

Theo gripped the girl by her shoulders and leveled with her. "Listen, I could take you in to the station. Destruction of property and trespassing are misdemeanors, and you've been at this for months. We'll need to get your parents involved, and it will be a whole *thing*."

Tears welled in Mara's eyes. "Come on! I was just trying to get him to go to you guys. I thought if he knew someone else knew, he'd turn himself in, and Grace could come home."

"I'll make you a deal," Theo said. "Tell me what was going on with Grace when she left, and I'll pretend the burning bags never happened. And it *never* happens again."

"What about her?" Mara thumbed at the officer on Miller's doorstep where Bishop was trying to pull herself away from Miller's exaggerated talk.

"I'll handle it. Get in my car, and I'll drive you home."

Mara grabbed Theo's cane from the middle of the road and returned it to her. Theo watched her go to the car, then dug deep within herself to walk without showing the pain in her side. She met Bishop in the driveway.

"Jesus, Theo, I thought we'd have to send a search team out for you. You okay?"

"I'm good." Theo arched an eyebrow toward her car. "I got this part if you can handle Miller."

Bishop looked over Theo's shoulder to the girl outlined by the streetlight. "I'm not sure this is a fair trade."

"I'll make it up to you."

In the car, Mara directed Theo through the twisty neighborhood streets.

"Grace never would have done it, you know? It was just talk."

Theo didn't take her eyes from the road. "Tell me about it."

"Grace said she was going to kill herself. She said she would cut her throat with one of her mom's razors. She read online that the neck makes you bleed the fastest, and it doesn't hurt as much as the wrist."

"Did she try to do it?" Theo riffled through the case notes in her mind. There hadn't been any hospitalizations or emergency room visits reported for Grace.

"No, but it scared me. She was incredibly sad until she wasn't."

Theo pulled off to the curb and put the car in park. She needed a place to talk to Mara without the pressure of her parents.

"This isn't where I live," Mara said.

"I know, but I need to hear more. Why did Grace want to kill herself?"

Mara reached into the pocket pouch of her hoodie and pulled out a phone. She scrolled through the saved images before selecting and enlarging one. She held out the screen for Theo. "I swore I'd never tell, but I just want Grace to come home."

Theo took the phone. The photo was taken in a bathroom. The edge of a bathroom sink was lined with three pregnancy tests. One inconclusive. The other two positive.

"She drank a bottle of water between each one to make herself pee."

"Are you telling me Grace left because she was pregnant?"

Mara groaned and grabbed the phone away from Theo. "She didn't *leave*! Aren't you listening to me? Grace wouldn't run away. And she'd never leave her phone."

"You said that something changed," Theo challenged her.

"Yes, but I think that's because she decided to keep the baby."

Theo took that information in. She tried to imagine how a sixteen-year-old might conceive of caring for a baby. Theo could hardly understand the concept at fifty-three. "She talked to you about this?"

"Not exactly," Mara said. "Grace didn't want to have an abortion. She told me that. She wanted to have the baby, so she went to the free clinic to see a doctor. She just couldn't figure out how to do that on her own. She knew her mom would never let her keep the baby."

"The free clinic? Out on Main Street?"

"Yeah."

Theo reached for her phone and pulled up two photos. Henry Nerra and Sam Polanski. "Which of these men followed you?"

Mara held the phone in her hand. She carefully examined them both. "I've seen them both with her. But this is the one she talked to most." She pointed to Sam.

"What does he have to do with all this? What aren't you telling me, Mara?"

Mara shook her head.

"All right." Theo threw the car in reverse. "I can take you in."

"No!" Mara sighed. "He was her secret, okay?"

"Who? Sam?"

Mara nodded. "She met up with him a few times. That's how she knew he was bad."

"Was he the baby's father?"

Mara paused, thinking. "She thought he could help her. Now Grace is gone."

Theo looked through the windshield into the night. She digested the information. It always had seemed like it might be a sexual assault or grooming case with Sam and Henry Nerra involved. But what if this was never about sex? What if Sam had only been the guy Grace went to for help?

"It was you, wasn't it? On the tip line?"

Mara picked at her nails. She gave the slightest nod.

Theo reached into the console and scribbled her phone number on the back. "Call me anytime. If you think of anything that might help us find Grace, I need to know about it, okay? Anything at all."

She pulled the car back onto the street, and as they neared the house, Mara asked to be dropped off on the curb. "The headlights, you know? They'll wake my mom."

"Mara?" Theo called as the girl stepped out of the car. "Did Grace keep a journal? Did she write anything about what she was going through?"

Mara shook her head. "She didn't have to. She had a counselor."

"Where?"

"At the clinic. Grace liked her, I think."

Mara shut the door gently behind her. Theo waited for the preteen to slip inside the front door of her home before pulling into the quiet neighborhood street.

Theo sat down on the bed beside Bree and pulled the blanket up over her bare shoulder. Bree stirred, caught a glimpse of the clock, and rubbed her tired eyes. "I can't believe it's this late. I just fell asleep."

"It's almost midnight, babe. Good thing you have the night off," Theo said. "You need the rest."

Bree caught a glimpse of Theo's hair. "You were with Lyle." She sat up. "I love it."

Theo grinned. "Lyle was going for professional and a whole lotta hip. Abby Wambach style."

"He nailed it."

Theo turned her head so that Bree could trace her fingertips along the buzzed sides and perfected edges of the mohawk. Lyle had gelled the trail of longer hair and styled it so carefully, you could see the comb's grooves.

Theo had been blessed with her mother's coal-black hair. Her mother's thick mane turned stark white by the time she was in her early fifties. Theo heard her mother describe that transformation time and again as if it was a dream.

"I went to bed one night," her mother had always said in her storyteller voice, "and woke up with a head full of feathery-white hair."

Theo remembered her endlessly winding her fingers through her long strands looking for silver, as if she could will it away.

Theo's mother had been gone for a few years, and Theo was forever grateful she hadn't lived to see her daughter wounded on the job. It had been her mother's greatest fear, losing Theo to a bullet.

Theo let Bree trace her fingertips along her jawline. Since the shooting, Theo's face had lost much of its softness due to weight loss from the surgeries and medicines that stole her appetite. It left the defining bones of Theo's face harsh and unforgiving. They were both still getting used to that.

"There's my Detective Theo." Bree kissed her softly.

"Move over." Theo nudged her. "It's so warm and dark in here. I've missed you today."

Bree laughed, and soon Theo pulled her in close against her body. She buried her face in Bree's long, curly hair. With an arm wrapped around Bree's waist, Theo held the baby with her wide-open palm. "Any movement today?"

Bree took Theo's hand in hers and moved it to the upper left side of her bump. "He gave me a hard kick right here this afternoon. For whatever reason, he likes this side."

"A little warrior."

"*Our* little warrior," Bree said.

"Yes, *our*." Theo smiled into her warm mess of hair. Bree never missed an opportunity to remind her the baby was as much Theo's as it was hers. These reminders always left Theo's stomach churning. Was she really ready to be a parent?

Since the shooting, Theo felt her age creeping up on her. She'd been reminded of it again when she tumbled in the neighborhood street. Another reminder came when Lyle had finished with her hair. She had scooped up a collection of clippings and let the hair float into her lap. Theo held the soft fine strands in her hands and let them fall between her fingers. That was when she saw it. A few silvery-white strands scattered among the dark.

"Earth to Theo. How was work today?"

"Same old, same old."

Bree wound her fingers through Theo's and held on.

Theo closed her eyes and took in a deep breath. The smell of Bree, the smell of love. They lay this way together for a while. Breathing together. Holding on to one another.

"There's a missing teen in a suburb near Cleveland. I'm driving up there in the morning."

Bree drew a sharp breath. "Tomorrow? What about the test for the baby?"

Theo froze. She'd forgotten. "It's just an ultrasound, right?"

Bree pulled away and sat up in the bed. "Are you kidding me? Were you even listening at the last appointment? It's the nonstress test and an ultrasound."

Theo shrugged. "Nonstress? Can't you do this without me?"

Bree shook her head. "Of course I can do it alone. I just wanted you there. But if this is a big development..."

"It is."

"Cody? Is he going with you?"

"He's working another case."

Bree's brow furrowed. "I thought the two of you were in on this one together."

"We are. Bull doesn't think this case has legs. Cody and Bishop have a Dayton caseload to work."

"Alone? Are you sure you're ready for this?"

"It's one day." Bree's question annoyed Theo. Did she really think she couldn't manage driving on the highway or visiting another police department? "I'll be back after dinner. Maybe before, depending on how things go."

"It's much more than just one day," Bree said, cutting through the bullshit. "And you know it."

When their relationship began, Theo regularly left Bree notes, saying she was checking on a lead and would be back in X number of hours. Bree liked to refer to detective work as a prairie dog hunt in a vast forest. It was no use trying to track Theo down, she'd said, and she'd learned that if she just waited in one place long enough, Theo always found her way back. "It's the golden rule for those lost in the wilderness, you know," Bree'd told Theo one time when she returned to her from a long day searching empty prairie dog holes. "Stay in one place and scream for help."

Bree had kissed Theo then, eager for more. "Do you feel lost?" Theo had asked. "Stranded in the forest?"

"No," Bree said, the tip of her tongue trailing down Theo's chest. "Not with you by my side."

All those notes and texts stopped once Theo had been shot.

"Bree," Theo said to her now, "I have to go to Brecksville. It's important."

"It always is. Do you feel steady enough?"

Theo nodded, but her belly tightened. She didn't want to admit she was nervous about taking so much on herself. But nothing mattered more than bringing Grace and Annabelle home alive.

"You have nothing to prove, Theo. I wish you wouldn't go."

Theo pulled Bree into a hug tight against her chest. Theo felt like she had everything to prove, most of all to herself.

CHAPTER FOURTEEN

Annabelle dozed in the dark. The sharp edges of the metal chain gnawed against her lower shin. Despite the heat, she shivered uncontrollably, falling in and out of a light sleep. A memory tore through the sheath of Annabelle's mind, a time so clear she felt like she was living it once again.

Annabelle sat on the rocky overhang of Deer Lick Cave in Brecksville Reserve. It was her favorite place in the park, like it was for so many others. She liked it best on cold and rainy days when hikers took other paths.

When Annabelle was younger, she'd come to Deer Lick Cave with Gran looking for white-tailed deer. Gran said the entire area used to be covered by ocean, and the salt from the water had sunk into the layer of sandstone beneath. Deer needed salt in their diet, and they flocked to the cave to lick the rocks. Gran loved to use the word *flocked*, but the truth was, in all the times they'd gone together, there were no deer flocking. Annabelle only remembered seeing these majestic deer a handful of times.

Deer Lick Cave was also the place she'd first met with Daniel alone. They had gone to school together for years. Once, on the school bus to a class field trip in second grade, Daniel told her she was pretty. She remembered that, always, tucking those words from him into the back corner of her heart. The truth was Daniel had never really been her friend. He was athletic, popular, and one of those kids that everyone wanted to be around. He was the best football player their school had seen in decades and had been talking about playing for Ohio State University since toddlerhood.

Annabelle was not the kind of girl guys like Daniel fell for. She wasn't even the kind of girl guys like him befriended. Maybe that's why Mrs. Allen paired the two of them up in English class for a long-term class project.

English was Annabelle's best subject, and Daniel soon realized she could carry them both into a great grade. They shared numbers, and soon Annabelle regularly obsessed over contacting him. She managed to restrict her texts to once every other day and kept the content about their project. He always texted her back. Sometimes his texts had nothing to do with the English project.

The first time Annabelle met Daniel at Deer Lick Cave, the rain poured in steady sheets. Her umbrella caught on branches along the path. He'd shown up without one, soaked to the bone.

They met regularly, always in the reserve and hidden away from their world. Daniel always brought fresh doughnuts from a nearby bakery, and they talked about school and parents while Annabelle did his homework. They even saw a few white-tailed deer.

Daniel had kissed her first, and Annabelle reminded herself of that constantly. He'd been the one to lean in over his algebra textbook and press his lips to hers. She'd held on to that, even if he'd followed the kiss up with extracting a promise to keep their friendship a secret. He continued to extract that promise for weeks, even after they'd gone much further than kissing.

"Friendship?" Annabelle asked after they'd had sex in the woods. She never would have referred to him as a friend.

"Or whatever." Daniel smiled. "It's just the guys. They don't understand. And we have the season ahead of us. I can't lose them."

"They matter that much?"

"It's football," Daniel had said. "The team's my ride or die. They're more important than my family."

Ride or die. What she wouldn't have given in that moment for him to think of her in those terms.

After they'd gotten their A on the project, Daniel ignored her messages for weeks before he replied.

When they finally met, Annabelle sat on top of the rocky overhang and watched Daniel walk along the trail. He wore his letter jacket, something he rarely took off at school, and his fancy Timberland hiking boots that crunched along the trail. When he looked up, she waved to him.

"The rocks are slick," he'd called up to her. Daniel was always thinking about injuries that might put him off the field. "Come down here."

The two sat on a park bench not far from the cave, a place meant for hikers to rest along the trail. He tried to keep the conversation light and avoided Annabelle's questions that began with *Why haven't you returned my calls?* and eventually evolved into *What did I do that was so wrong?*

"I'm just not ready for how much you need me," Daniel said.

Annabelle looked down at her boots that gaped at the ankles. Ruby had left them behind a few weeks back when she showed up for a random night of shelter. She missed seeing her cousin every week. Ruby had found a life somewhere in the city, and it didn't include Annabelle.

"I can stop texting," she offered and hated herself for needing this boy beside her. This happened every time to her, friendships, relationships, you name it. People generally backed away from Annabelle once they realized they couldn't fill the gaping hole inside her. She just needed someone else to be there.

"You told me I was pretty once."

Daniel chuckled. "You've told me. I sort of remember it."

"You were the first boy to tell me so," she said. "The only boy to ever say that to me."

"It's true," Daniel said. "You are pretty."

Annabelle stared at him.

She had to say it, just blurt the words out. "I'm pregnant with our baby."

"What?" Daniel laughed at first. "No way."

"It's not a joke, Daniel."

He shook his head. "That's not possible."

When Annabelle didn't respond, he let loose. "No, Annabelle. No." He stood up, furious, and turned to look down at her on the bench. "Have you been to the doctor? Those pee tests are always wrong."

"I'm pregnant, Daniel."

Neither of them said anything for a while. Daniel eventually returned to his seat beside her. Birds cawed around them. A collection of ducks rounded the edge of the creek looking for food.

"How do you know it's mine?"

The question knocked the wind out of Annabelle. She'd expected him to deny the pregnancy but not to accuse her of sleeping around.

"Oh my God," she nearly spat at him. Tears filled her eyes. "It's yours, Daniel. Yours and mine."

The finality and certainty of her words sucked the air out of the space between them. Daniel's body tightened next to Annabelle's. His hands fisted as his energy coiled.

"It's not mine," he said again. "It's not. I'll help you because you're my friend, and you need it."

It was Annabelle's turn to laugh. "What a good guy," Annabelle had mocked him, surprising even herself. "Player of the year, right here."

"Stop it," Daniel said. "Just stop. I have some money saved up."

Something about his offer of money spoke to her. She thought he meant they could make a go of it. Maybe they could do this together. Start something real and solid for all three of them to hold on to.

"It's a girl," she told him, the edges of her mouth quivering with hope. "Our girl. I can feel it."

"It's nothing, Annabelle." Daniel shook his head in disbelief. "Nothing more than a few cells. We need to get rid of it."

Annabelle hadn't expected the conversation to immediately turn to abortion. Her hand settled over her flat belly where the baby grew inside her.

"We have to give our baby the best of us. The very best that we can possibly be," Annabelle told him. "I want her to always know deep in her heart that we did right by her."

"What are you saying?"

Annabelle turned to face him. "I'm telling you I'm keeping her."

Daniel stomped his boots against the earth. He stood and was already halfway to the trail that led back to the parking area before he turned back.

"I should have listened to everyone, Annabelle," he hollered at her. "They all told me to stay away. I felt sorry for you. The poor, sick girl. This is what I get for being nice."

Annabelle sat on that park bench for hours after he left, staying long after the sun had set. She made the baby a promise. No matter what Daniel did or didn't do, she would keep the baby and find the very best parents for her. Annabelle swore she'd do everything in her power to keep the baby safe.

Rage boiled inside her for weeks. The more Daniel ignored her, the more she wanted to tell everyone. Yet there was this part of her that also wanted to protect him. She knew so much of Daniel's future rode on the scholarship he'd hoped for from OSU. Annabelle had wanted him to tell her she was more important than his friends, football, or that scholarship. She'd wanted him to tell her he loved her, that they'd be a family, and he'd protect her.

She remembered everything about the way Daniel walked away from her that day: the cloudy sky, the smell of creek water, and that biting fear of knowing she'd have to face her future alone. Now Daniel was dead, and that promise she'd made to the baby from the lonely park bench was the only thing that kept Annabelle's heart beating.

CHAPTER FIFTEEN

Theo bypassed downtown Cleveland and drove toward the wooded bluffs of Brecksville.

"One of my friends in college grew up in Brecksville," Bree had told her. "They pay to protect all that green space around them."

Bree's comment intrigued her, and Theo discovered that the average household income in Brecksville was more than she made in two years of work. The Cleveland suburb showcased the perfectly landscaped settings where children walked with their parents and the family dog to school every day while police parked on street corners to give a friendly wave. Parents felt safe letting their kids play in the neighborhood unattended, and every family seemed to own a Lab or golden retriever. Brecksville, on its shiny surface, was the kind of place where nothing bad ever happened, especially to its children.

Dayton was only about a three-and-a-half-hour drive from downtown Cleveland, but a world away with its spacious woodlands and ponds. It wasn't until Theo pulled off the interstate that she marveled at the difference in the landscape. While Dayton had some fantastic metro parks and hiking trails, it couldn't compare to the wooded bluffs and ravines of the Cuyahoga Valley National Park that shouldered the Brecksville city limits.

Theo pulled into a parking space at the Brecksville PD. Another wave of anxiety struck, and she second-guessed herself all over again. At that very moment, no one other than Bree knew she was there. While she'd already spoken to Detective Maxwell Weston and arranged to meet at the station, they hadn't discussed the details of the cases yet. Theo still had time to change her mind. The second she set foot inside the building and asked to speak to Detective Weston, there would be no turning back.

Theo wasn't sure she was ready to take this on. She'd come to Brecksville on her own time, yes, but she didn't have the department backing her in the investigation. If push came to shove, she knew Bishop would support her choices, but the fact remained that Theo was representing Dayton Police without clearance.

"I have a bad feeling about this," Bree had said earlier that morning, giving up on the resistance band exercises.

"It will be fine. I'll be back this evening."

Bree gave Theo a long look, her eyes still puffy with sleep, and rubbed her round belly. "I wish you'd let me go with you."

Bree had offered to go along the night before, and Theo had scoffed. "Bree, I'm a big girl. I don't need you to be my chaperone. Besides, I really need to do this on my own."

Theo tried to ease her mind. Bree had enough on her shoulders already—she didn't need to understand what a long shot this would be.

Theo took a deep breath and stepped out of the car. She leaned on her cane as her body tilted a little to the right, then a lot, before catching hold of the car behind her for extra support. These bouts with balance didn't happen much anymore. But she'd been sitting in the car too long, ignoring the advice of her doctor to walk and stretch every hour.

As Theo walked the small parking lot, a red sign in the entrance window caught her eye, reminding drivers that the police and fire departments were there to help with proper child seat placement in vehicles. Soon she'd be strapping a young one into a car seat and angling her rearview mirror to get the perfect view of the baby.

"Tell me about your missing girl," Theo said, following Weston into a media room. "There have been reported sightings of her, correct?"

Weston offered Theo the roller chair in front of an oversized computer screen. "Nothing confirmed, but we have a few videos sent in by folks who swear it's Annabelle Jackson. All were recorded in the downtown area of Cleveland."

His pale yellow golf shirt reminded Theo of a country club regular, particularly with his perfect smile against summer-tanned skin. Paired with stylishly cut thick salt-and-pepper hair, Weston didn't look like he belonged in any police station on a Saturday morning when he could be out golfing. He fiddled with the aviator sunglasses perched atop his head. A distinct tan line ran across his nose and under his eyes.

"The thing is," Weston said, "those images aren't clear. Her own mother can't be sure it's her."

"What do you think?"

Weston shrugged. "I don't believe it's her, but your guess is as good as mine. It's incredibly frustrating. Just when I think we might be getting somewhere, another unconfirmed video or photo turns up." Weston sat down beside Theo. "Let's start with a confirmed video of Annabelle. This is the last known image, two days before she went missing."

Rose Jackson had recorded a clip on her phone of her daughter Annabelle walking along a forested trail.

"A-Birdie," her mother teased her from behind, "turn around. Give me a smile! Come on. Humor your mother!"

"Mom! Turn it off."

Theo observed the teen's back. Slender build, no more than five and a half feet tall. Annabelle's shoulder blades pushed against the fabric of her thin T-shirt. She walked with her head down and shoulders rounded, which gave her the look of someone much older than sixteen. Thick dark blond hair hung down her back and swung from side to side with her every step.

Three minutes and twenty seconds into the video, Annabelle finally turned and faced the camera. "There. You happy?" Annabelle held her arms out as if to say, *What do you want from me?*

"Pause that," Theo said.

She leaned in toward the frozen computer screen, studying Annabelle's long white neck and the tight edges of her mouth. There was so much about the girl she recognized and so much she did not.

"She's Grace Summers without the braces," Theo said. "The hair color, the slight build. No makeup. The whole girl-next-door vibe."

"They could be sisters," he agreed.

Theo grasped at any sort of hope the two girls were still alive. There was an athleticism to both teens, despite their slim builds. Theo hoped that might give them some sort of edge against their attacker. Maybe he didn't realize how strong they really were or how fast they could run, but strength and adrenaline went a long way in saving a life.

"Where was this video taken?"

"Brecksville Reserve. According to Annabelle's mother, it was her favorite place. She spent a lot of time there, hiking the trails and fishing. Park security cameras recorded her leaving in her car that afternoon, and that's it. She hasn't been seen or heard from since."

It didn't escape Theo that both girls frequented and were last seen in popular local parks.

"We have a lot of outdoors enthusiasts and park patrons visiting us year-round," Weston said. "Cuyahoga National Park gets most of that foot traffic, but the locals spend their time in the Brecksville Reserve. It has fewer visitors."

"That's probably why she liked it so much." Theo pressed play and watched as Annabelle turned away from the camera. She broke into a run, and Theo heard the sound of Annabelle's shoes pounding against the trail.

Her mother called out, "Slow down! Let me catch up!"

Annabelle only laughed. That haunting sound lingered as the teen disappeared from view.

Theo couldn't get the image of Annabelle running on wooded trails out of her mind. What she wouldn't give to be able to run a trail again. To cut loose and run, the dirt path beneath her feet, the foliage brushing against her body as she zoomed past. What she wouldn't give to be in her old body once again.

"Detective Madsen."

Weston's voice brought Theo back to the room and back into her current body. "I'm with you," she said, rubbing her eyes.

"It's a lot to consider, I know. What makes you so sure Grace Summers didn't run away?"

Theo considered his question. "What makes you so sure Annabelle didn't run away?"

Weston chuckled. "Touché."

Theo smiled. "I did get some interesting information yesterday. We had a tip that Grace was seeing a counselor." She pulled the file from her bag and watched Weston read the report.

Client Name: G
Age: 16
County: Montgomery
Visit 1

Counseling Notes: Client came to clinic for a reliable pregnancy test. Positive. Nurse requested intervention when client became emotional and said she couldn't stop crying. Client wanted assurance our talk would remain confidential. Concerned about others finding out about pregnancy. Knows identity of father, but hinted it was nonconsensual. Father won't speak to her. Feelings of abandonment, isolation. Single mother at home, only child. Led client through different options re: pregnancy. Talked about her short- and long-term goals and how this may alter them. Client left with homework to think over options and begin to draft an action plan. Agreed to meet 3X.

Client Name: G
Age: 16
County: Montgomery
Visit 2

Counseling Notes: Client's affect brighter, more talkative. Client created and brought pros and cons list for pregnancy options. Thoughts of abortion but wants baby to have "a happy life." Feels "torn" by the decision. Hasn't told mother. Spoke of friend who listens, someone who told her this could be a fresh start. Friend suggested she could use baby to build the big family client always wanted. Client said it's not what she imagined—wanted to be a part of a big family but not produce or mother it. Client half completed action plan. Will complete for next visit and continue talks w/friend about pregnancy/life goals.

Client Name: G
Age: 16
County: Montgomery
Visit 3
    Counseling Notes: No-show. Called number on file. Number no longer in service.

"Interesting," Weston said.

There was a knock at the door. "Look at you two, working hard on a Saturday. Brecksville taxpayers are getting their money's worth."

Another middle-aged man who looked like he belonged on a golf course joined them.

"Hey, Doug," Weston said. "This is Detective Theo Madsen from Dayton. We're looking at the footage of the Jackson case."

"Doug Clayton, chief around these parts. Good to have you in our house." He pumped Theo's hand up and down, his gaze settling on Theo's cane. "Well, have the two of you solved whatever there is to be solved?"

That was all it took for Theo to understand Weston's position in his department. Just as she had worked so hard to convince the Dayton PD there was more to Grace's story than a runaway, Maxwell Weston fought the same battle with the Brecksville PD about Annabelle.

"I was just about to show her the interview," Weston told Clayton.

"With who?" Theo asked.

"Daniel Holtzman."

Clayton groaned. "These teens. Way too old for their years and full of games."

Theo picked at her thumbnail while Weston cued the recording. She'd heard about teens dismissed by law enforcement most of her career, and it bothered her. Some detectives dismissed them outright as unreliable due to hormones. But that hadn't been Theo's experience. She wanted to be the detective teens felt safe to talk the truth with, safe to seek out for help.

Chief Clayton filled Theo in on Daniel's statement. "He claims he wasn't Annabelle's boyfriend or involved with her, but we have a witness who saw the two of them together two days before Annabelle went missing." He used air quotes for *went missing*, as if Theo needed anything more to understand he didn't believe this was a real missing persons case.

Theo remembered reading something in Annabelle's file. "The secret boyfriend."

Clayton nodded.

A couple of Annabelle's classmates told police she might have been meeting someone. Her friends hadn't met him, and Annabelle refused to talk about it, but they all thought it had something to do with the school's star football player. They'd been paired together for some sort of class project.

"Where were they last seen together?"

"In the reserve," Weston said. "Some kids from the high school saw them walking the trail near Deer Lick Cave."

Theo watched the monitor. The young man and his mother sat with Weston in an interrogation room. Daniel began by admitting he met Annabelle near the cave but only because she sounded anxious.

"She wasn't my girlfriend or anything," he said, wringing his hands under the table. "We knew each other from school, and she was upset."

"Why would she call you, Daniel?" Weston asked. "If you only knew each other from school and weren't close friends, why wouldn't she reach out to someone closer?"

Daniel shrugged and finger-scrubbed his short hair. "She always wanted more from me, I guess."

"How so?"

"She wanted me to be her boyfriend. She texted all the time. Annabelle can be a lot to deal with, you know?"

"Girls can be like that," Weston agreed. "Daniel, from what I'm hearing, it sounds like the two of you had much more of a relationship than just friends at school."

Daniel kept his eyes trained on his hands, popping his knuckles one by one.

"Annabelle is missing, Daniel. I need you to tell me everything you can remember about that meeting in the Brecksville Reserve."

"She just said she was lonely and missed me. I told her I couldn't give her what she wanted." Daniel shrugged and adjusted his jacket. "I mean, I feel really bad. If something happened to her..."

"What exactly did she want from you?" Weston asked.

Daniel's mother touched his arm. "Why don't I know about this? I've never seen you with that girl."

"It was school stuff," he said to her. "We were working on a project."

"So you were dating Annabelle," Weston interrupted.

"Not dating. Not really anything. We were working on an English presentation together, and things kind of went too far," he explained. "I never felt the same way about Annabelle as she did for me."

"Did she say anything about leaving Brecksville? Did she mention a new friend, someone she might be talking to?"

"No," Daniel said. "She only talked to me about feeling sad and lonely. I suggested she talk to someone about it, an adult who could help—maybe her doctor. She had a lot of medical appointments because of lupus. You know about that, right?"

The discussion turned to Annabelle's struggle with lupus and her daily medications before Daniel's mother ended the interview. "I need to get him to practice," she told Weston. "My boy has told you all he knows."

Theo watched the monitor as the two filtered out of the interrogation room.

I suggested she talk to an adult who could help.

This phrase from Daniel struck Theo as odd. She rolled it around in her mind. So formal. So practiced and perfected.

Daniel was hiding something.

CHAPTER SIXTEEN

When Annabelle first learned of Pearle Oliver, she didn't think much of the stranger who was at least ten years older than her own mother. Annabelle had been clear. She wanted to find a *family* for her baby, not a single mother who lived in the middle of nowhere Ohio. She wanted her baby to have a different experience than her own. Ruby promised The Handler would deliver for her little one.

Other than Daniel, Ruby was the only one Annabelle told about the baby. Ruby, with her worldly ways, knew exactly what to do. "I know the perfect person to help," she'd said. "Leave it all to me."

Within a few days, Ruby had given Annabelle a list of names with profiles. Ruby said someone known as The Handler brokered deals with people hoping to purchase healthy, pure newborns.

"Pure?"

Ruby gripped the rearview mirror and applied a fresh coat of lipstick. "Yeah, you know. White kids. Healthy and free of all Western medicine."

"But all babies see doctors," Annabelle said, confused.

Ruby ignored the comment. "The Handler is really interested in yours. Your baby will become part of the New Nation. You've heard me talk about them, right?"

Annabelle knew very little about the group. She'd heard Ruby talking to her mother about it, this group with beliefs her mother did not agree with. Annabelle had listened to their debates at a distance.

In the last two years, Ruby had gotten more involved with them—she called them *the family*—and Annabelle's mom worried about her niece.

"Look, I wouldn't get you into this if I didn't think it was best for you." Ruby puckered her lips and wiped the edges clean with her pinky. "You need the money, and you'll make bank. Promise."

Annabelle was curious about this person brokering a deal with her baby's life, but it was clear these families would have so much more than she could ever offer her baby. And then there was the money, the amazing promise of a fresh start. Annabelle dreamed of starting over in a new town where no one knew her as the sick girl or the charity case or the girl without a dad or any other way she'd been known in Brecksville. She'd already been given five hundred dollars in cash for agreeing to the terms and conditions of the deal.

Ruby told her Pearle Oliver shouldn't be discounted right away. "Yeah, she's older, but she's a fantastic parent. She's also a great friend of the organization. Don't toss her out just yet."

Annabelle wanted to be extra careful, though, so she scoured the list of names and checked all their social media. She became a voyeur into these people's lives, examining photos and posts for hours. She could dissect a profile pic of a couple grinning at a fresh garden bloom and think, *Could this be them? My baby's parents?* Soon she would move on to the next name on the list, unable to see her baby with anyone so disingenuously happy.

While Annabelle wanted her baby to end up in a wealthy home, the white suburbanites who posted more vacation photos of themselves than anything else with phrases like *God, I needed this vacation to Hawaii* or *I've worked so hard to get a few days with the fam* annoyed her. Annabelle had never been to the places these people photographed, and she couldn't imagine her child there, either. She certainly wanted a life for her baby that was financially abundant and stable, but Annabelle also wanted a family that regularly did things together, not one who tossed their kids off to day camps and babysitters whenever possible. Or, worse, left alone. Maybe that was why she kept coming back to the name her cousin suggested: Pearle Oliver.

Pearle had no social media footprint, or any other digital connection for that matter. Annabelle found this strangely comforting. She imagined someone who went against the societal norm and kept her life private. The more she looked at Pearle's picture, the woman seemed ageless, an Earth Mother who only used all-natural and home-grown materials.

Plus, Pearle somehow reminded her of Gran. Both women seemed to have the same sensibilities, and there was a physical resemblance there that made Annabelle's heart hurt. Pearle's name moved quickly to the top of her list.

A few days later, Ruby met Annabelle in a Quick Stop parking lot. She smiled and pocketed the list. "Great choice. I know it's hard, and you didn't have much time, but you're doing the right thing. Pearle will be thrilled—you have no idea. She wants a newborn baby, like...yesterday."

Annabelle was so happy to see Ruby. She hugged her cousin, letting her hand close around Ruby's red ponytail. Named for her fiery red hair, Ruby had always been the one Annabelle looked up to. Ruby was the cooler older cousin who always had friends around and money in her pocket she was willing to share with Annabelle. Gran always said the two of them would need to look after one another like sisters.

Annabelle had been worried about her cousin since Gran passed away. In the last few years, Ruby disappeared for weeks on end. It wasn't a secret—Ruby worked as a prostitute. While she'd stayed with Annabelle and her mother sometimes, it never lasted. After a few weeks of sharing Annabelle's room, Ruby would disappear once again. Annabelle always relished the time her cousin was home with her, the times when she felt like she truly had a family member who loved her since Gran had gone.

"I worry about you, Rubes. How do you know these kinds of people?"

"*These kinds of people?*" Ruby laughed. "Annabelle, you're one of us now."

"You know what I mean."

"I know that the New Nation wants to save America's future. I know that we will be a part of that."

"Ruby, I'm just worried for you. That's all."

"You sound like your mother."

Annabelle heard the contempt in Ruby's comment and recoiled. She'd heard these words before, this same tone meant to hurt her. Images flashed across Annabelle's mind from the day she walked into the shared bathroom to find Ruby in the tub, the water pink with blood, and tiny cuts running up her arm. Slashes in a long row, bleeding but not deep.

"Ruby," she'd screamed and ran to her cousin.

Ruby had said those words then before kicking Annabelle out of the bathroom: *You sound just like your mother.*

"Hey!" Ruby grabbed Annabelle's hand. "I'm fine, okay? Remember when you used to braid my hair? All those french braids and pigtails?" She laughed. "That was a long time ago."

"Much too long ago," Annabelle said. "I miss it."

Ruby leaned back in the driver's seat and shut off the engine. "So, you want to know how it works? Because some mothers don't want to know anything."

"I do."

Ruby explained that she would deliver the chosen name to her contact, who would then pass it on to The Handler. A burner phone and detailed instructions on how to proceed would soon follow.

"Who is The Handler?" Annabelle asked. "Have you met this person?"

"It's a secret, but he's the one who brokers all the deals. He takes a cut from the payment for the child, so you'll be sharing the money fifty-fifty with The Handler."

"Fifty-fifty?" This was the first Annabelle had heard of splitting anything. Fifty-fifty sounded like too much, particularly since she was the one carrying the baby and giving birth.

"Annabelle, this is against the law. You get that, right?" She reached over her shoulder to hand Annabelle a hair tie. "No one will do this for free. Besides, you'll walk away with more than enough to start a new life anywhere you choose. That's what matters, right?"

"It just seems…excessive."

"It's not, though." Ruby turned to face Annabelle. "I've heard of the Handler taking up to seventy-five percent."

For a moment, Annabelle thought about calling the whole thing off. Ruby's words about the New Nation alarmed her, and she wasn't sure she wanted to be a part of this. She'd made an adoption plan for herself online before Ruby stepped in. But Annabelle had already spent the five hundred dollars on her phone bill, gas, and food. For once, her phone bill was paid two months in advance, and she'd bought a new school uniform to replace the one she'd been wearing for almost a year.

Annabelle reached into her pocket for the plastic tube. There was just one last thing she needed from her cousin. "I need your help."

"Everything is done, cuz."

"Not quite." She held the DNA testing tube out to her cousin.

Ruby finally understood. "You want me to take the test for you?"

Annabelle nodded. "You have to. They only want mothers in perfect health."

"You're making the assumption I'm healthy," Ruby said, taking the clear tube from her cousin. "Besides, I'm not clean."

"This isn't that kind of a test. It's only looking for your DNA," Annabelle said.

Ruby picked up the cotton swab and looked in the rearview mirror. "You're overthinking this, A. They'd need a blood draw to test for autoimmune. This isn't that big of a deal."

Annabelle shrugged. "Let's not take that chance, okay?"

Annabelle held her cousin's gaze until Ruby finally said, "This is fucked up, you know? Seriously fucked up."

Annabelle agreed and laughed in a sad way. She'd already thought of that. "My baby is going to be really special," Annabelle said. "I can feel it in my bones."

"What about Daniel? Has he given you any money?"

Annabelle shook her head and looked out the side window.

"I told you he was a piece of shit." Ruby smacked her open palm against the steering wheel. The sound of it made Annabelle jump. "I told you to stay away from him."

"He's not a terrible guy, Ruby. He's just so focused on college and football."

"Right. It has to end, Annabelle. You cannot see him anymore."

"I know," Annabelle said. "I want the baby to have the very best life. I can't provide that, so…let's do this."

"Have you considered that I may be a carrier?" Ruby asked. "These diseases run in families. I might even have it." Ruby searched for her cousin's eyes. "What I'm saying is that it could be just as bad for me to take this as you."

Annabelle shook her head. "I'll take my chances."

Even though autoimmune diseases tended to run in families, particularly among the women, Ruby hadn't shown any symptoms.

"Open wide," Annabelle told Ruby and watched her swab her cheek.

Annabelle packaged up the tube and used a marker to write her name on its label. Then she pulled her cousin into a tight hug. Annabelle needed more than anything for The Handler to believe there was absolutely nothing wrong, even if her fiery-red cheeks told everyone exactly what was going on inside her body.

Ruby turned to her. "You'll have to say good-bye to your mom."

"I know. Maybe in the future she'll understand, and we can see each other again."

Ruby took a deep breath. "That's not possible, A. You get that, right? You cut ties with your old life. Everyone. It's part of the deal when you enter this family."

Annabelle heard her cousin, but she didn't fully believe this part of the contract. How would this *family* know what she did three years from now? Or ten?

"You didn't," Annabelle said.

Ruby closed her fist over the testing tube and stepped out of the car.

CHAPTER SEVENTEEN

Detective Weston's radio broadcast the latest call as he drove Theo through the winding roads of Brecksville. They came upon a horse farm nestled into the landscape. She smiled at the German shepherd who ran along the fence line beside their car with a tennis ball in its mouth.

"That dog is always out," Weston said. "It seems like he runs every inch of that land every few hours."

"Picturesque," Theo said.

"That's Brecksville," Weston said. "On the surface, we are a bunch of happy bees." He nodded to the high school mascot on a road sign.

"Well, at least you aren't the happy beavers."

Weston laughed. "Good God, is that a real high school mascot?" She assured him it was. "Ohio. You never know just what you'll find, do you?"

Her phone buzzed against her thigh. Again. She'd forgotten to send Bree a text once she arrived at the station, and Bree was blowing up her messages.

Theo thumbed out, *Sorry :(fine. En route to first interview with detective*

Bree shot back a quick response, *You're lucky I didn't call the cops!*

"Everything okay?" Weston asked.

Theo thumbed back, *I am the cops* and inserted the blowing kiss emoji. *Appt go ok?*

Bree sent back the thumbs-up.

Theo slid the phone back into her pocket. "Checking in at home."

"To be honest, I'm surprised Dayton sent you. I didn't get much of a response from your squad. What finally caught everyone's interest?"

"I can be very convincing, Detective," Theo said. "My chief thought we needed to find out more about your case and make certain they aren't connected."

Weston nodded. "I'm glad someone else sees more to these cases than just me."

"Which is why I'm happy to do the interview with you."

Weston thanked her again. "Annabelle's mother hasn't been the easiest person to deal with."

Theo chuckled. "I have experience with difficult parents. I wanted to speak with her, anyway. You said Rose Jackson works long hours. Our girls come from very similar households."

Weston agreed. "He goes for teen girls from single-parent homes for a reason."

"Both of these young women seemed lonely and alone. There wasn't anyone watching them closely, and that made it a lot easier for our perp to get inside their heads."

Weston turned down a neighborhood street. "Annabelle has some street smarts, and that makes her different from a lot of kids around here. Most of them have the book smarts but have been sheltered, to their detriment."

"Wealth to an excess."

"We have the extremes of the spectrum here in Brecksville, obviously," Weston said. "The lavish wealth built next to Section 8 housing units. That's where Annabelle grew up. She's an only child, and her mother is head server at a fancy steak place in the city. We don't know much about Annabelle's father other than he hasn't been in her life since she was a toddler. By all accounts, her grandmother raised Annabelle and her cousin Ruby."

Weston eventually pulled into an apartment complex with boxy buildings lining the street. He checked his phone for the correct address and pulled into a parking spot that looked just like all the others on the street.

"Rose Jackson has really struggled since Annabelle disappeared. Depression, trouble at work, all that. She says we aren't doing enough to find her daughter," Weston said. "She's convinced Annabelle didn't leave on her own."

Theo stepped out of the car and thought about how the longer Grace's case went on, the more her mother wavered in her insistence that Grace was taken. *Maybe*, Mary Summers eventually conceded, rubbing her brows bald and raw, *maybe my kid ran off.* It was a real kick in the teeth after all the noise she'd made in the press.

Weston knocked on the ground level apartment's door until Rose Jackson cracked it open just enough to catch sight of the detectives.

"Detective Weston," she said, as if her heart had sunk into her stomach. "Please say you have good news for me."

"I wish I had some news," Weston said. "Instead, I brought someone to talk with you. This is Theodora Madsen. She's the detective working on the case of the missing teen in Dayton."

The door slowly opened.

"Call me Theo, please. Do you have a few minutes to talk about Annabelle?"

Rose Jackson looked her up and down until her eyes eventually settled on Theo's cane.

"Tell me this," Rose said. "Have you found your girl? In Dayton?"

Theo shook her head. "Not yet."

Rose Jackson held Theo's gaze a moment, as if analyzing her. Finally, she waved them in.

They followed Rose through a congested hallway into a small kitchen where a table was piled high with takeout menus and unopened mail.

"Have a seat." She motioned to them. "Sorry for the mess. Mind if I smoke?"

Theo shook her head and considered Rose. Fine lines settled in her upper lip and around her eyes. Life had not been kind to her, and she wore that in her face.

Theo accepted the chair, the basket-weave of the seat frayed from what looked like a cat's claws. As she sat, she noticed the photograph on the refrigerator. Theo stood, moved closer. "Is that...?"

"Hmm?" Rose turned to the fridge. A sudden blush covered her cheeks. "He's my guy."

Theo examined the picture. The man's beefy arm hooked around Rose's neck in the photo, possessive, demanding. He grinned at the camera as if he didn't have a partner and mother currently missing him in Dayton.

CHAPTER EIGHTEEN

Annabelle knew her mother was dating again. It wasn't that her mom had had lots of relationships—in fact, it was the opposite. Even though Rose Jackson was very social at work and had many acquaintances, she didn't date them. Annabelle could only name two men her mother had been with. One was her father, who Annabelle couldn't remember, and the other was Rick, who had been gone for a few years. Her mother had kept Annabelle away from Rick, which was easy to do since Annabelle was basically living with her grandmother. Sometimes, when Ruby was also at Gran's, the two girls shared a bed, giggling late into the night. Sometimes they'd overhear the arguments between her mother and Gran about Rick.

"How long will you put up with this?" Gran asked. "Think of Annabelle. For once, think of your child."

"I am thinking of her, Mom. She cannot be around him."

"Look at you…"

Voices hushed, and Annabelle knew that meant Gran was inspecting her mother's body, taking stock of the bruises and marks on her skin. Annabelle had noticed them, too, even though her mother tried to hide them under thick sweatshirts and scarves.

"I'm saving her from all this," her mother said. "Don't you understand that?"

"Your daughter needs you," Gran said. "I won't be here forever, Rose. You know that."

"I'm saving her, Mom."

No matter how many times Annabelle's mother insisted she was saving her, Annabelle didn't see it that way. Her mother had abandoned her. Again. This time it wasn't for her job but for a man. A man who beat her. How could her mom choose that over her? It made no sense, and that knowledge burned her insides. She tried to quell the fire before the rash came, before the flare that would put her in bed for a few days.

Eventually her mother's relationship with Rick ended, and Annabelle heard it was because he'd gone to jail. She'd asked Gran what happened but was told it was for adult ears only. Annabelle knew Rick had done something very bad.

"Is it because he hurt Mom?"

"No, child. Although he deserves jail for that, too." She spread her wide-open hand over Annabelle's head and pulled her close. "Don't worry. He's gone, Annabelle."

But Annabelle worried. Just because Rick was in jail didn't mean her mother was coming back to her. It screamed the truth to Annabelle, a truth she'd always feared from the bottom of her heart. Her mother didn't want her.

That was many years ago, but suddenly the signs of a man hanging around had returned. For starters, her mom had begun wearing lipstick. Maroon, a dark red that matched her blush, both of which looked garish on this woman who had gone without makeup for years.

"Who is he?" Annabelle asked her mom when they finally crossed paths in the kitchen one morning.

"Who?"

"Come on, Mom." Annabelle grabbed the box of cereal. "You met someone. Who is he? Are you getting married?"

Rose laughed. "Married? What is this, the 1940s? Marriage isn't in the cards for me. You know that."

Annabelle did know. Her mom preferred to be alone. When she walked out the door from the bar at the end of her shift, she was done with people. As Annabelle saw it, that sentiment included her daughter as well.

"You're right, though," Rose said. "I did meet someone. Let's just see how things are in a few weeks, okay? Maybe I'll introduce you."

"What's his name?"

Rose dug through the cupboard for a clean mug. "Sam. Okay? His name is Sam."

Annabelle spooned her cereal. She doubted Sam would still be around in a few weeks. It didn't really matter. She was leaving, and in an odd sort of way, knowing her mother might have someone to be with once in a while made her feel a little better about her decision.

As the days rolled by and her belly began to bulge, Annabelle obsessively checked her burner phone for calls. It lay quiet in the bottom of her backpack, but Annabelle was more than ready for the signal. She wondered what Pearle was doing. Preparing a space for her? Lining up medical services for the birth? She'd been told she'd give birth with a midwife and not in a hospital. In the back of her mind, Annabelle worried about what might go wrong. The baby could be breech or the umbilical cord could be wound around the baby's neck. Everything about this plan was a gamble, and she'd accepted that. She reminded herself of the article she'd read online—birth traumas were almost nonexistent in teen moms. She wouldn't be that rare statistic that scared everyone to death.

As for her new life with Pearle, there were many more rules than Annabelle ever anticipated. She had only begun to understand the stakes, both legal and personal, for everyone involved. As the days passed, her anxiety escalated. She fell in line and agreed to bring nothing to Pearle's home other than the burner The Handler provided, a change of clothing, and her car.

Everything physical was replaceable, Annabelle reminded herself. She could always buy new shoes or books. But as the days wore on, Annabelle began to chafe at that rule. Her heart tugged at the thought of leaving certain items behind. Little tiny things that meant something only to her.

Annabelle considered a few keepsakes, small trinkets no one would notice. Gran's treasured brooch. An Ohio State University pen in the shape of the Buckeye mascot. Mrs. Henderson, her ninth-grade teacher, gave her that pen and said that nothing could hold Annabelle back from a college degree at OSU but herself. The rock in the shape of an oblong heart that she found at Brecksville Reserve from one of her and Daniel's secret meetings.

If she was honest, Annabelle treasured the rock most. They'd been walking together along a hiking trail, Daniel in his bare feet because his new boots were giving him blisters. He was jumping around to protect the tender soles of his feet when they came upon a rocky area. Daniel stumbled into her to save a step full of pain, and she stumbled into a patch of darker rocks. They laughed together as she bent down to examine them, and that was when she found it. The heart-shaped rock. It almost sparkled at her, as if the rock had been waiting its whole life for Annabelle to find it.

"Look, Daniel! This rock was made for us."

He turned to see what she had found. His fingertips grazed the dark rock. It wasn't black, but a dark marble of maroon and gray. "Yeah," he said. "I guess so."

"I'm keeping this," Annabelle said, but Daniel had already moved on. She fisted the rock, their rock, and tucked it safe into the pocket of her jeans. Before she'd even taken a few steps, she'd already decided the rock was validation sent from a higher being, fate in the form of a physical object.

Soon Annabelle would meet Pearle for the first time. Although the deal had already been brokered, Annabelle couldn't wait to see the woman who would raise her child. A tiny part of her worried that Pearle would take one look at her and drop the deal.

As the days rolled past, it struck Annabelle as almost funny how sentimental she found herself. She felt the impending moment of her escape only heartbeats away, that moment when the burner would buzz and the screen would glow with the code word of where to meet. Even with all that excitement and wonder, there was a small part of her reaching back. Maybe her mom really didn't mean to hurt her. Maybe she really was doing what she thought was best for Annabelle, working all the time to keep her in a good school and a good neighborhood. Maybe her mom didn't realize how lost Annabelle was without her grandmother. All of these maybes crept into her mind at the oddest times.

In the last few weeks, Annabelle struggled to focus. Her usual ultra-awareness of the world around her dimmed and left her frightened. Doubts nagged at the corners of her mind. She told herself not to feel guilty about leaving her mother. Annabelle promised herself she'd always maintain some sort of tie with her mother, even if it was as thin and delicate as a cobweb. Rose Jackson, if nothing else, was the embodiment of strength.

CHAPTER NINETEEN

According to Rose, Sam Polanski knew how to make himself scarce. She hadn't heard from him for over a week, and he wasn't answering his messages. Sam had been living with a friend of Rose's, one of the cooks at the restaurant where she worked.

"He's like that," Rose said. "Hot and cold. I never know what version of Sam I'm going to get."

Rose sat across the small table from Theo and Weston. She rubbed her eyes and groaned. Theo noticed the bloating of her face, the dark swell under her eyes from late nights.

"What did Annabelle think of Sam?" Weston asked.

"She hasn't met him. At least not in person."

"Why not?"

Rose shrugged and lit a cigarette. "I figured she wouldn't like him. Annabelle can be tough on anyone who comes into my life."

Theo watched Rose. She refused to make eye contact, and Theo couldn't tell who Rose was trying to protect more, Sam or Annabelle.

Theo pulled a business card from her wallet. She scribbled her personal number on the back and handed it to Rose. "I really need to speak to Sam. We're checking in with everyone who had anything to do with Annabelle or your family at the time she went missing."

"Brecksville PD already did that. Right, Weston?" Rose blew a stream of smoke toward the ceiling fan.

The detective winced. Her dig at him hit home.

"Yes, but it's been a few weeks," Theo said. "Memories change."

She wished she could tell Rose so much more without jeopardizing the case. Rose and Mary Summers had more in common than a missing daughter. They both were romantically involved with Sam Polanski. Theo had a strong feeling those relationships were fueled solely by Polanski's desire to be around the women's teens. She needed to find Polanski before she could divulge that information. Otherwise, she risked the very real chance that he'd go underground.

Rose stood and snapped Theo's card to the fridge with a Myrtle Beach magnet. The same magnet held a photo of a young woman not much older than Annabelle.

"Beautiful girl," Theo said. "I always wanted to be a ginger."

"Right? That's my niece, Ruby." Rose reached up and ran her fingers through the edges of her thin, shoulder-length hair. "She's always had the best hair in the family. Might as well be Annabelle's sister."

"Where is she now?"

Rose rolled her eyes. "Ruby's twenty-one and thinks she's grown."

Theo and Weston laughed at that description.

Rose nodded to Weston. "He knows my Ruby. She's been in some trouble. She hasn't stayed here in a few months."

"What kind of trouble?"

"Cleveland PD picked her up once for prostitution," Rose said. "Ruby's always looking for a quick way to make cash."

"Have you talked with her about Annabelle's disappearance?"

"She swears Annabelle didn't tell her anything."

"And?"

"I believe Ruby. They've hardly seen each other since the holidays. Besides, Ruby checks in with me on occasion. She shows up here every now and again with some food and beer. It's been hard on us both."

Theo remembered that Ruby had been one of the initial interviews Weston conducted. Her alibi checked out. She'd been working with her aunt at the restaurant all day cleaning. Ruby had told Weston she needed the extra money to pay off a medical bill. She even had a selfie she'd snapped of her and Rose working at the restaurant that day.

While Weston talked to Rose about the case, Theo took some notes. Weston had told her Rose appeared to be traumatized by her daughter's disappearance. All the reports Theo read, however, indicated Rose regularly left her child on her own or with her grandmother. When Theo read that, she assumed Rose had been a young mother who wanted to continue to live a childless lifestyle. Now Theo wondered if the caretaking arrangement with the grandmother had been about something very different.

"Annabelle's a great kid." Rose shifted in her seat, this time catching Theo's eyes for a few seconds before looking away. "She's smart. She wants to go to the local community college and transfer on to nursing school at OSU. She's certainly spent enough time with doctors and nurses for her lupus."

"Tell me more about that," Theo said. "Does she take daily meds?"

Rose pushed hair out of her eyes and looked past Theo. A small window was open over the sink, and a cool breeze slowly cleared the cigarette smoke from the kitchen. "She takes meds twice a day. Hydro-something. I can't say those fancy long names. It's the same med my mother took. Something for malaria, but it fights inflammation. Annabelle says it doesn't always work, but her joints swell and ache without it. It's one of those things. The meds don't make her feel a hundred percent, but when she's off them, she flares."

Theo scribbled in her notepad. She recognized how much information Rose had on her daughter's medical condition. This wasn't a mother who didn't take interest in her child. "What's a flare?"

Rose knocked the ash from her cigarette and twirled the end of it in her fingers. "Nothing good. Something triggers the immune system to kick in to overdrive. It could be an allergy or the flu. Could be as simple as heat or stress. Her body fights itself all the time. The doctor puts her on a steroid treatment to get the inflammation down so that lupus doesn't destroy her organs." Rose rubbed her tired eyes. "Annabelle really needs her meds."

Theo nodded, making a note to ask Weston about Annabelle's doctor. What surprised Theo was that Rose was known at work to be the caretaker of fellow employees and regulars at the bar. It didn't make sense she'd leave her only child alone for long shifts, particularly a child who struggled with a serious medical condition. Theo guessed Rose had to work so much to cover the medical bills.

"Could Theo take a peek into Annabelle's room?"

"Sure," Rose told Weston. "I haven't moved anything since that day."

Rose's small home was built like a trailer, one long rectangle. The bedrooms sat at one end, a family room at the other, and the kitchen in the middle. Theo and Weston followed Rose down the narrow hallway toward the bedrooms and a shared bath.

Annabelle's room was surprisingly stark for a teenage girl's. There were no posters of rock bands or Hollywood celebrities. Her walls were painted a pale yellow, and her bed took up most of the room with a small desk in the corner.

Theo let herself get used to the thick carpet in the room, stepping from side to side a few times. T-shirts and jeans spilled out of an open closet door. A collection of gym shoes scattered from beneath the bed.

"There was nothing out of place," Rose said. "She left her laptop on her desk along with all her schoolbooks."

"What do you make of police finding her phone and ID at the Brecksville Reserve? Does the handprint mean anything to you?"

Weston reported that the DNA for the handprint matched Annabelle's blood, just as Grace's handprint had in the Dayton case. The two girls had somehow cut themselves and used their own blood for these prints, almost as if they'd left a small wave good-bye. Both Brecksville and Dayton had worked hard to keep the handprint details out of the press, but it eventually leaked. Both disappearance scenes were in public areas, and the handprints were an easy element of the case to copycat.

Rose sat down on the edge of the bed. "I can't make sense of it. She'd never do this to get attention. That's not Annabelle."

Theo moved over to the desk and picked up Annabelle's laptop. She'd plastered stickers over any free space on the lid of the computer, colorful swaths of singers and her high school logo mixed in with cute dogs and outdoor gear stores. Theo opened the lid. Next to the mouse pad, Annabelle had a large sticker for the Women's Movement, a hot pink fist inside the symbol for woman.

"Was Annabelle locally active with the women's movement?"

"It was a focus of one of her classes, I think. Annabelle talked a lot about hashtag #MeToo and joined a feminist reading group for a while at her school. The group fizzled out. I don't think the kids wanted to do the reading."

Theo opened the top desk drawer, scanning over the collection of paper clips and memory sticks. "That's impressive for a teen. Annabelle must have related."

Rose shook her head. "She's sixteen. She relates to everything for a few minutes before her attention goes somewhere else."

Rose explained that her daughter's interest in the group probably had more to do with who was involved. The cool kids were all doing it, she said, and the group was led by a popular teacher.

"Annabelle always wants to be with those kids at school who live in large homes and drive Jeeps or loaded SUVs," Rose said. "She's ultra-impressed with money, and those are the people that started this reading group."

Weston commiserated with Rose about teenagers as Theo surveyed the rest of the room. A wooden chair sat in the corner with clothes draped over it. A few T-shirts hung over its back. Theo picked up a lavender and white spiral tie-dye and held it up toward the light from the window. The women's movement symbol covered the front of the shirt. The back had a tiger, Annabelle's high school mascot, along with five signatures in a black permanent marker.

"Do you know these people?" she asked Rose, holding up the signed shirt. "Annabelle's name is here. Who are the other four?"

Rose took the shirt. "She loves this shirt. I think it was from the reading club. I'm not sure about the names. Wait, this looks like the name Cadi Melton. She's the teacher that started the group."

"Do you mind if we keep this for a while? I'd like to track down some of these other names."

"Sure. Anything that might help."

Theo tucked the T-shirt under her arm as they made their way to the front door. Once they were outside, Rose surprised Theo by reaching for her hand. "My Annabelle is alive. I can feel *her*. She needs me, and there's nothing worse than not being able to do anything when your baby needs you."

Theo had never really been one to trust in the proverbial mother's instinct. All that changed when Bree became pregnant. With their own baby on the way, Theo understood this concept better than she ever had before.

"We'll do everything we can to find her," Theo promised, struck once again by the connection Rose had with her daughter.

Rose gave Theo a weak smile. "You know, Annabelle has always been afraid of the dark. When she was a baby, I loaded her room with night-lights. She used to get this look of pure terror when it was bedtime. Her eyes would fill with tears, and her eyeballs bulged out of her tiny head. Then she'd shiver. She'd shake and shake like a little bird. My A-Birdie."

Tears rimmed Rose's tired and swollen eyes. "That's how I feel all the time now. Eyes bulging out of my skull, tears threatening to run down my cheeks as I frantically shake. Darkness. That's all I see when I think of my little girl."

CHAPTER TWENTY

Annabelle kicked the flat tire again as if it could change things. At least she'd gotten the car over to the highway's shoulder. The afternoon traffic wasn't heavy. She groaned in frustration before popping the trunk for the spare, an ancient foot pump jack, and wrench. She tried to hold all of them away from her clean shirt and the brand-new black jeans she'd been forced to buy because of her growing baby bump.

Today was a big day. She'd meet Pearle for the first time.

Annabelle had already been running late, but this flat would push her back even further.

They'd picked a Waffle House in Akron as their meetup spot, a place far enough away from Brecksville that Annabelle wouldn't happen to run into anyone she knew.

The pebbles and rocks along the highway shoulder dug into her knees as she knelt with the wrench to unscrew the lug nuts. Annabelle had changed more that her fair share of tires in her lifetime. Gran seemed to find any nail and every piece of glass on any given road. Annabelle later learned that it was because her grandmother's tires were almost worn through, but she kept patching them. Once Annabelle had the lug nuts off and the foot pump jack was placed, she stepped away from the car. Her hands fell against her hips that had recently become prominent. Even so, no one would ever guess Annabelle was pregnant. She loved keeping this secret. In an odd way, it made her feel powerful.

"Sorry, little one," she whispered to her belly and thought about Pearle. She imagined the woman already seated in a corner booth with a menu spread out before her. She imagined Pearle's long hair loose and below her shoulders, her bright eyes filled with excitement for the first face-to-face meeting. Then Annabelle thought, *What if she leaves or gives up on me? Am I really doing the right thing?*

Annabelle had already tried the burner number, but Pearle wasn't answering. Pearle wasn't known for keeping track of her phone. Annabelle had tried to call several times before with no luck. Most likely she'd forgotten it at home.

With a thick Doc Martens boot, Annabelle stomped the lever that slowly raised the edge of her car until the dead wheel was off the ground. The key to getting the old jack to work was getting it into the perfect position. It could be tricky, but Gran had shown her how to angle it just right.

Annabelle knelt again, curling her body toward the tire and spreading her back to the traffic behind her. She couldn't stop thinking about Pearle. She'd spent so much time getting ready, picking out the perfect shirt that matched the color of her painted nails, a true rarity for Annabelle. She'd spent even more time on her makeup to hide the rash that had begun to spread across her cheeks only yesterday. Annabelle wanted to arrive at the meeting early so she could impress Pearle. She wanted this woman to see that she was a good mother, that she cared about doing all the right things for her baby.

"She's going to think I'm such a screwup," Annabelle told the tire, her eyes glazing over with angry tears.

That's when a semi slowed as it passed Annabelle, its brakes screeching along the shoulder until they hissed as the truck came to a halt.

Annabelle had the flat off and walked it back to her trunk. Her heart raced when she saw the trucker jump down from his rig and walk toward her.

She slammed her trunk and rushed to put on the spare. She didn't want anyone to see her, and this trucker was tampering with her plan.

"You okay?" the trucker asked. "Need some help?" The worn soles of his cowboy boots scraped along the gravel along the shoulder.

Annabelle struggled to get the wheel lined up with the tire. "Thanks, I got it. Just a flat."

The driver came closer. "Sure?" he asked. He looked closely at Annabelle, evaluating her and the tire.

"Thank you," Annabelle said, dropping two of the lug nuts. His gaze unnerved her, and she let her long hair fall across her face. She'd be leaving soon. The last thing she needed was someone who had seen her in this area.

She heard the trucker chuckle behind her. "I'm sure you can handle this, but I used to change tires for a living. You're looking at an ex-mechanic."

Annabelle looked up at the man for the first time. She felt his kindness and appreciated the distance he kept from her, giving her space. "Okay," she finally said, surprising herself. "Your help would be great."

Annabelle backed away from the car. She turned her back to the traffic speeding past as he took her place beside the wheel.

"Ah, I see the problem," he said, pulling on the straggly edges of his gray beard. "Your wheel is bent, and it's causing the tire to wobble. I don't think this spare will last you more than fifty miles or so. It'll blow just like the tire."

She watched as he secured it and screwed in the first lug nut. He advised her on what to do to get the wheel fixed and what kind of tire to buy. "It'll cost you, but worth it in the long run. You won't have these breakdowns anymore."

As he screwed the rest of the lug nuts in place, he asked, "Where are you headed?"

Annabelle's stomach tightened at the question, but she told him, mostly because she was taken off guard by his directness and hadn't thought of another town fast enough.

"Akron's a great town," he said, "and not too much farther. You'll be fine to get there." He spun the sad little wheel to be sure it was secure and stood to release the jack. The trucker looked at her again, really seeing her. "Everything okay? Can I help you get to Akron?"

"No," Annabelle said too fast. "Thank you, I'm fine." She took the wrench and small jack from him and tossed them in her passenger seat. "I appreciate all your help, but I'll be on my way."

"Okay, then. You be safe out here, young lady."

The trucker walked back to his rig. Annabelle knew he'd turned around to watch as she climbed into her car. She just wanted to get back on the road and away from his prying eyes. She watched through her rearview mirror as he opened his cab door and climbed in. When Annabelle sped off, he gave her a quick beep of his horn.

Annabelle pushed through the double glass doors as a bell jangled above her. The Akron Waffle House bustled with the late dinner crowd. The smell of fresh coffee and waffles engulfed her. Annabelle's stomach growled.

Slow down, Annabelle reminded herself. *Take a deep breath. Or three.*

She tipped her head forward and let a patch of hair fall across her face as she walked past the hostess and into the seating area. She kept her head down as she scanned the booths. The last thing she needed was Pearle to recognize the pinkish-red butterfly on her face. Anxiety made Annabelle's rash ten times worse, and the glean of sweat over her face only highlighted it. She'd spent the last ten minutes furiously reapplying makeup over her cheeks and eyes in the perpetually cloudy rearview mirror under Waffle House's glowing yellow lights.

Pearle sat alone in a back booth reading a newspaper. As Annabelle approached, Pearle looked up at her through a pair of half readers, red and gold speckled, and her face broke into a huge smile.

"Annabelle!" Pearle stood and met her in the aisle.

"I'm so sorry. I had tire trouble," Annabelle gushed as Pearle pulled her into a quick hug. She smelled of fresh-baked bread and clove cigarettes. This woman she'd been imagining for weeks was solid and whole underneath her touch. Annabelle felt her knees give for a moment under the weight of expectation.

"Please, no apologies. Car trouble, you say? I'm just glad you're here and safe." Pearle stepped back from Annabelle, holding her at arm's reach. "As I live and breathe, Annabelle! You are more beautiful than I imagined."

Annabelle blushed so hard, she felt it in her feet. She wanted to curl up in this woman's arms like a child, feel Pearle's warmth and solidness against her, and tell Pearle how hard everything had been these last few months. Annabelle knew this seemingly ageless woman would understand everything. She'd have all the answers.

"You're doing the right thing, Annabelle," Pearle said. "I'll love your baby to the moon and back."

Pearle took Annabelle by the hand, leading her to the booth. Annabelle let her shoulders fall away from her ears. She was here now with Pearle. Everything would be okay.

That's when she saw the second coffee cup alongside a plate streaked with syrup. The bathroom door swung open, and a hulking man in an oversized pea-green coat stopped at their table. His breath came in short heavy blasts, and Annabelle smelled him—a murky lake with a heavy dose of body odor.

"I knew you'd be in the bathroom when she arrived," Pearle said, sliding into the booth.

"Sorry," he mumbled as he clamored into the booth. His large belly pressed against the edge of the table.

Pearle gave a forced smile. "I'm sorry, Annabelle. This is my son, Emmett. He lives with me on the farm and helps tend to the property."

Annabelle greeted Emmett, but he didn't look at her, his dark eyes darting everywhere but her face. His thinning hair hung around his shoulders in clumps. A thick scraggly beard hid most of his face. The shape of his old T-shirt had long been lost, and small holes lined the collar.

"You need to know something about me, Annabelle. I'm a mother that accepts all kinds of children at any age."

Annabelle smiled, though she wasn't exactly sure what that meant. She accepted a hot cup of coffee from the server.

"I had Emmett when I was sixteen," Pearle said. "My parents hated me for it, but they eventually accepted me back into their lives. Emmett's my most beautiful mistake." She leaned over and kissed Emmett's full cheek. "I know what it's like to be in your position, Annabelle. It's really scary, but you are brave."

Tears filled Annabelle's eyes as she wrapped her hands around the warm mug. Just as she suspected, this woman understood. For the first time in a long time, Annabelle slowly let down her guard. She noticed the way Pearle's left eyelid drooped when she laughed. Just like Gran's. But there was something more—Annabelle couldn't quite put her finger on it. Now that she saw Pearle in person, she had the distinct feeling she'd seen her before.

"Have we met?" Annabelle asked.

Pearle shook her head. "I can't imagine where, darling. Trust me, I'd remember a gorgeous face like yours. Please eat," Pearle encouraged her.

Annabelle ordered a waffle when Emmett ordered a second plate of them.

"I always wanted a houseful of children but couldn't have any more of my own," Pearle said. She wore a thick red and black checked flannel, her shirt open at the collar to show a small golden cross necklace. "I've adopted two other children who are grown and out in the world. Our nest is empty now," Pearle said, looking at Emmett. "It's time for another little one."

Annabelle was curious about the farm. "Do you have cattle? Goats? Horses?"

"Not anymore," Pearle said. "It used to be a working dairy farm, but we sold off the cattle. We have over fifty acres of land. We're truly in the middle of nowhere."

"I bet it feels good to be away from everything. From everyone."

"Absolutely," Pearle said. "We used to have more land until my great-grandfather sold off a large chunk when he fell on hard times. We share a property border with Charles Mill Lake Park, so it feels even more isolated." Pearle winked at Annabelle. "It takes a lot to keep a place like ours running. We'll be glad to have you around."

Annabelle ate her food and listened as Pearle explained how nature would be the best mother to Annabelle during her pregnancy. She and Emmett had recently redone the space where Annabelle would be staying. "Updates to die for," Pearle added.

Annabelle grinned, but the truth was she'd be happy anywhere with a warm bed, good food, and a safe place to hide out for her pregnancy.

Pearle set her coffee cup down. "Now, about that car of yours. Tell me what happened."

As Annabelle filled them in on the constant struggles with her car, Pearle turned to Emmett. "Alternator, possibly?"

He shrugged and continued to chew his waffle. "Or starter."

"It runs," Annabelle said. "But there's a tire issue now."

"Honey." Pearle pulled her handbag from the seat and opened her wallet. "Let me give you a number. One of my best friends, and he's a whiz with any kind of motor. He's not far from you, so don't worry about that."

Pearle scribbled a name and number on the back of an old receipt. She pushed it and a fifty-dollar bill across the table to Annabelle. "This will get you home. Don't worry—I'll cover the cost of the repairs."

"Thank you," Annabelle said.

She hadn't expected money or the promise of car repair. She certainly hadn't expected Emmett. She didn't really know what she'd been expecting. But the feeling she got around Pearle, that energy of *I can take care of everything*, flooded Annabelle. Her breath caught inside her throat. She recognized that energy. It was her grandmother's. For the first time in a long time, Annabelle didn't have the slightest doubt. She'd chosen the perfect person to mother her baby.

Annabelle drifted in and out of thin sleep. A sheen of oily sweat covered her skin. Her scalp itched with the filth of the past weeks and the stink of blood. Her ankle had swollen tight against the metal clamp, and she wondered if she'd broken it. She'd charged against the container's opening at least three times, only to have the ankle chain yank her back to the floor. The metal bit into her skin. She tried to ignore the throbbing bloated pressure of the bruised and torn skin.

After hours of screaming, Annabelle had a raging sore throat to show for it and the metallic taste of blood. When she finally collapsed to the floor, Tillie was beside her.

She woke again with the wet scratch of Tillie's tongue against her arm. Annabelle looked up at the container's ceiling and tried hard not to move in the dark. Her body hurt too much.

And then she remembered. She *had* seen Pearle before.

They'd crossed paths outside the free clinic. Pearle had her hair hidden beneath a baseball cap that day. She'd been standing with her back pressed against the side of the building, handing out flyers. Annabelle steered away from her, but there was a moment when their eyes caught. Pearle's steel-blue eyes didn't look *at* her that day, but *through* her.

On Annabelle's second visit to the clinic, a random flier blew against her. She held it out, remembering the woman who had passed them out before. The symbol for the women's movement anchored all four corners of the flier.

Don't kill your baby! it screamed in handwritten letters. *Adopting healthy newborns. Make $.*

Later, when Annabelle left the building, the woman was a block away, wrapped inside a black leather coat. She was huddled around two girls. Annabelle stopped a moment and watched. The girls were small-framed with long hair down their backs. One might have had glasses. The other wore a tattered jean jacket with a #MeToo patch. Girls so ordinary, they could have been her.

CHAPTER TWENTY-ONE

The Brecksville Reserve felt to Theo like stepping into a picture-postcard of nature and serenity. Weston offered to take her to the park while they shared an early dinner, and Theo was anxious to see it before she left town. It was the perfect time to go—the setting sun glistened on the creek. Theo watched two teens grasping for minnows and crawdads, their silhouettes blacked out against the sun. She sat with Weston at a picnic table to review their notes. The field behind their table burst with spring wildflowers and reminded Theo this was one of her favorite times of the year, the edge of summer.

"Well," Weston said, "this is it. The place where Annabelle disappeared. From what we've gathered, this is where she met Daniel before they headed out on a trail."

"I can see why. It's really beautiful here," Theo told him.

"You don't expect it, do you? All this nature tucked away so close to Cleveland proper."

The size of the park helped to keep visitors spread out, and Theo guessed the two teens met at low-traffic hours to keep their relationship private. Theo wondered which of them insisted they be kept a secret and how much that person was willing to do to keep it that way.

She and Weston had had a productive day, and she was exhausted. She hadn't walked or moved so much in one day since the shooting. While her hip and leg ached, it was a good ache, one that felt well-deserved.

They'd run into a few roadblocks that afternoon. They'd tracked down the high school teacher who'd led the reading club. Cadi Melton told them that the administration had strongly encouraged her to end the group meetings. "It was the football team's fault. Those kids were trying to be so…What do they call it now? *Woke*. But there were too many players and cheerleaders missing practice for our meetings. The games suffered, and Booster Parents were angry. And that was the end of it."

While Cadi couldn't add anything to what Theo and Weston already knew, she promised to speak to each of the participants individually for more information.

Ruby, Annabelle's cousin, was nowhere to be found. They'd checked in with her last known residence and at a friend's where they heard Ruby was crashing on the couch. Nothing. Theo left Ruby a note, but she doubted the young woman would call. Ruby's record didn't bode well for trusting the police.

As they navigated their way through Annabelle's possible contacts in Brecksville, they stopped at Daniel Holtzman's residence. He'd been quiet since the police last spoke to him. Weston had followed up with him, but his mother immediately referred the detective to his lawyer.

Weston told Theo he found the entire exchange odd since it was his first contact with Daniel. "He was wound up, you know? Anxious and angry."

Theo understood that anger. She thought about Henry Nerra and the way he'd reacted at Castleton Motors. "Daniel knows something. I just can't figure out why he's so determined to keep her secret if Annabelle didn't mean anything to him."

Daniel lived in a large home with a towering front door made of glass. When no one answered two rounds of the exquisite chimes, Theo slipped her card into the door with a note. *Tell us what you know, Daniel. Help us find Annabelle.*

Weston opened the case file and pushed three photos across the picnic table to Theo. "I know you've seen these, but I feel like there's something we're missing. I can't put my finger on it."

She spread them out before her, side by side. The photos highlighted the location where Annabelle's partial bloody handprint and phone were found. She'd pored over them ever since Bishop told her about Annabelle's case. She shared Weston's frustration—there was something there, something more than just a handprint that connected these two cases.

"Why the handprints in their own blood?" Weston asked. "It has to mean something."

Theo agreed. "It's one of two things. The kidnapper cut them and used the prints to show his power over the girls. Or they cut themselves to show everyone they made the choice to leave on their own. My bet is on the latter."

Weston nodded. "It's like we have all these separate pieces that are important, but they aren't connecting."

Theo drank from her water bottle and then said, "But *someone* lured them out of their lives. Someone else has a plan for them."

"Sam Polanski, possibly," Weston said. "He's significant."

"He could be our lynchpin. Other than the handprint and the missing teens, he's the only other connection."

Theo had spoken to Polanski's latest parole officer while she'd been working on Grace's case. Polanski had served time in the Montgomery County Jail as well as one of the state prisons with Nerra. The PO didn't have much to report on Polanski. He kept his nose clean and served his time.

Theo's phone vibrated against her hip with a Cleveland area number she didn't recognize.

"Madsen."

"Hello," a woman said, apprehensively. "You don't know me, but I just got your message. Daniel Holtzman is my son."

The caller had Theo's full attention. "Thank you for calling. Is everything okay?"

"It's Daniel," she said, her voice catching with her tears. "He's gone."

❖

Priscilla Holtzman, Daniel's mother, was reed thin and red-faced from crying. She crossed her arms over her chest as if she was trying to hold herself together. She looked like a different woman than the confident version of herself on the interview recordings with her son. "My husband travels a lot," she said. "He's in Chicago right now but agreed it was time to call you."

"How long has Daniel been gone?" Weston asked.

"Two days. I didn't want to report it because I thought he ran away. I figured he'd return any minute. Then I got your card."

Priscilla sat across from Theo and Weston on a white leather couch. Silent tears ran down her cheeks. "Nothing's missing," she said, "except for his phone, wallet, and Jeep."

"I'm glad you called," Theo said. She didn't say that Daniel's disappearance reminded her a lot of Grace's and Annabelle's. In its attempt to look normal, everything appeared staged to Theo. Her first thought was Daniel and Annabelle had agreed to leave a few weeks apart and meet up somewhere. But there was something about Daniel's disappearance that was different from Annabelle's. It felt sudden, unplanned. And they hadn't found a bloody handprint.

"Daniel is still seventeen. Will you put an Amber Alert out for him?"

"We don't have enough evidence he's in imminent danger for the alert," Weston explained. "We've already reported him in the LEADS database. The whole country has access to the missing teen report. We'll also put out a BOLO for his Jeep. He's had the time to put some miles between us, but we'll do all we can to find him."

While Priscilla found the Jeep information for Weston, she pointed Theo down a hallway to Daniel's bedroom. His bed was expertly made with matching throw pillows. A laptop sat open on his desk. Theo tried to access files, but it was password protected.

Priscilla stood in the doorway. "Detective Weston is calling in the information," she told Theo. "I'm sorry I didn't contact you sooner."

"We'll do our best. Has he asked for more money than usual lately? Or asked for more chores for cash?"

Daniel's mother shook her head.

"Does he have a bank account or a debit card? How does he access cash?"

"The account has been empty all school year. Daniel hasn't worked because of the football team's time constraints. If he has money, it's because I gave it to him."

Theo made a note. Daniel had to have access to cash, even if it was only enough for a full tank of gas and some food.

"It's just the two of us here during the week. I've tried to get him to talk about Annabelle." Priscilla wiped away a tear. "A large part of me thinks he's gone off to try to find her."

"Why would he do that?" Theo asked.

Priscilla shrugged. "I know my son. He thinks if he can find Annabelle and bring her home, then everyone will believe he had nothing to do with it."

"Did he? Have something to do with it?"

"His friends all think so. They've turned on him."

"What do you mean?"

"He didn't exactly tell me that, but I know. The football players and the cheer team always hung out here on the weekends and after school. Since Annabelle's been gone, there's no one here but Daniel, and he hides in his room like he's done something wrong."

"Do you think he has done something wrong?" Weston asked, joining them.

"I know my son," Priscilla said again.

"But...?" Theo said when the woman hesitated.

She sighed. "These last forty-eight hours...I'm not so sure."

Daniel and Annabelle had gone to school together for years. Priscilla had even met Annabelle's mother a few times at school functions. She'd never heard Daniel talk about Annabelle or known her to be in his group of friends.

"All of this came out of nowhere," she told Theo. "I thought he was dating Stacy Adams. She was over here every weekend and after every game."

Theo scribbled down the name *Stacy Adams*.

"Since you pay the phone bill, you technically own Daniel's phone. With your permission, we can track it. We'll be able to tell if he's had any communication with Annabelle since she left." Weston explained Priscilla needed to come to the station to make a formal report so the BOLO could be issued.

Priscilla took in a shaky breath. "It all feels so real now," she said, rubbing her arms as if she was cold. "It feels…so certain. Where is my boy?"

"Can I call someone for you? Your husband? A family member?"

"It's okay," Priscilla shook her head. "I'm okay."

Gone.

The word Priscilla had used echoed in Theo's mind as she waved good-bye to Weston and made her way out to her car.

Gone.

Theo rolled onto the interstate, headed toward Dayton, and mulled over the day's findings. It fascinated her that these teens could simply step out of their lives and vanish without leaving a trail behind. Two of them left with their own vehicles, and that should have made the process of finding them much easier. It was hard enough for an adult to vanish without leaving clues, particularly with a vehicle, but teens? It's didn't seem possible unless the teens had help. A lot of help.

Chapter Twenty-Two

Annabelle pulled into the Cleveland auto repair shop, maneuvering her Hyundai through the parking lot trying to avoid the potholes. Annabelle wasn't so sure about this place. There were other businesses closer to her home and ones she'd used before. But Pearle had been adamant. She'd pay for the car's repairs only if Annabelle brought it to Castleton Motors. Since Annabelle had already spent all the money from The Handler, she needed this.

The main door of Castleton Motors welcomed customers with a sign that explained the small business was under renovation.

"Please excuse our mess!" The receptionist had a smile plastered across her face. "I'm Brittany. I heard you'd be in." She watched Annabelle sign in. "Have a seat. Sam will be right with you."

Annabelle asked for the Wi-Fi code and sat down. She was already thumb to screen and scrolling through social media. A few minutes later, she felt eyes on her and looked up. The receptionist had been watching her the whole time. A chill shivered up her spine.

A side door opened. "You Annabelle?" an older man called out to her, his long dark hair pulled into a ponytail.

"Pearle sent me?" Annabelle hadn't meant for it to come out like a question.

"Right." He nodded, waving her to him. "Walk with me out to the car so I can see what's going on."

Sam held the door wide for her. As she passed, she felt his eyes looking her up and down until finally settling on her belly.

He *knew*. Annabelle looked around the garage full of mechanics. Were they all part of the New Nation?

Annabelle opened her car door to pop the hood. "Before you do anything, I need to be sure Pearle is paying."

Sam grinned. Annabelle could see the white gum parked along his lower teeth. "Relax, honey." His voice made Annabelle wish she could shower. "Pearle's footing the bill, so let's get to it."

She showed him the tire and started the car so he could hear the engine sounds. Then Annabelle grabbed her backpack and handed Sam the keys.

"Hold on there, speedy. That bent rim could mean alignment problems." Sam popped his gum. "This will take over an hour. You have some time to wait?"

"I've got my homework."

Annabelle found the waiting area, a small room off to the side of the garage. A tall wall of windows looked out over the auto bay, and Annabelle sat beside it. She watched as Sam drove her gray Hyundai onto an open lift.

The Hyundai wasn't the car she'd wanted. All the popular kids drove Jeeps to school, and Annabelle's jealousy grew each time a new one appeared in the school parking lot. Daniel's was bright yellow, the color of summer sunshine. Annabelle could see it coming a mile away, and she wanted her own cherry-red one with oversized tires to match his.

Pearle promised Annabelle the Jeep. After the baby was born, Pearle swore Annabelle would have a new ride to wheel off into her new life. Annabelle had already decided she would get a hula dancer for the dashboard and a sound system that could stream any music to match her every mood. She liked to think about that hula girl on the dash, her hips swaying with each bump of the road, and loud songs spilling from the speakers. She wouldn't have a care in the world.

Her mother had given her the Hyundai the day after she received her driver's license. She arrived home from school, and a gray four-door she didn't recognize was in the driveway next to her mother's truck. Annabelle was surprised. She hadn't seen her mother in days.

"Hey there." Her mom sat on the front stoop, blowing a stream of smoke out of her nostrils. "How was school today?"

Annabelle shrugged. "Who's here?" She thumbed over to the car.

"Just us." Her mom tossed the butt of her cigarette into the nearby bush. "I figured you needed a car to drive."

Annabelle froze in her tracks. She waited for her mom to laugh. When she didn't, Annabelle turned to look at the car again, this time with a whole other view of what that car could be.

"It's mine?"

Rose nodded, walking toward her. She dangled the keys in front of her before dropping them into Annabelle's hand. "All yours."

Annabelle squealed and jumped to hug her mother. She knew her mom could hardly make the monthly bills. They wouldn't have been able to stay in Brecksville if it wasn't for her overtime shifts at the restaurant. Yet there was this car—just for Annabelle. A gift that made her heart feel as though it could burst. Annabelle climbed in behind the wheel.

"It's nothing special," her mom said, watching her in her new car. "It runs like a tank, and that's all that matters."

"Get in," Annabelle called out.

Soon the engine hummed underneath them, and the road rolled below them. She opened the windows to let the spring wind blow though their hair. Her mom reached for the radio and turned the dial until she found a Tom Petty song. They sang at the top of their lungs as Annabelle drove through the winding roads of Brecksville toward downtown Cleveland. She had to share her new treasure with Ruby. Annabelle thought she knew where her cousin was staying, and she wanted Ruby to be a part of the family celebration.

The memory brought tears to Annabelle's eyes. It had been one of those rare instances when everything was different. Her mother surprised her with something completely unexpected, and it felt like the deepest kind of love she'd ever known. But soon—always—that love vanished. Her mom went back to work, and Annabelle went back to being all alone.

Annabelle's phone vibrated with an incoming message from Ruby.

How was new baby mama?

Annabelle emojied back with a thumbs-up and a red heart. *She paid to fix my car.*

Told u. They'll do anything for healthy white baby. Emoji laughing with tears.

Annabelle took a quick photo of her car on the lift and Sam working on it. *Who's this guy?*

The dots told Annabelle that Ruby was examining the image. *???*

He knows I'm pregnant. Part of Nation thing?

A few seconds passed. Annabelle wasn't sure if her cousin would tell her anything.

Then, *Paranoid much? He don't know shit.*

Annabelle noticed her cousin didn't answer the question.

Baby mama give you $?

Some. She worked it out with the garage.

Gurl!!!! Demand cash next time.

Annabelle sighed. It was just like Ruby to look for an angle, a way to take more and more. Annabelle never wanted to be like that, always unhappy with what she had.

Ruby added, *Most breeders demand cash.*

Breeders?

Smiley emoji with tears. *What they call pregnant women.*

Annabelle rolled her eyes. Not very original. *They?*

The organization. The Handler.

Annabelle groaned. Eyeroll emoji.

Ruby sent back an emoji of a woman shrugging.

What is the New Nation anyway?

Dots from Ruby again.

How many people are in on this thing?

Ruby answered, *I only know what I need to. Don't ask questions.* Dancing dots.

After a minute or so, Ruby typed again, *Take what they give you and run. K?*

Annabelle looked up from the phone and watched Sam through the glass. Ruby had never used the word *run* when speaking of Annabelle's new life.

Don't ask questions A. Better that way.

Annabelle sent back a thumbs-up emoji and closed the text. Until that moment, she'd felt safe with the plan and this group her cousin had brought her into. She believed her cousin would protect her. Since meeting Pearle, Annabelle had so many questions. Her mind ran a thousand miles per minute. There was no settling it down, no time when curiosity about the New Nation didn't plague her.

A *breeder*.

She questioned once again whether she was doing the right thing. Did she really want to sell her baby to a stranger? No matter how kindhearted she might be?

Pearle had been so genuine. They'd both felt the connection during their meeting at Waffle House. Later, in a brief phone conversation on the burner, Pearle told Annabelle more about her life with Emmett.

"I was so young when I had Emmett," Pearle said. "He was my everything. Still is. The doctors told me he was delayed. They said he might have speech problems. But I always knew he wouldn't. He couldn't! Not a boy of mine. I promised him we'd work through it together, and we did."

Annabelle held the burner against her ear, listening to the deep calm of Pearle's voice.

"I understand the fear," Pearle told Annabelle. "I understand, and I can help you."

Sam tapped on the window, pulling Annabelle out of her memory. He motioned for her to meet him at the bay door. Her car had already been moved to the open garage.

The heavy steel door swung open. "You're all set," Sam told her. "I changed the oil for you. It was running low."

"Thank you."

Sam held out the keys, and when Annabelle took them, Sam wrapped his hand tight around hers. "You've made the right decision," he told her. "Pearle will take care of you. We all will."

Annabelle pulled her hand away. She fisted her keys. The smell of oil and chemicals and steel bit at her nostrils. Annabelle hurried to her car with a protective hand spread over her growing belly.

CHAPTER TWENTY-THREE

Theo killed the engine in her driveway and leaned her head against the seat rest. It had been a long day, and her leg ached something fierce. She rubbed the knot in her hip, digging fingertips into the tender flesh. She was certain she'd be feeling the trip to Brecksville for at least a few days.

Weston had called two hours after she left Brecksville. His team had been through Daniel's phone records. Most of the numbers were accounted for, but there were four calls coming from an unknown number, a burner. Weston had someone working on it, but burners were notoriously hard to track. Neither of them put much stock in that lead going very far.

"On the day Daniel went missing," Weston had said, "the very last call was made from Brecksville to a small town along Interstate 71 called Redhaw."

"Redhaw?" Theo had never heard of it.

"Looks like he was headed toward the Mansfield area. The call is only three minutes and fifteen seconds. Then the phone goes black."

The burner was most likely destroyed.

Bree had left the porch lights on. She rarely worked Saturdays since she'd become pregnant and spent them curled up with her rom-com books and films. Theo usually loved Saturday nights with Bree. Tonight was a different story. Not only did Theo arrive later than expected, after ten p.m., but she'd spent the day avoiding Bree's texts. It felt like Bree was checking up on her as if she was a child.

Once Theo knew Bree's test had gone well, she didn't see the need for more communication until she got home.

Theo leaned more heavily on her cane than usual as she opened the front door. She found Bree in the TV room snuggled under a blanket. She was relaxing on the couch in her usual Saturday night gear, comfy pajamas and old leather slippers.

"It's warm in here, hon. You okay?" Theo cracked open a window.

It was always warm whenever Bree was in the house. It didn't matter the room's temperature—pregnancy hormones left her chilly and goose-pimply, an oddity that her obstetrician liked to point out at their appointments. "Most of the women I see are sweating buckets at this stage of pregnancy," he'd told them. "Your chills are one for the books."

Bree paused the movie. When she looked up, Theo saw the red around her eyes and recognized the sniffles. "I was worried you weren't coming home."

"Come on, Bree." Theo leaned in and kissed her. "It's only a little after ten. My whereabouts are known."

"Ha ha." Bree smiled despite her irritation.

Theo collapsed on the couch beside her. A frozen scene from *Imagine Me & You* filled the screen. "It's the movie, huh?"

Bree pulled another tissue from the box on the corner table. "Every time."

It had been almost two years since their first real date. Bree invited Theo over for a home-cooked meal and a movie. A rom-com, of course.

"From the looks of your kitchen, you don't cook much," Bree had told Theo one morning when they emerged from Theo's bedroom. They were not technically together at that point, but they couldn't keep their hands off one another.

That description of Theo's kitchen was accurate. It might have been possible to find a jar of peanut butter and some cups of yogurt in the fridge. If you were lucky, some granola bars or a bag of chips in the cupboard. Theo ate out most days, grabbing something on her way to and from work.

On that first real date, Bree had made a slow-cooked beef stew, and the scent struck Theo the minute she stepped inside the house. Homemade biscuits baked in the oven while Bree showed Theo her home. When the kitchen timers finally went off, they feasted. Once their bellies were filled with good wine and even better food, Bree popped in the film.

"I'm a sucker for romance," she'd said, grabbing the box of tissues from the kitchen.

"You cry at romance? I thought these were supposed to be funny. Cute." She air-quoted *cute*.

Bree shrugged. "Of course, but I cry every time. I love it when people get what they've always wanted in the end."

"But how do you know the way it really ends? The movie always cuts off at the happiest moment."

"Such a realist," Bree said. "Just let me have this one thing, okay?"

So two hours later, as the tears spilled down Bree's cheeks, Theo held her close.

"The thing that gets me about all these romantic movies is in real life there are no easy answers," Bree said. "Nice people always get hurt, you know?"

"Is that some kind of omen for our relationship?"

Bree smiled. "Relationship. That word sounds good on us, don't you think?"

Theo agreed. It definitely did.

Now, a couple years after those initial dates, Bree turned to Theo. "Tell me about your day."

"Long, but I'm glad I went."

"Are the cases connected?"

"I believe so. Too many similarities. I just need to convince Bull Michaels of that."

Bree dropped the remote on the table beside her. "Theo, tell me what's going on."

Theo let her head fall back against the couch. "It's a politics thing, I guess. Bull isn't willing to work with Brecksville on this one because, like us, they have no hard evidence anything has happened to their girl. Bull told Bishop to end it after this initial consult."

"But you won't let it go." Bree tossed the blanket off her legs and stood. "How long are you going to chase this, Theo? What about our new family? I needed you there today."

"We're close, Bree. I can feel it."

Bree knew all about Theo's spidey sense. "You weren't there. You didn't care enough to call. You didn't even ask how things went when you came home. I'm terrified that you'll do nothing but work once the baby is here. Please don't be the absent parent, Theo." She stood up and grabbed her empty tea mug and potato chip bag. "I swear, I cannot raise this kid alone."

"I'm always thinking about us. That's not fair, Bree."

"Isn't it?" Bree headed for the kitchen.

Theo remained on the couch while Bree banged the cabinet doors and slammed her mug into the dishwasher.

"Bree!"

Theo listened to Bree's slippered feet moving down the hall, and a wave of exhaustion rolled over her.

Theo had meant it with her whole heart. She *was* always thinking about Bree and the baby. But it was hard for her to grasp that this child would be someone she'd help raise and bring up in this world. What kind of world was this for children, anyway?

Theo saw the worst parts of human nature and the ways an innocent being could be eaten whole. It scared her to think of the responsibility a child would bring to her life and the worry that, even at her best, she might not be able to protect them. She'd told Bree how worried she was only a few weeks after the pregnancy had been confirmed, and Bree hushed her.

"You aren't doing this alone. *We* aren't doing this alone. It's a village, remember? We have family and friends and teachers and doctors and neighbors who will help us. Trust in that."

One of Theo's greatest fears was that one of their lifelines would go rogue, the devil they didn't see coming until the damage had been done.

Theo found the envelope Cody left with her name scrawled across it. When she ripped the end open, two photos spilled out. One featured Sam Polanski behind the wheel of an old truck in a local grocery parking lot. The black-and-white photo showed his features clearly: new growth of beard stubble, longer hair pulled back in a greasy ponytail at the nape of his neck. The second photo was of Polanski sitting in that same truck, parked along the edge of a sidewalk. As Theo looked at the photo, she realized she recognized the location. The single paved walkway, the grassy fields along both sides. In the distance, Theo could see the large gray base of the bell tower. She flipped the photo over and found the date. Two days before, near the site of Grace Summers's disappearance.

Theo checked the envelope and found a small note, scrawled in Cody's messy script. *Polanski's in Dayton. Planning something or revisiting the scene of the crime?*

CHAPTER TWENTY-FOUR

The thick tree line finally broke at a sliver of a dirt road. Annabelle missed it twice and had to backtrack along the two-lane state route, checking and rechecking her paper printout of directions. She'd never followed directions this way before, but she didn't have her phone for navigation.

Pearle had said their property backed against a large reservoir, Charles Mill Lake. Annabelle didn't know a reservoir could be so large until she crossed over its bridge and landed in a dense forest. Pearle had warned her it would look as though she was driving into the middle of nowhere, but Annabelle hadn't exactly expected this level of nowhere.

Annabelle had stopped at a large gas station when she exited the highway outside of Mansfield. She wanted to be sure of her directions, and she needed some chocolate. She grabbed a candy bar, a pack of gum, and a new toothbrush. She'd been worried about leaving her own toothbrush behind. With her fresh new smile after two years of braces, she wasn't willing to chance whether Pearle would have a toothbrush available.

"Do you know this address?" Annabelle asked as the clerk bagged up her things. Her nametag said *Vera*.

"You're headed to the thick of the woods," Vera said. "I grew up around the Charles."

"The Charles?"

"Yeah. It's what we call the reservoir around here. You need to get across the bridge to find this property."

Annabelle scribbled some directions on her receipt, but she was distracted. The wall of burner phones and batteries behind Vera made her ache for the phone she'd left behind. She heard Pearle's directions clearly in her mind: *Leave anything electronic. I have new things for you, a phone and laptop for your new life.*

"I'll take a phone," Annabelle said, surprising herself. She wasn't one to break the rules, and just the thought of it caused a sudden shallow breath. "Do I need to sign up for a network if I prepay minutes?"

"No, but the second the minutes run out, you're done." Vera reached back and pulled one of the plastic packs off the shelf hanger. "We sell a ton of these, and folks just toss 'em when the minutes are gone. How many you want? I can load you up right here."

Annabelle wanted to buy five hundred minutes, but she knew that was tempting fate and her wallet. This would only be used for emergencies. Most likely she'd never need it, and Annabelle promised herself she'd toss the thing as soon as her new life began.

"Thirty," Annabelle said and watched the woman cut open the plastic wrapping with industrial strength scissors. Annabelle fidgeted as the woman loaded the minutes, anxious about where she could hide the phone.

"This is a dumb question," Annabelle said, "but can you trace one of these phones? I always heard you can't."

"Not dumb at all," Vera said. "I use these all the time. I don't want the NSA tracking me or reading my messages."

"They do that?"

"Hell yeah!" She leaned over the counter to show Annabelle the back of the phone. "These phones are hard to trace, but it happens. Here's the deal. You have to use the phone for them to trace it. That's why everyone dumps them once the minutes are used up." She looked up at Annabelle and dropped her voice. "I've been playing with this model. There's a wire in the mix that seems to block that signaling for triangulation if you cut it, or at least it slows it down. Want me to snip it for you?"

"Does it stop tracking?"

"I think so. Nobody's showed up at my house yet."

Annabelle considered Vera. She had no idea what triangulation was, but it sounded like something she didn't want. What did she have to lose?

"As long as the phone still works, go for it."

Near the base of the Hyundai's back seat, the cloth had come away from the plastic molding. Annabelle slipped her fist inside to hide the phone behind a pile of torn seat foam. Then, just to be safe, she also tucked inside the seat the sandwich baggie with the remainder of her prescription pills.

Pearle had been very clear. Along with no electronics on her property, she insisted on no medications, including vitamins and supplements. Pearle believed that all medicine must come from the earth, not some white-coated laboratory. Annabelle hoped that once Pearle understood the truth about her condition, she'd want Annabelle to have her pills. And if Pearle never understood, Annabelle would have her small hidden stash of meds in her car.

Annabelle tucked the fabric into the base of the seat as best she could. Then she sat in the driver's seat, looking through the rearview mirror to see if she could detect the break in the fabric. She ate the candy bar. The chocolate had already begun to melt over her fingertips. She chewed fast, as if Pearle might see her already breaking a rule by eating sugar and chocolate.

Annabelle told herself the burner had been a smart purchase. Proactive and safety-conscious. After all, no one knew where she was but Ruby and The Handler. As she pulled away from the store's lot, Annabelle wished for Ruby by her side. She truly was on her own now, and she wasn't sure she really wanted to be.

The cashier had given Annabelle a brief sketch of where to go, and Pearle had advised Annabelle to look for two heart-shaped balloons tied to a mailbox. When Annabelle finally saw the red amidst the variant dark greens of the pine, she couldn't believe it was really a road. Technically, it wasn't anything more than a long winding driveway.

Annabelle's Hyundai bounced over the gutted areas of the dirt path that wound like a ribbon through the forest. Annabelle was convinced she'd taken a wrong turn until the car drove over the lip of a ridge. The bark-patched roof sat against the forest of trees.

Finally, the full house came into view, white and weathered, sprawling and flat. It looked to Annabelle as if small additions had been made over the years to the original house. The stone walkway led to a few steps carved from larger rocks and ultimately to a navy-blue front door with a multicolored welcome mat.

Annabelle took a deep breath. She was only about ninety minutes from home, yet it felt like a different country. Brecksville's nature was planned. Every trail was carved out and made safe for families. The lakes had lifeguards on duty during swim times and play areas were combed for poison ivy and any animals that might not take kindly to kids. But here, the land around Annabelle felt wild. Unruly. Overgrown and out of control. There were no lifeguards, no planned family fun in the woods, or safety measures carefully put into place. There were no floodlights in the tall trees or safety alert boxes that automatically contacted the police. Everything about the area held the strong twinge of danger.

The front screen door swung open, and out stepped Pearle Oliver. A red bandana pulled stone-white hair away from her face. She waved a long thin arm over her head. "Welcome home, Annabelle! Supper's not more than an hour away." A black and white collie circled Pearle's legs. "Tillie's been waiting all week for your arrival. She can't wait to have another female in the house."

The dog barked her agreement.

Pearle hugged Annabelle tight and held on. Over Pearle's shoulder, she caught sight of the large figure looming inside the screen door. Emmett's face emerged, his eyes hooded with shadow. He watched as his mother welcomed Annabelle before he slipped back into the darkness of the house.

CHAPTER TWENTY-FIVE

Early mornings in Dayton brought a steady stream of folks into Partial to Pie Bakery. Theo couldn't get enough of their strawberry rhubarb and found herself there at least once a week. She collected her pie and steaming coffee. Cody sat huddled at a corner table with a large brownie.

Cody took a bite. "Best brownies ever."

"Which is why the place is called Partial to Pie."

Cody chuckled. "Whatever. They're fantastic."

Theo set her phone on the table. She forked pie in her mouth with one hand and scrolled through the photos Cody had recently sent her. Mary Summers had verified for Theo that morning that Sam Polanski was back in Dayton and staying with his mother. According to Mary, he'd been almost everywhere in the Dayton area since he arrived but hadn't made time to see her.

"It's over," Mary had told Theo. "I never want to see him again."

There was enough hesitation in her voice that Theo didn't believe her. If Sam showed up on her doorstep, Mary would welcome him in as if nothing had happened between them.

Theo took another bite. She wanted to know what Polanski was up to. He knew something about the missing girls, and his actions would be a better source of information than any of the lies he would probably tell them during questioning.

"Let's keep up the tail," she said. "We'll see where he leads us."

"I'll never understand how a guy like Polanski convinces women to trust him," Cody said. "I mean, if anyone should be on high alert, it's a single mom of a teen daughter."

"Oh, he's convincing. Mary Jackson said this was the first relationship she'd had in years." Theo leaned back in her seat. She gauged the length of the line for pie and considered purchasing another slice. "Polanski plays the role of the reliable guy, the one you can lean on for everything. He takes care of the everyday things like paying bills on time and grocery shopping. For a single mom who works a lot of overtime, this is a dream."

"Mr. Nice Guy who steals your kids."

An employee called out that they'd sold the last slice of quiche.

Theo watched two people leave the line. She knew Cody had been watching Woodland Cemetery and Carillon Park for possible Polanski sightings. "How long have you been watching the bell tower?"

Cody shrugged and wiped his mouth with a napkin. "On and off. I've been doing a lot of drive-bys. I haven't mentioned it because there hasn't been anything new until the other night."

A trio of teenage girls sat down in a booth near them. They looked as if they'd just come from the swimming pool with their hair in air-dried clumps from the sun and chlorine. Their thin sleeveless arms reached for the shared quiche in the middle of the table. They giggled with freckles spread across their noses and the day's sun still red on their shoulders. Theo wondered if they knew Grace. She wondered if her story scared them at all.

"Thanks for keeping an eye out, Cody. I'll talk to the chief about adding a detail to the park at night. Or at least have officers on duty drive through the area regularly."

For the first time in months, Theo felt like she was working with a partner again. Nothing could compare to the magic she and Bishop had as a team, but Cody held his ground well. The two tossed around possibilities for Polanski, but it felt like they were swinging at the low-hanging fruit. Polanski and Nerra might not have appeared to be worth much in the grand scheme of things, but Theo saw them as her way in. Polanski, just like Nerra, was a link to something—or someone—higher in the food chain.

Theo had a similar feeling about Daniel Holtzman. He was also low-hanging fruit. His impulsiveness led him to use his phone to talk to either Annabelle or someone involved with her disappearance. Grace and Annabelle had been schooled by someone on how to evade detection, but Daniel hadn't. Polanski and Nerra didn't have much schooling in evading detection either. If anyone would lead her to Annabelle, it was going to be one of those three men.

Cody pushed his empty plate away from him. "I can't stop asking myself why these girls wanted to leave their lives so much. I mean, that's ultimately what we're saying here. They chose to leave. From the outside, they both appeared to have opportunities a lot of others don't. It's just…why?"

Theo shrugged. "They're sixteen. Everything looks terrible at that age until it gets even worse. It doesn't help that their brains aren't even fully formed."

Cody laughed, reaching for his empty coffee cup. "I guess I got lucky with my half-formed brain. I made it out of my teen years relatively unscathed."

"I heard about you over many beers. You were an angel, Detective. At least in your father's eyes."

Cody blushed as he stood to refill his coffee. Sometimes they both forgot how far back their relationship went. Theo had been there for all of Cody's formative birthday parties with a gift in hand. She'd been there for the high school graduation party and when Cody got his first badge. She watched him pour the coffee and, for the first time, thought about how odd it must be for him, too.

CHAPTER TWENTY-SIX

After a long dreamless sleep, Annabelle awoke to the smell of bacon and hotcakes sizzling on the skillet. She rolled over in the plush sheets, finding a softer spot on the down pillow. She hadn't slept this well in weeks. Pearle's guest bed felt like a cloud, and Annabelle sank into the soft linens. The baby had been pulling at her lower back for the last few days. Those tight muscles had released overnight, and Annabelle felt like she did before the pregnancy.

It was already after ten, and the delicious smells from the kitchen pulled her from the cozy bed. On her way to the shower, Annabelle stopped by the window to look out over the front of the house. Her car wasn't where she'd left it. The Hyundai was nowhere to be seen. She picked up her jeans off the bedroom floor and checked the pockets. Her keys were gone.

A soft knock at the door surprised her. "Annabelle?" Pearle's voice called from the hallway. "There's a fresh change of clothes hanging in the closet for you."

"Pearle? Where's my car?"

Pearle was silent, and then Annabelle heard her weight lean against the closed bedroom door. She was about to call out to her again when Pearle said, "We're all safe, darling, I promise. We'll talk over breakfast."

Annabelle thanked her and listened to Pearle walk away from the door. Then she turned and stepped inside a bathroom to die for. The space was three times larger than the bathroom she shared with her mother, and this one was decorated in colorful tiles and sparkling glass.

Annabelle could have stood underneath the three-headed shower all day, but the scent of breakfast eventually pulled her out. Wrapped in a soft oversized towel, Annabelle found the closet. The carpet under her bare feet was thick, a plushness she'd never really experienced before, as her bare feet sank with each step.

The closet had only one item to choose from, a button-up denim shirtdress. It was large on her small frame, and she tied it off with a colorful belt she found on the floor of the closet. There were no shoes, so Annabelle slipped her own gym shoes back on, cringing as they rubbed against her bare feet. She felt cleaner than she had in months, almost as if she'd been power-washed inside those shower jet streams, and the shoes felt filthy. They were a remnant of the past she desperately wanted to lose.

Annabelle flipped her still-wet hair over her shoulders and offered to help Pearle in the kitchen. She was already lifting the food, and Annabelle took a seat next to Emmett around the large oak table. The old farmhouse was comfortable, and Pearle had spent a lot of time updating her kitchen with the latest appliances and decorating the place with a rustic-chic flare. The wooden floors were real, not the laminated fake sheen Annabelle was used to, and there were places in the walls where the original wood grain filtered through. Everything was bathed in soft sunshine through multiple skylights. The warmth and smell of home-cooked food settled Annabelle into the memories of her grandmother. Certainly, Gran never had a home like this, but it was the *feeling* of the place that was so familiar.

Tillie came to Annabelle's side, her warm head resting on Annabelle's foot. She leaned down and slipped the pooch a bit of bacon under the table.

"Anything yet?" Pearle asked Emmett over her pancakes.

He shook his head.

Annabelle gave Pearle a questioning look.

"Someone reported you missing, honey," Pearle said. There's a BOLO for you and your car."

"BOLO?"

"Be on the lookout. The order has been issued statewide. Don't worry, Annabelle. They can't issue an Amber Alert without proof you're in danger. You're safe here with us."

"Oh." Any other words escaped Annabelle. Her mother had gone to the police. She must have been worried. Annabelle hadn't expected that.

"Emmett hid your car late last night. We can't have it sitting out in the open right now."

"I understand," Annabelle said. She focused on her eggs and bacon. A painful knot developed in her chest at the thought of her mother. She had the sudden urge to hold her own car keys.

"Don't worry. Everything will be over soon," Pearle said, passing her the syrup. "These things tend to die down in a week or so. We just need to stay diligent. The Nation depends on it."

Annabelle nodded.

"I know you haven't had much to do with The Nation yet, Annabelle, but you will in time. You've found yourself the family you've been dying for."

"And The Handler? Is he a part of this, too?"

Pearle and Emmett shared a long look.

"My cousin told me." Annabelle felt the need to explain herself. Why were they staring at her that way?

"Well." Pearle eventually gave Annabelle a big smile. "When you need to know, I'll tell you all about it. Don't worry now, honey. You've got a baby to eat for."

Evening landed gently at the Oliver home. After Annabelle had all the fried chicken and sweet tea she could drink, Pearle announced the surprise of the day was upon them.

"How about we get you settled, Annabelle?"

"Settled? What do you mean?"

Emmett came down the stairs with Annabelle's backpack.

"I promised your own place, Annabelle." Pearle smiled. "I always keep my promises."

Annabelle followed Emmett and Pearle out the front door, but she was confused. She didn't realize that Pearle meant her own space would be separate from Pearle's home. No one spoke as they followed the slip of a path into the thick woods. The deeper they walked, the darker it became with the dense tree coverage.

In the distance, Annabelle caught sight of the edge of a lake. An old pontoon boat sat hitched to a dock, and the water lapped against the boat's edges.

"Where are we?" Annabelle asked. "Is this the reservoir?"

"Yes, it's the Charles."

Annabelle jumped at Pearle's voice. Pearle had been in front of her for most of their walk. Somehow she managed to fall behind Annabelle, so close Annabelle could hear her breath.

"We're lucky to have the protected state park in our backyard. Emmett loves the water, and he takes the boat out all the time. You can swim here, Annabelle. The water is clean and cool."

"That sounds nice."

She followed Emmett, sandwiched between him and Pearle, until they came to a clearing of sorts. A dark green storage container was hidden within the trees. Emmett led them past it and down another footpath to where a matching storage container sat, tucked away inside the forest.

Pearle stepped closer to the storage unit's closed door.

"This is your place," she said.

"I don't understand, my place?"

Pearle smiled. "Don't judge a book by its cover, young lady. The outside might not be much to look at, but give it a chance."

Pearle unlocked two padlocks with different keys. She bent over and rolled up the container's accordion door like a window blind.

Annabelle's jaw dopped. The inside of the storage container was the last thing she'd expected. LED string lights lined the top of the container, showcasing the inside. A plush queen-sized bed was tucked into the back of the container, complete with puffy pillows and the to-die-for thread count sheets she'd slept on the night before. Pearle had strung rainbow LED lights through the metal headboard's slats, and there was a reading lamp beside the bed. An oversized leather

La-Z-Boy chair was set closer to the door with a small writing desk and a new laptop, still in its box. That same plush carpet from the guest bedroom lined the storage container's floor. What surprised Annabelle most was the intricate plastic chandelier hanging from the ceiling of the container. Battery powered, it shone bright with all its little crystals spraying rainbows throughout the container.

"Pearle, it's beautiful!"

"Come on." Pearle waved her inside. "I won't bite."

Annabelle stepped inside the transformed nine-by-fourteen storage unit. Her feet sank into the carpet. Pearle had stacked a pile of books for her near the big chair. "I thought you might like to read," Pearle told her. "I bought some books you might be interested in."

Annabelle walked to the bed and ran her hands over the soft blankets and linens. Tears filled her eyes. "Pearle," she started, but the tears came on fast. "This is the kindest…"

"Now, now." Pearle pulled Annabelle into a hug. "You're family. This place is for my kin."

Pearle and Annabelle sat down on the bed, as Emmett brought in her backpack, a large bucket, and a shopping bag. In the small space, Annabelle detected Emmett's murky lake odor. Warm air collected inside and hardly moved despite the open door and two small open vents at opposite sides of the top of the container.

He grumbled past her and headed out of the container while Pearle unpacked the shopping bag. Watermelon colored towels and washcloths. Pajamas with puppies all over them. Another pair with palm trees and smiling suns. Soft fuzzy slippers, white and shimmery with a purple unicorn head stitched over the toes.

"I tried to think of everything you'd need," Pearle said. "Toiletries are under the bed in a tote. I know it's a small space…"

"Pearle, this is too much."

"Nonsense. You're carrying my child! I want you to be comfortable. Everything out here runs on battery, but I can bring out a small generator if you need it."

Annabelle pointed out the jugs lined against the bed.

"Gallons of fresh water," Pearle said. "Running water is the one thing we don't have for you."

It dawned on Annabelle exactly what that meant. "There's no toilet."

Pearle held out the bucket. "I'm sorry, love, but you're in the middle of a forest. No one can see you. There's a bucket if you wish." Pearle slid the bucket under the bed. "We'll bring you meals three times a day and some snacks along the way."

"Oh." Annabelle reached for her throat, scratching a rash developing on her skin. "I can't come into the house?"

"I want you to have your independence, Annabelle. This is your little place away from the world. Of course, I'm always here for you. You can come to me with anything you need."

Annabelle's fingertips rubbed the edge of her collarbone. "I understand." She looked at the new stack of towels. "Where can I shower?"

"The lake, of course. It's a fresh water source. Emmett uses it, too. It might be chilly at first, but it will feel great when the high summer temperatures hit."

Pearle seemed to be one step ahead of Annabelle, and always, it seemed, with her best interest at heart. Annabelle knew it was really about the baby, but it felt good to have someone—anyone—think about her needs. She loved the idea of having her own place, even if it was a moving and storage container with no running water in the middle of a forest.

Annabelle let Pearle wrap her in her thick, warm arms. "You're home now, darling," she cooed. "It doesn't matter what's happened in the past. I will take care of you."

Annabelle rested her head against Pearle's chest and took in her smell, a mixture of soil and lavender and sky. It felt good to land in this woman's arms and on her property. Almost like Gran's.

Then Emmett was there with a full plate of after-dinner snacks for Annabelle. Fat juicy green grapes, slices of yellow cheese, and a spread of crackers, salami, and an apple. He'd also brought her a plastic bottle of flavored fizzy water.

While Emmett set the plate on the desk, Pearle reached for Annabelle's backpack. She emptied it onto the bed. "I told you to pack light, dear."

"I thought I did." Annabelle watched Pearle root through her change of clothing and extra shoes with astonishment. Pearle was very serious about her rules, but this seemed excessive. She thought about the phone and medication she'd hidden inside the stuffing of the back seat of her car. If Pearle was this careful about searching her backpack, what would happen if they found the phone or pills? A shiver ran down her spine.

Emmett stood at the container's opening, his heavy work boots banging against the container's steel floor. He watched them intently.

"I'll take your shoes," Pearle told Annabelle. "There's no need for them here."

Pearle held out her hand, waiting for Annabelle to step out of her old sneakers. "It's summer, and you're heading into the final weeks of your pregnancy. Feet swell, you know. Trust me, you'll be happy I've taken them."

Annabelle stared incredulously at Pearle. "Where are you taking my shoes?"

Pearle smiled and cooed once more. "Oh, Annabelle. This is how things work here. I've perfected my methods over time with the others. Trust me, sweet one. I know what I'm doing."

Others? Annabelle wanted to ask how many other pregnant girls had been through here, but she couldn't find the words. Slowly, she stepped out of one worn sneaker and then the other. Annabelle curled her toes into the carpet. Her feet felt so naked, so vulnerable. For a split second, the image of her mother's face appeared in Annabelle's mind. Her mother's smile that made the corners of her eyes crinkle.

"I know you're scared," Pearle said as she collected the shoes. "What you are doing is very brave, Annabelle. Your baby will be part of the New Nation."

Annabelle nodded. "Ruby told me about that."

Pearle stiffened just for a second, but the shift was enough for Annabelle to notice. "It's been years since I've seen her."

Years? Annabelle puzzled over this statement. Maybe Ruby hadn't been involved with Pearle because The Handler took care of everything.

"Last item on the list," Pearle told Annabelle, changing the subject. "I need to make sure you don't have any contraband on you."

Contraband? What was this, the military?

"Quick! Untuck your pockets for me. I'm going to pat down your bra area and waistband just like TSA does in an airport."

"I don't have anything. I promise."

"Then this won't take more than three seconds. Spread your arms."

Annabelle did as she was told and turned to face the opening of the container. Emmett was still there, watching her.

"I'm really embarrassed about my baby bump," Annabelle said. "Please don't make me show my body in front of Emmett."

Pearle's fingertips felt along Annabelle's back. "Darling, I won't. But there's no need to hide the pregnancy here," she said. "This oversized shirt gives the baby the space it needs to grow." Her hands lowered to Annabelle's waist and circled it, then down to her hips and thighs.

Annabelle pulled away from Pearle and folded her arms across her chest. She crossed one thin leg over the other.

Pearle cooed once again how happy Annabelle would be on the property. "It's the start of a brand-new life. It's exciting to be so close to the change, isn't it?"

"The change?"

"All new things in time, darling. For now, rest and replenish yourself." She pointed Annabelle to her plate of snacks. "Tomorrow is another big day."

Twilight disappeared before Emmett finally left them alone in the container. Annabelle was grateful for the small lights scattered throughout the space. Without her phone or a clock, she was lost for time but guessed it wasn't any later than nine p.m.

"What's the password?" Annabelle nodded to the laptop. When Pearle gave her a confused look, she added, "For the Wi-Fi."

"Oh, I thought you understood. There's no internet out here."

"You said—"

"Honey, don't worry"—Pearle smiled at her—"you aren't a prisoner. We're taking extra precautions because people are looking for you. In a few days, everything will blow over. Then you can come and go from the property as you wish."

Annabelle took a deep breath. "I can leave anytime?"

The cute little container felt so free…so independent. Annabelle told herself she could live without a toilet and running water if this meant that she had a place all her own. She could even live without Wi-Fi.

"Of course. Annabelle, you have my word. If you don't like it out here after a few nights, you can come back to the guest bedroom. Agreed?"

Annabelle looked around her and nodded. She preferred smaller spaces. She imagined this could be like glamping without a toilet or shower.

"Agreed. The door stays open?"

"You're in charge of the door," Pearle said, and they shook on it. "It gets cold out here at night, so you might decide to pull it closed."

Once Pearle left, Annabelle sat down in the oversized chair and listened to the sounds of the forest. Frogs and crickets sang along with the cicadas. An owl hooted every few minutes. She heard a small animal clawing its way up a tree. This new world was going to take some getting used to. So was this overpowering feeling of *alone*.

Annabelle felt a warm weight against her foot. A wet lick of her big toe.

"Tillie!" Annabelle leaned over to give the dog a good back rub. Tillie rolled over and allowed Annabelle to pet her soft belly. Annabelle dropped to her knees beside the dog. "I think we're gonna be fast friends."

CHAPTER TWENTY-SEVEN

Theo found Bree at the kitchen table in her comfiest pajamas. She'd wound her thick dark hair into a makeshift bun planted on top of her head. It was well after midnight, but Theo wasn't surprised to see Bree awake on her night off. With a sleep schedule that was scattered at best, Bree regularly stayed up until two or three a.m. when she wasn't on shift.

Theo walked past Bree on the way to the refrigerator, hoping to catch her eye. Bree didn't look away from the screen.

"Come on, Bree. I'm sorry." Theo reached for the orange juice. "I know the appointment meant a lot to you, but…"

Bree typed something into the keyboard. "I know. The case won out. It always does."

Theo grabbed a glass from the cupboard. "It's a strong lead, Bree. Besides, I was trying to protect you."

Bree finally looked at Theo. She watched as Theo poured the juice, probably surprised she wasn't drinking directly from the carton. "I don't need you to protect me. I'm a first responder, remember? I know how this shit goes down."

Theo drank her juice. The citrusy acid bit at the back of her throat. It had been two days since her trip to Brecksville, and Bree's chilly presence hadn't softened. She sat down in a chair across the table from Bree. "Then why are you so upset?"

Bree shut the laptop. "Seriously? Don't you see it?" When Theo didn't respond, she added, "It's the baby, Theo. Our baby. We are a team here, and I need you to step up."

"I'm sorry. I didn't realize the appointment was so important."

Bree stood to refill her tea, and Theo took the opportunity to change the subject. "Besides, I'm stepping up. See that basket of fresh laundry? Yeah, I did that."

Despite herself, Bree giggled.

"I thought I'd do a load since this is my last relatively clean T-shirt."

"Tough times call for heroic actions."

Theo grinned. At least she'd cracked Bree's hard casing from the last two days.

For the first few months after Theo came home from the hospital, Bree took care of everything—laundry, cooking, cleaning, you name it, all on top of her usual work hours and a new pregnancy. As Theo's strength allowed, she'd gone back to taking care of herself and doing her best to help Bree out where she could. Injury or not, laundry was always the chore shoved to the bottom of the list until it became a crisis.

"What are you doing, anyway?" Theo asked.

"Mom's been on me to get a gift registry together. I'm making one now on a few different sites."

Theo smacked the heel of her palm against her forehead. She'd forgotten Bree's mother was throwing them a baby shower. "When is that? Two weeks?"

"Next Saturday. I was going to email this to see if you wanted to change or add anything." She pushed the laptop toward Theo. "How about you check the virtual list now?"

Theo scanned through the selection of baby items. Everything was pale yellow or a soft green. "You're the expert in all this stuff. I can't really add anything."

Bree groaned and crossed her arms over her chest. "Theo"—her voice held warning—"step up."

Theo balked. "You're kidding, right?" Bree's words stung. "I painted the baby's room. I even put that insane crib together."

Bree scooted her chair closer. "And I thank you for all of that. It's all amazing, and I know the baby will love the room. I want you to help me with everything else, though. I want us to do it together, this parenting thing."

Since the shooting, Theo hadn't done much to prepare for the baby. It was easy to forget what was coming because Bree went about her daily life as if she wasn't pregnant. She took everything in stride. If something needed doing, Bree did it. That was one of the things Theo loved most—she rolled with whatever came her way and adjusted accordingly.

"I'm sorry." Theo felt like Cody, apologizing at every turn.

"Take part, and I'll be happy."

Theo pulled the laptop closer and tried to concentrate on the baby. She scrolled through some more items, unable to picture the pacifiers, onesies, and tiny socks in their house.

Everything in the last few months had been about Theo and her recovery. She hadn't even imagined what it would be like to have an infant living in their home. A person that needed *her* to survive.

"We haven't talked about this in a while," Bree said, "but have you given any more thought to what you want the baby to call you?"

"We still have time." When Theo tried to think about it, she became completely overwhelmed with thoughts of the new addition to their family. "Have you decided?"

Bree beamed and rubbed her small belly bump. "Yeah, I'm Momma or Mom. If you want the same, we could do something like Momma Bree and Momma Theo."

Theo pulled up an image of the baby stroller Bree had selected and enlarged the photo. It gave her eyes somewhere to be, somewhere other than eye contact with Bree. This discussion always made Theo feel uncomfortable because her role was undefined. The term *mother* didn't seem to apply to her. She wasn't carrying the baby and giving birth. Bree clearly owned that title. But Theo didn't really feel like a *father*, either. So where did that leave her?

"Mom wants to announce us at the baby shower by our parenting names." Bree reached for Theo's hand and wound her fingers through Theo's. "I know this is hard for you," she said. "But you are going to be the best parent our kid could ever have."

Theo shook her head and nodded down to her leg. "Yeah, a fantastic gimp of a parent. I won't even be able to coach the kid's T-ball team or run with them in the park."

"You are getting so much stronger, Theo," Bree soothed. "Besides, you don't even know whether our kid will want to do those things."

"What if I'm a jobless parent?"

"You are a protector, Theo, through and through. You'll always have that job, no matter who's writing your paycheck," Bree said. "Besides, DPD won't let you go. You're a legend around these parts."

Theo scoffed. Bree had expressed sentiments like this before, but Theo struggled to believe them. "What if it doesn't heal?"

Bree shrugged. "Our kid's gonna love you no matter what. I love you no matter what."

Bree always knew just what to say. Her words had a way of seeping inside Theo and prying her open. "I don't want to be called Mother, Mommy, Mama, Mom, or any other version of the word. I want a name that isn't gender specific and laden with all kinds of expectations."

"I understand. So what should we call you?"

"*T.*"

"T," Bree said and then again, letting the letter roll around in her mouth. She grinned. "I love it." Bree pushed back her chair and sat down in Theo's lap, careful to put her weight on Theo's good leg. Bree wrapped her arms around Theo's neck and leaned down to kiss her.

Theo's open palm spread over Bree's belly.

"T and Momma and baby." Bree brushed the hair away from Theo's eyes with her fingertips, then gave her a long kiss, gentle and warm. Theo tasted the toothpaste on Bree's tongue. "Thank you for coparenting with me, T. I know this wasn't exactly your dream, and you're doing this for me. I wouldn't want to take this journey with anyone else."

Theo's lips trailed the long length of Bree's neck. She unbuttoned Bree's top as she leaned into Theo. Soon it was all skin and breath and warmth.

Theo wrapped her arms around Bree and tried to stand. She struggled, trying to leverage her elbows against the arms of the chair. Her thighs shivered. Her knees locked and then gave way. She sat down hard. Frustration filled her. "I want to carry you to bed, like I used to."

Bree stood and reached for Theo's hand. "You will again, T. I know it in my heart." She led Theo to bed, letting her pajama top fall to the floor.

CHAPTER TWENTY-EIGHT

Annabelle woke somewhere in the middle of the night to the sound of metal clanking against metal. She'd didn't know exactly how long she'd been on Pearle's property. Time twisted and stretched in ways she'd never known before. It had been at least a few days, possibly a week. She'd been inside her container most of the days, sometimes going out for short walks. It felt like she was constantly waiting on Pearle to return, Pearle who kept her fed and hydrated.

She lay on her back and listened to music, faint but audible. She recognized a guitar riff from a song her mom liked to play when Annabelle was younger, something by Led Zeppelin.

Slowly, she elbowed herself up. She'd turned off all the lights except for the LED string around her headboard. The chandelier's battery had already died, the string of lights around the top of the container had burned out.

Bare feet against the plush carpet, Annabelle edged along the side of the container. Her eyes were far from adjusted to this level of darkness, but given the lights from her bed, she could see the edge of the container, the place where it went from inside to outside. Her slippers were tucked under the oversized chair close to her, and she slipped her feet into the unicorns.

Step.

Another step.

A dim light came from the other storage container's open door. Annabelle hadn't seen or heard anything from that closed container since she arrived. She'd been curious about the matching container, particularly because Emmett and Pearle never went inside it.

Three padlocks usually held the container door down, and Annabelle couldn't reach the vents to see inside. There was something different about this container even though it was the same size and color as hers. Inching closer and sneaking a glimpse around the side, Annabelle expected to see Pearle. Instead, Emmett grunted over a toolbox and grumbled about the bad lighting. Hiding behind a patch of trees, Annabelle listened. There was another light, farther through the trees, and it took her a moment to realize it was coming from Emmett's pontoon boat.

As Annabelle inched closer to the container, she could make out a brown tarp covering a car. She understood immediately. It was her gray Hyundai, stored in that container.

"Git, dog!" Emmett's holler was followed by a high-pitched whine. Tillie slinked out of the container and found her way to Annabelle's side, her wet nose pressing against Annabelle's knee for comfort. Annabelle buried her hand behind Tillie's ears and smelled the distinct odor of gasoline. Damp paws. Tillie had stepped in it.

Emmett moved around the car. He'd popped the hood and clattered away underneath it. What the heck was he doing? The car had just been serviced on Pearle's dime.

Emmett had parked the small four-wheeler next to the container's opening. He brought out a large box and dropped it into the four wheeler's bed. Before climbing into the driver's seat, Emmett turned off the light in the container and pulled the door closed. Soon the bright headlights of the vehicle swept past Annabelle as the four-wheeler turned toward the lake's edge and parked alongside the dock.

Emmett's hulking frame collected the box. Soon the fiberglass dock swayed and kicked up water until Emmett dropped down into his old boat. The pontoon jumped to life, and Emmett untied it from the dock. He gassed the engine and headed for the center of the lake.

Once Emmett's boat had gained some distance, Annabelle made her way down the trail. She stood at the edge of the floating dock, the moonlight allowing her to see much farther in the open area. The dock settled in the boat's wake. Emmett's boat turned out of the channel and disappeared.

"Where's he going, Tillie? What's out there, anyway?"

The dog scratched her neck with a back paw and waited on Annabelle.

Annabelle had assumed Emmett lived in the house with Pearle. She now realized everything about that welcoming had been for show. Emmett didn't have any more rights to Pearle's house than she did. She figured Emmett lived on his boat, but where did he go when he disappeared from Pearle's property? Where did he go on the Charles?

Together, Annabelle and Tillie made their way back toward the storage containers. Annabelle stopped and wrapped her thin arms across her body to keep warm—she was shivering terribly—and listened for any sound. Cicadas and crickets and the sounds of Tillie's panting filled the night, along with her own heartbeat inside her throat. Annabelle took a deep breath, knowing there might never be another time. Under the light of the moon, she ran to the other storage container.

Emmett had left the door wide open. He'd stripped the battery from her Hyundai, hollowed out the car in an essential way. Emmett had left her nothing more than a skeleton. He wanted her to know. Pearle wanted her to know. There was no hope of leaving. She was pregnant and stuck on remote land with no car, phone, Wi-Fi, or shoes.

Talk about a bad Lifetime movie.

Inside the Hyundai's container, darkness enveloped everything. Her unicorn slippers padded along the steel bottom. She inched along the trunk of the car with her fingers splayed wide until she came to the passenger-side door with its closed window. She yanked the handle. Locked.

Annabelle moved to the driver's door. It was locked, too, but the window was partially down, just the way she'd left it. She reached in and pulled the door handle open, one of the blessings of having an older car, and slipped into the driver's seat.

The smell of her car. The fit of the cushion beneath her. It all felt so safe, and she wanted nothing more than to start the car and drive as far away from this place as she could get. More than anything, she wanted to go home to her mother.

Annabelle leaned between the front seats and used her fingertips to find the loose section of material on the base of the back seat. It took some time in the dark, but her hand eventually found its way inside the cushion. The phone was still there, and her hand closed around the cool plastic case. She realized she'd been holding her breath. She reached in a second time for the baggie of pills. Sweat ran down the sides of her face as she left the car, making sure to lock it behind her, and using its shape to guide her to the lip of the container.

Fresh air, finally. She stepped into the cool grass and took a deep breath. Tillie had been waiting for her, but now the dog's nose was against the earth, rooting for something. Annabelle took a step toward Tillie. There was something sticky on the bottoms of her slippers. Annabelle reached down. Her fingertips settled into something thick and cool, probably the gasoline that covered Tillie's paws.

Annabelle looked down at her palm. Tillie left a streak of darkness across her skin. She turned to get a better look inside the container. In the moonlight, she saw the uncovered steel floor, which held thick rivulets of something dark. Blood that had congealed. Tillie had found even more of it on the land surrounding the container, her paws furiously digging at a patch of ground that held the blood of someone else.

CHAPTER TWENTY-NINE

Theo waited for police to wave her through Carillon Park's main entrance. At eight a.m., the park was busy with its usual morning walkers, moms with toddlers, and joggers. The long winter had finally collapsed, and everyone wanted a piece of the warm sun. That made it difficult for DPD to clear the park, particularly once people caught on to the idea that something was going on. Something terrible.

Theo followed the long drive until she met other emergency vehicles. She parked on the grassy shoulder, thinking about Grace Summers and her handprint at the foot of the bell tower.

Time had a way of eddying around Theo. She measured everything against the date Grace went missing. In some respects, it felt like it'd been forever since she'd caught the opening of the case. Sitting there in her car looking at the looming tower now, it felt like Grace had only been gone a few days. Theo cut the engine and set out toward the river, at the opposite end of the property.

Theo's phone buzzed with an incoming message from Hannah Bishop.

Where are you?!!

She replied, *Just arrived.*

River. Now!

It had been about an hour since Theo received Bishop's initial call. She'd just showered. Sunlight streamed through the half-open curtains of the bedroom, and the smell of Bree's fruity shampoo still hung in the air. She'd already left to fill in for an emergency shift.

When the image of Bishop in a New York Mets baseball cap and jersey covered Theo's phone screen, she knew it wasn't good.

"Madsen."

"Theo, I need you. We have something."

"Address?"

"Carillon Park."

Now, in the distance, Theo saw the collection of law enforcement scattered across the park lawn. A red tarpaulin was up, and Theo knew that meant they'd found evidence. Forensic material needed to be kept dry and safe. The sinking feeling in Theo's gut told her that material was most likely a body.

DPD officers were stationed along the river walkway and all park entrances to minimize the chance of photographs and recordings hitting social media right away. Theo's cane clicked along the sidewalk. She wanted to run toward the team, but her hip didn't agree after her long day in the Cleveland suburbs and her night with Bree. It demanded she slow down or threatened to give out under the pressure, the exact thing Theo feared might one day happen in front of her colleagues.

Cody Michaels waved, and Theo's chest constricted. Not long ago, she would have been the first called to the scene, the one directing everyone else. Now she'd been low on that inflated phone tree. She'd been an afterthought more than an essential member of the homicide unit.

Theo met the attending officer and reached for a pair of gloves. She stepped into shoe coverings and a disposable bodysuit, catching a glimpse of the chief's stern face while he barked orders. Everyone was in motion, yet there was nothing more than a controlled level of chaos.

She joined Cody as the coroner, Steve Spain, arrived in his white van. Theo hadn't seen him since the shooting. He slowly backed toward the tarpaulin, his van beeping wildly. There was a squawk of excitement from the crowd and Theo heard, *Someone's dead.*

"It's her, isn't it?" Theo asked Cody.

He stared at her, his face ashen with a touch of green. Theo sidestepped him and made her way toward the crime-scene photographers. The young woman lay on her back in a cotton sundress. Her pale feet nearly glittered in the morning sun. Dark blond hair haloed out from her head. Her stiff arms held an olive-green blanket. Theo balanced with her cane and leaned over the blanket. She lifted its edge with the end of a ballpoint pen. An arm held a baby nestled inside the crook of her thin elbow.

"Can you make the ID, Theo?" Bishop asked, now at her side. "Is it Grace Summers?"

Theo wanted to kneel beside the young woman, but she knew her hip wouldn't allow her to stand back up. She bent further at the waist and inspected the body. The girl was bone thin, which made her cheekbones and nose more prominent than Grace's features in photographs. Her eyeballs bulged against her closed lids, a far cry from the images of the smiling teen that had circulated on social media since Grace went missing. The young woman's mouth was slightly ajar, and Theo saw the flash of metal. Grace still had her braces.

"It's her."

Bishop's exhale sounded like it was part horror and part relief.

The cameras snapped all around Theo as crime-scene techs zoomed in on every aspect of the two bodies before her. Tears pricked Theo's eyes. She knew from all of Bree's pregnancy books and charts that this baby couldn't have been more than three months old. Long blond eyelashes rested against pale puffy cheeks. The infant looked too thin, malnourished. Tiny, fisted hands rested against his chest. The baby looked like a sleeping doll against Grace's bone-thin body.

"It's all about the baby, isn't it?" Bishop finally said.

"If it's all about the baby, this is an epic fail."

Theo and Bishop stepped aside while Spain investigated and moved around the bodies.

"Who found them?" Theo asked.

Bishop blinked a few times, hard. She looked exhausted. "Two joggers along the side of the river. They called 9-1-1 and told dispatch they found a young woman sleeping beside the river with her baby."

"Jesus."

"I know. The officers who took their statements said they choked back tears as they called for homicide."

Theo wondered why the killer brought the bodies back to this very public location, even if it was in the middle of the night. It was a huge risk to use a massive public park with a well-used paved trail along the river, not to mention the heavily trafficked roads that cornered the park. Why was it so important to return Grace to the same public place where she disappeared? And what exactly was Polanski's role in all this? She and Cody hadn't been able to track him down since Cody photographed him sitting in his truck at the bell tower.

"Let's get a closer look, shall we?" Spain sat down cross-legged on the walkway, next to the baby, and signaled the tech to take more images. With gloved hands, he gently unwound the baby from Grace's arms. He then slowly unwrapped the blanket and pulled it away from the baby's stiff body. Spain turned the tiny nude child over in his hands. There were no blemishes or signs of abuse on the baby boy's skin. It looked like he had simply frozen during sleep.

"He's dehydrated," Spain said, "and malnourished." He gently set the baby on his back and opened its miniature mouth with his pinkie finger.

"He's been this way for some time," Spain said.

"How long has he been dead?" Chief Michaels asked.

"Off the record, I'd say three or four days. Five at the most."

Dr. Spain moved and knelt next to Grace's head. He reached a finger into her mouth which displayed the same sores over her tongue and cheeks. "She's also malnourished and dehydrated," he said. "Someone took the time to bathe and wash her hair."

"Before or after death?" Bishop asked.

"I can't make that call right now." Spain pulled the fabric of the dress away from the body. "The clothing appears freshly laundered."

The scene had been staged. Why?

Possibility one, the killer cared for the victims and wanted them found. The killer couldn't stand to see the bodies decompose in the open air, and so they were placed in a location they'd be easily noticed. Two, the killer wanted the media blitz. No matter how hard the police worked to keep the press away, someone always had photos and videos. And there was always the third possibility. The killer was giving law enforcement the finger. *I've had them all along, and you never found us. I had to bring them to you.*

"The young woman hasn't been dead as long as the baby," Spain said. "Maybe forty-eight hours."

Bishop groaned. "Lord, she watched her baby die."

"Cause of death?" Bull Michaels asked. It was well known that Spain hated that kind of pressure. True to the chief's nature, he always pushed the coroner for any answers he could get.

Spain sighed but gave in. "The preliminary findings indicate strangulation, but there's a lot going on here."

"Can you give us any more to go on?"

"I need to run some tests before I make any formal conclusions. Give me a few hours, and I'll have more answers for you."

While Spain and his assistant bagged the bodies and loaded them into his van, Theo walked the perimeter of the scene. She circled out wider and wider, taking in all the sights as the crime-scene unit wrapped up and the area thinned of law enforcement.

Bull Michaels eventually called Theo over, and she met him alone near the walkway. She stood tall, both hands resting on the cane, her gaze trained on every movement of the chief's face. She wanted him to acknowledge she'd been right all along, but that was too much to ask for. Instead, he rubbed his chin and asked, "How you been feeling?"

"Good."

"Glad to hear that." Bull rolled up onto his toes and back to his heels. He had a habit of doing that. "I don't mean to push, Theo, but we really need you to run point on this one. If you're ready, that is."

"I'm ready, Bull," Theo said. "I've been ready."

"Work with Cody." Theo turned, the end of her cane dragging on the cement. "And Theo? Bring this girl home alive. Hear me?"

Her eye caught Bull's before she turned away. The department needed Annabelle's survival story to counteract the tragedy of Grace and her baby's murders. But the clock was ticking toward Annabelle's due date. Soon they would be too late.

CHAPTER THIRTY

The afternoon sun streamed in through the opening of the container. Annabelle lay on the carpet with Tillie against her side. The dog's breath had gone long and deep with sleep.

There'd been no sign of Pearle or Emmett on the property all day. Annabelle had even gone to the house and knocked on the heavy wooden door. The entire place was latched up tight.

Annabelle took advantage of the quiet day, grateful Emmett hadn't come back with his boat. She walked into the water, its coolness rising up along her legs until she sank beneath its surface. She swam in the crisp water before scrubbing her hair and body with shampoo.

With her hair still wet and body wrapped in a sun-warmed towel, she lay beside the dog while her stomach growled. She missed TV. She missed her phone. She missed noise.

The silence made her think, giving her the space to spool out every nuance and thought tick of her brain. She couldn't let go of the dried blood in the other container, the way it had gathered and pooled in the rivets of the steel floor.

Daylight made it easier to explain away. It was possible Emmett had killed a deer on the property and used the open container to hang the animal. Perhaps he hadn't hosed out the container after cleaning the animal. Or it could have been Tillie. Maybe she'd cornered a squirrel or groundhog into the container and ripped it apart. Annabelle reached over and rubbed Tillie's soft ear. She knew deep down that wasn't possible. This dog wouldn't hurt anything.

Annabelle's thoughts continued to spool. She hadn't thought to check the flooring of her own container. It was carpeted in the same thick, soft plush of the house's guest bedroom. This carpet felt brand new, not something that had lined the container for long.

Annabelle dressed quickly and then ran her fingers along the edges of the carpet, feeling the rough fabric cut where it met the seams of the steel container. She pushed out the large chair and a storage box of paperback books. Annabelle moved to the front of the container and rolled the thick carpet back toward the bed.

It wasn't long before she found markings on the floor of the container. Maybe it was the way the light hit, but she saw lines scraped into it. Hash marks. Letters, maybe.

Tillie sat outside on the grass looking in, curious. Annabelle shoved against the heavy carpet. She held it back with the weight of her, as if she was halting a wave from crashing.

More hash marks. More letters. Then names, clear as anything in the daylight.

Paige

Kate

Penny

Grace

Annabelle forced the carpet back a few inches more. She found one last message alongside the side of the container. A message left for her: *RUN*.

Annabelle's foot lost purchase with the steel floor. The carpet unrolled with such force it shoved her out of the container and perfectly laid itself back in its place. She lay facedown in the grass. Tillie's wet nose nudged her shoulder and neck.

"I'm okay," she told the dog, lifting onto her wrists.

Annabelle's breath caught in her throat. She stifled a scream.

Emmett towered above Annabelle. One hand clenched a fresh gallon of water and a bag of food. The other held container locks.

CHAPTER THIRTY-ONE

Theo examined Cody Michaels's whiteboard. He'd drafted every detail for the team while she'd been working the desk. He'd even included photos of suspects and timelines for both Grace Summers and Annabelle Jackson. Theo leaned against the corner of her desk with her arms crossed over her chest. It felt good to be back in her own department and on her own territory.

"Interesting tip came into Brecksville," Theo told Cody. "A long-haul trucker reported seeing Annabelle Jackson a few weeks before her disappearance. She had a flat along the interstate and he stopped to help. Annabelle wasn't too receptive to him but did say she was headed to Akron. He remembered the specific part that Annabelle needed to order. Weston's looking into garages in the Brecksville area."

"Was she alone?"

"Yeah. He said she was nervous. Skittish," Theo said. "Maybe he spooked her, or the car damage upset her. Either way, the driver felt like she couldn't wait to get away from him."

Cody marked a place on the timeline for the truck driver incident. "They were together for a few minutes. She had every opportunity to ask for help if she needed it."

"She didn't know she needed help yet."

He leaned against his desk and reached for his phone. "Meaning?"

"Meaning this happened in the last week Annabelle was home. Maybe she still believed all the bullshit someone had fed her."

Cody cleared his throat. "You think she was tricked into leaving on her own. Then she couldn't get herself out of a bad situation."

Theo nodded. "It rings true with what we have so far."

"Wait a minute. You said she was headed to Akron?" Cody scrolled through his phone until he found what he was looking for. "The phone company reported Daniel Holtzman's phone lost all service in the town of Stowe." He looked up at Theo. "Stowe is only ten miles from Akron."

"Annabelle met someone in that area," Theo said. "Someone she trusted."

Weston had already put Akron PD on alert, but Theo decided to message them about possible sightings in the area. Most likely Annabelle had met someone in public—at a coffee shop or a restaurant. Theo hoped the PD up there could do a little digging.

"It's after eight," Cody said. "I'm calling in for delivery. Join me?"

"Twisting my arm, right?"

Cody grinned, and for a moment, Theo felt like the shooting at Castleton Motors was a million miles behind them.

Theo's phone vibrated against the desk.

"Theo? It's Sarah. Bree's squadmate."

"Sarah, hi."

Something wasn't right—Theo felt it like a kick to the gut. Sarah's voice was controlled with only the hints of fear a first responder could hide well.

"What's going on?"

"It's Bree. She wanted me to call you. We've transported her to the ED."

"ED?"

"They're checking her in now, and the doctor will be here soon. She's having severe pelvic pain, Theo."

"What?" Theo struggled to hear what was said and couldn't process Sarah's words fast enough.

Bree had been at home, preparing for her shift. She called her own team for help when the pain became too severe.

"She's stable, but we can't be sure what's going on," Sarah said. "Bree needs you."

If Theo hadn't been sitting when she got the call, she would have collapsed. This development came out of nowhere. Bree was uncomfortable and ready for the pregnancy to be over, sure, but everything had been going so well.

"Is...is she losing the baby?"

It was Theo's biggest fear. Bree was the strongest person she knew, but the loss of the baby this late in the pregnancy would tear Bree apart in ways Theo feared she wasn't strong enough to endure.

"Bree needs a doctor. We've already called her obstetrician, and the attending doc is in with her now."

"On my way."

Warm summer rain splattered across the windshield as Theo pulled into a parking spot near Miami Valley Hospital's emergency department. She sat for a minute, watching the wipers swipe to the left and then the right. She felt as if she wasn't really there. She felt trapped inside a nightmare she couldn't wake up from. Her throat squeezed as her chest filled with a tornado of emotions. She ruptured into tears and ugly crying.

What scared Theo most was that Bree had been in dire pain and didn't call her. The fact Bree hurt too much to drive herself to the hospital terrified Theo to the bone.

The wipers swished across the windshield once more before Theo killed the engine. Everything would be okay, she told herself, if she could just get to Bree's side.

Theo sloshed through the parking lot puddles. Rain soaked her hair and shoulders. Theo had been trying to protect Bree for months from the truth about her feelings about the shooting and the baby. It had been an attempt to save her from any additional stress. Now, sloshing her way into the ED, she wondered, what if, all this time, *Bree* had been trying to protect *her* from something?

CHAPTER THIRTY-TWO

E mmett!"
Annabelle looked up at him, a giant standing above her. She hadn't heard his boat engine while she'd been moving the furniture and carpet.

Annabelle crawled on her hands and knees and looked for Tillie. The dog had vanished into the woods.

She slowly found her feet. Emmett's silence and pointed stare disarmed her. She babbled nervously about her bath in the Charles, as if that could explain why she'd moved the lounge chair and other furniture outside the container.

"I was worried," she told him. "Where's Pearle? I don't want to be out here all alone."

Emmett set the food and water down. He bent over the lounge chair and lifted it in one swoop, carrying it back into the container. His hulking frame turned to face Annabelle. He jutted his chin out, motioning her back inside.

She picked up the gallon of water and the food before moving into the container. "Where's Pearle?"

Emmett offered her the chair. "Comes and goes."

It was the closest Annabelle had ever been to Emmett. Underneath the scraggly facial hair, his teeth shone white, in strong contrast to his dirty skin and hair.

"It's lonely out here, and I thought you would be around more." Annabelle took the bag of food from him. Steam drifted through the opening of the bag. "I'm just nervous. It's getting close now, you know? The baby." She looked down at her belly.

"You aren't alone." His voice had a whispery growl to it.

"And the lights"—she pointed to the ceiling—"the batteries are all dying. Only the strand along the bedframe has any juice left."

He took a few steps closer to her bed and reached for the dim strand of LED lights.

"Emmett?" Annabelle reached into the bag for a plastic spoon. Her mouth watered at the smell of fried chicken, mashed potatoes, and gravy.

"The other girl. The one from Dayton," Annabelle said. "Grace was here, wasn't she?"

Her question seemed to give Emmett pause, his dark hooded eyes assessing her. He pulled the LED string and the last of lights went out.

"Did Pearle adopt her baby? What about the other girls?"

"Eat up." Emmett walked past her on his way out of the container.

"You'll bring me new batteries, right?"

Emmett stood at the lip of the container, facing her. For a few seconds, Annabelle thought he wanted to tell her something. His eyes searched her, pled to her. Then he reached up and slammed shut the accordion door. All the outside locks slid into place with the final click of the padlocks.

Darkness slammed over Annabelle. She sat very still and pretended she'd only shut her eyes. When she opened them, she told herself everything would be different. Outside the container, Emmett's footfalls crashed through the foliage until she couldn't hear them anymore. Annabelle wanted to scream. She wanted to slam her fists against the steel walls. Instead, she sat with the bone-heavy weariness and the ache of her entire body. Her heart beat loud in her ears, the *thrush thrush thrush* of it pumping faster. Her breath caught, and she gasped for a full breath. A growing awareness settled on her. *I've been so stupid.*

She collapsed to the floor, curling herself into the fetal position. Eventually, her breath evened out. She could have been in that position for five hours or five minutes. It all felt the same. The panic attacks always landed harder when she was off her lupus medication.

She had hidden the pills under the elastic band of her underwear. Now, she held the sandwich-sized baggie in her fisted hands, her fingertips metering out each tablet of medication, counting them to herself in the dark: one, two, three, four. Four pills. Enough for two days.

The darkness of the container unnerved Annabelle. Even scarier, her body seemed to be unraveling from its very core, as if her spine let go of all that held her together. She felt the fiery burn from the rash over her cheeks, the butterfly she was never happy to see, and a sign she'd tried to hide from Pearle since the moment they met.

These pills. They'd helped to save her. Annabelle really needed a round of steroids to break down the lupus flare, but she'd have to make do with what she had. She really needed two pills a day, but she could get by on one…couldn't she? The small round tablets felt like safety against her fingertips, and she remembered Gran saying to her, *If you lose your health, you lose everything.* Annabelle needed the strength from those pills if she was ever going to get out of this mess alive. Four pills—hardly a drop against her raging lupus.

I'm in big trouble.

The jug of water felt cool against Annabelle's palm. She uncapped it and swallowed all the pills, their powdered edges sticking to her throat. Then she crawled toward the bed, reaching with her fingertips until she felt the burner under the mattress. The lights of the phone's face gave the container a familiar blue glow.

Annabelle dialed nine and then her fingertip hovered over the one. Everything inside her screamed to call for emergency help. She needed police, paramedics, anyone who could respond. Then an image of her mother shot in the chest flashed before her eyes, followed by an image of Ruby dead beside her mother. Annabelle couldn't let that happen.

She hadn't dialed numbers on a phone in years, and it took more than a minute to think of the digits. Even then, she wasn't sure she had the right number when the factory-recorded voice announced the generic voice mail message.

"Ruby? I know, I'm breaking the rules. I don't want to get you into anything. But I need you." She detailed where the container was on Pearle's property and begged Ruby to come for her.

After she ended the call, Annabelle held the phone in her hand and listened for Emmett. He'd left her, hadn't he? What if he'd heard her on the phone? She stood motionless with only the shallowness of her breath moving her chest.

She heard nothing save the wildlife around her coming out for the night. The occasional rustling of brush and sticks near the container, most likely a squirrel or some other small creature.

Annabelle dialed more numbers from memory, took a deep breath, and waited for the connection.

"Daniel?"

CHAPTER THIRTY-THREE

The emergency department's sliding doors swooshed open. Theo's hip and thigh muscles burned, but the adrenaline powered her through to Miami Valley Hospital's reception.

"Checking in?"

Theo shook her head. "I'm here for Bree Adams. EMS brought her in about forty-five minutes ago."

The receptionist attacked her keyboard with a barrage of key strikes.

"Are you a family member?"

"Yes. Bree's pregnant and I'm the coparent." Theo left out the part about them not being married.

"Have a seat. I'll check her visitor status."

"Is she okay?"

"Someone will be right with you." The woman turned away from Theo, which had the same effect as a door slamming shut.

Theo understood no one could release information about Bree's health or the baby's, but that certainly didn't help to quiet the fear growing inside her. There were no open seats in the waiting area. Theo was so anxious she couldn't sit, anyway.

She paced. Her mind raced. Her heart pounded inside her ears as she tried to regulate her breath. Bree was in the exact place she needed to be at the moment. Theo reminded herself to trust in that no matter how hard.

"Theo!"

Bree's mother, Julie Adams, pulled Theo into a quick tight hug. She felt Julie's warm tears against her neck.

"My girl," Julie said, pulling away from Theo. "She has to be all right."

Julie had welcomed Theo into their family the moment Bree introduced them. Bree's parents were divorced, and Bree had had minimal contact with her dad since he moved to the East Coast while she was in high school. Even though Bree saw her mom at least once a week, Theo rarely joined in when the two of them met for lunch or a visit. While Julie had been nothing other than supportive and helpful during her recovery, Theo guessed she'd heard everything about their relationship and then some. Theo wasn't exactly sure how she felt about that.

"She wants this baby more than anything in the world," Julie said, wiping her eyes. "It will crush her…"

Theo reached over and rubbed her back. "Let's not go there just yet, okay?"

Finally, an aide—she introduced herself as Heather—called for Bree's family. When Theo hesitated, Julie grabbed her arm. "You're coming, too." Together they followed her through the corridor toward Bree's cubicle.

"Is everything okay with my daughter and the baby?"

"I'm not a doctor," Heather reminded them, "but one will be with you soon."

After they walked a long hallway full of patients and staff, Heather pulled an isolation curtain back. Bree looked so small in the hospital bed, rolled onto her hip, her face red and puffy from crying. Theo rushed to one side while Julie took the other, each reaching for Bree.

"I'm still pregnant," Bree told them through tears. "I heard the heartbeat myself."

Both Theo and Julie exhaled long and hard.

"There are problems." Bree's back shook with her sobs.

Theo rubbed her shoulder. Theo knew from her work with hospitals that they'd never have left Bree alone if her life was in danger, or the unborn baby's.

"It will be okay, I promise. Have you seen Dr. Hartt?"

"Not yet. The doctor on call ordered some tests. They just took my blood for labs."

Bree reached out for Theo's hand. She sat down on the edge of the bed. "God, Bree. You scared me to death."

"I'm sorry," she said, her eyes brimming with tears, as the machines checked her vitals. "There was blood. I didn't know what else to do."

"You should have called me."

Julie jumped in to soothe Bree, assuring her daughter she'd done the right thing.

"What if the baby is coming now?" Bree asked. "It's way too early."

Bree had just crossed into her thirty-third week of pregnancy. Preterm labor was one of her biggest fears. She'd seen too much of it on her EMT runs and witnessed the struggles some of those babies had to survive.

"Let's not panic, okay?" Julie said, stroking her daughter's hair from her face. "You arrived preterm and did just fine."

"That's different! I was only two weeks early. This could be a lot worse."

Julie hushed her by recounting the numerous scares she'd had during her pregnancy with Bree. Julie's voice was soothing, and Theo watched the monitors as Bree's vitals moderated. She felt her own breathing ease, too.

Finally, the curtain pushed back, and their obstetrician, Dr. Hartt, had one of the biggest smiles Theo had ever seen.

"You've had quite a scare," Hartt said, after greeting everyone in the room. "You've got a few things going on, and everything peaked at once. You're not in labor—you're having Braxton Hicks contractions. My larger concerns are the pain and the bleeding."

Bree took a breath of relief and explained to Theo that Braxton Hicks was false labor, a way for the body to prepare for the upcoming birth. The pain that Bree described, however, was unusual.

"We usually hear that it's equivalent to menstrual cramps," Dr. Hartt said. "I'm concerned about the blood. It's more than spotting."

"Did the tests show anything?" Bree asked.

Dr. Hartt nodded. "You have a UTI, and a pretty nasty one. You're also dehydrated. I'm willing to wager you're stressed out as well. I hear you're still working full-time."

Bree groaned. "I want to work, Dr. Hartt. I need to keep busy."

"You also want to have a healthy baby." The doctor gave Bree a hard glance. "You've been taking care of everyone else these past few months, Bree. It's time to take care of yourself. I'm putting you on bed rest for the remainder of this pregnancy."

"Bed rest?" Bree asked incredulously.

The doctor smiled. "I'm estimating you have about three weeks to go. It could be sooner, but I'm really hoping the baby waits that long."

Three weeks. Theo struggled to wrap her head around that number. Less than a month.

"It's going to get very uncomfortable, even when the UTI clears up. You're carrying around an extra human, you know."

Julie consoled Bree while Theo thanked the doctor on his way out.

"I need you to watch Bree, Theo," Dr. Hartt said. "She knows what she's supposed to do, but she also needs to be reminded. Bree's a go-getter, and it's going to be hard to keep her down. She needs that rest and lots of water."

Soon a nurse arrived with a full bag of fluid for Bree. Another nurse had already gotten an IV site started. Everyone watched as the fluid dripped down into the line.

"We're going to fill you up," the nurse joked. "Let me know as soon as you need to pee." Before she left, the nurse started Bree on an antibiotic, shooting the liquid in through her IV.

After an hour or so, Julie needed to leave. "You're looking much better, darling. Your stepdad needs a ride home from work. Can I drop off some food for the two of you tomorrow? Some lasagna? I made some this weekend, and its more than enough for the two of you."

Julie kissed them both good-bye and promised to drop by every day to check in on Bree.

Bree closed her eyes. "I'm so tired."

"Sleep, baby." Theo listened to the monitors beeping around them and the sound of medical staff in the hallway.

Almost an hour later, Bree opened her eyes. She smiled at Theo. "You're still here."

"I'm not going anywhere."

"What are you thinking about?"

"You. I'm sorry, I've been a strain on you."

Bree shook her head.

"I have," Theo insisted. "The shooting. My recovery. Now that the case is heating up again. It's a lot, for both of us. It's time for me to take care of you."

Bree sighed. "It's not the case, okay?"

Theo broke eye contact with her on that statement, acknowledging that there was more to the story than she'd told Bree.

"It's the baby, Theo."

"Come on."

"You aren't ready."

"Bree..."

"No, this is my fault. I pushed so hard for this baby. I pushed you into a family."

"I want this baby, too. I'm in, Bree. I'm here. I don't know how else to say it."

"That's just it, Theo." Bree closed her eyes. "It's not what you say. It's what you do."

A technician surprised them, popping inside the curtain. "Sorry to interrupt," he said. "Dr. Hartt ordered one last ultrasound. This one's of the bladder."

Theo watched as the tech unhooked Bree's bag of fluid and laid it beside her on the bed. "We want the bladder full for this test," he said. "We'll keep those fluids pumping."

He unlocked the bed wheels with a thump. Theo squeezed Bree's hand tight before she rolled away.

Theo called after her, "I'm not going anywhere."

CHAPTER THIRTY-FOUR

Annabelle rested on the mattress, staring up into the darkness. She wished like hell for Tillie, the feel of her thick, soft coat against her hand. Emmett had locked the dog out of the container when he left, but Annabelle could hear Tillie's soft whine not far from the closed door.

What was taking Daniel and Ruby so long to find her? She spun scenarios in her head, each one designed to showcase how desperately they tried to find her but were stopped by something they couldn't control. Perhaps she hadn't had the correct number for Ruby. Her cousin went through phones and numbers like water.

But Daniel? He must have gotten her voice mail. He checked his messages every hour, sometimes more. Maybe he didn't care what happened to her. That was a hard thought for her to accept, but then she'd always known she couldn't compete with his friends. His *ride or die* crew. He'd even used the phrase with Stacy Adams, the cheerleader he'd dated on and off for the last two years. But never her. Annabelle was truly on her own.

Hot angry tears ran down Annabelle's temples and into her ears. It had taken far too long to understand what she'd gotten herself mixed up in. She'd thought she understood the terms of the contract with The Handler. *Harm may come to those you love if the contract is broken in any way.* The realities of what that meant haunted her. Her mother. Ruby.

She had to find a way out of all this without involving the police.

Tillie barked on the other side of the container.

"I'm here," Annabelle called out to her. She heard the dog push closer until she finally settled down with her back against the steel container.

"Did you know all those girls, Tillie? All their babies?"

She heard the dog panting on the other side of the steel wall. Annabelle hadn't expected all those names. The code for her had been the bloody handprint, and that was how she'd heard about the one in Dayton who went missing. Why hadn't she heard of these other girls? Maybe they hadn't left behind bloody handprints.

Tires crunched over the gravel drive. Doors shut.

Annabelle stood up on the bed. She reached for the open vents.

Pearle's voice drifted from a distance, but there were others. Voices she didn't recognize.

CHAPTER THIRTY-FIVE

Detective Hannah Bishop paced the waiting area of Montgomery County's morgue. Everyone was anxious for the autopsy to get going, but Bishop was particularly on edge, as the media clawed at her back for answers. Grisly details about Grace and the baby splashed across social media and the local news. DPD had been fielding all kinds of calls and visits from people demanding answers.

It was Cody's first rodeo at the morgue, his face ashen against his dark curls. With his hands stuffed into his pockets, he didn't take his eyes off his shoes.

Theo had spent the last thirty-six hours tending to Bree. It felt strange, this flip in their relationship, and Theo did her best to fill the caretaker role. "Am I as good at this as you are?" she'd teased, bringing Bree a snack of peanut butter crackers and banana in bed.

Bree had groaned as she tried to prop herself up in bed, complaining that the baby had been doing somersaults for hours on end. "You're better at this than you think. It's the baby. This little love isn't happy with me lying around."

Theo knew Bree hated to take leave from work. Bree understood intellectually why she had to do it, but she was reacting to her mandatory rest like a punishment.

Theo had sat down on the bed beside her and rubbed Bree's belly. "Our little one will thank you one day, and they'll be born knowing John Hughes's movies by heart."

Bree chuckled. "I hope so! I hope our baby is as much of an eighties fan as I am." Bree had mostly slept since she got home from the hospital, but when she was awake, an eighties movie was on.

Now, standing in morgue reception, Theo felt guilty for leaving Bree. Julie was keeping her company, but Theo felt that pull for home with a sense of unease.

Dr. Spain opened the door and welcomed them inside. "I'm sorry for the delay," he said. "It took some time to verify a few toxins."

"The wolves are baying, waiting for my report," Bishop said. "The media has been fierce with this one."

"These findings might do more to work up the public than calm them."

Bishop groaned.

"See this?" Spain pointed a gloved finger.

Theo and Bishop leaned over Grace's body for a closer look. Cody stayed where he was, his face even grayer than it had been in the reception area.

Spain pointed to a discolored area around Grace's neck. "It's a thumbprint, and a large one, from a fist hold. Someone strangled Grace to death with their bare hands."

Spain pointed out some bruising on Grace's neck from the killer's other hand. "Most people don't have the strength in their grip to choke someone out. It's amazing, really."

"The handspan," Theo said.

"Quite large! To give you some perspective, it's almost twice my own." Spain held up his open hand for everyone to see.

"Did the baby die in the same way?" Bishop asked.

"Yes. The killer was able to grip his neck in one hand and shatter the baby's spinal cord. It was a fast death for the baby, but the mother fought. Someone clipped her nails and cleaned underneath them."

"Destroying DNA evidence," Bishop said. "She must have scratched the guy to hell and back."

"Yes. She also bit the insides of her cheeks and lacerated her tongue gasping for air."

The group followed Spain around the separate tables, one for mother and one for baby, as he directed them through his findings.

Mother and son were dehydrated and malnourished. The bottoms of Grace's feet had been shredded and deeply bruised.

"It looks like she ran through a wooded area without any shoes," Spain said. "The cuts and bruising are consistent with heavy vegetation and loose gravel. Her soles are thin, so this wasn't a normal practice for her." He went on to explain that because both bodies had been so carefully cleaned, he didn't have any remnants of the earth to test for a possible location.

"I found another rarity. This case is shaping up to be one for the books." Spain led them to the baby's table.

"Uh-oh," Bishop mumbled. Such sentiment from a coroner was never a good thing for police.

Spain rolled the baby onto his stomach to reveal a bump the size of a Ping-Pong ball along the spine. "Myelomeningocele—a type of spina bifida. It's a very serious condition. These cases are usually caught in the ultrasounds during pregnancy, and many mothers choose to end the pregnancy because of it." He pointed to the bulge. "This sac is filled with nerves that should be enclosed within the spine. Chances are this baby wouldn't have been able to walk without significant medical intervention and surgeries."

"The child was born prematurely?" Bishop asked.

"I suspect that," Spain said. "It's hard to tell because he's so malnourished and significantly undersized. It's also very likely this mother did not have prenatal care and the usual ultrasounds and tests."

"You said they both were malnourished," Theo said. "Grace is thin, but I thought it might be worse."

"That's an interesting thing. Based on my findings, the malnourishment is recent. It began *after* the baby's birth," Spain said. "Someone kept her alive to give birth and then withdrew nourishment." Spain turned back to where Grace lay. "There's something else. This recent scar on the palm of Grace's left hand." He turned her hand over to reveal the raised vertical line about an inch long.

"The partial bloody handprint," Theo said.

Spain nodded. "The wound looks like it was deliberate, possibly self-inflicted. The clean cut appears to have been made with the blade of a small knife."

Theo recognized the placement of the scar. "That reminds me of the way kids used to cut their palms to be blood sisters or brothers." She held up her left hand. "My scar is faded now, and we only scratched the surface, but my best friend and I cut our palms in third grade to be blood sisters."

Cody spoke up, surprising them all, "It's a pact. To stand by each other, to always be there for each other, right?"

An image flashed in Theo's mind. The partial handprints and the way the blood had congealed at the sites where the two young women had gone missing. All this time and she'd missed it. The handprints served as the sworn secrecy sealed with blood.

The Dayton Police Department boiled over with activity. Theo and her team managed to find a creative path to the squad room without much interference. Every media outlet wanted a statement from them, and they weren't even close to releasing any details about the bodies.

Cody's color had returned. He brought Theo a steaming cup of coffee, and his eyes lingered on her desk. Grace's and the baby's clothing had returned from the crime analysis unit. Techs had been over the clothing, searching for the slightest hair or any minute clue that could give them an edge on where the two had been before their death.

"It's hard to look at." Theo nodded to the clothing. "I'll take it down to evidence after our debrief with the chief."

Cody's eyes lingered on the clothing. "How do you do this, Theo? Case after case? Doesn't it get to you?"

"It does." Theo leaned back in her chair and met Cody's gaze. "I learned to turn it off a long time ago."

"It?"

"The blood, the bodies, the violence. It's the only way I've survived."

Cody nodded, and his brow furrowed as if he was trying to make sense of it all.

"You have to remember—this is not the typical case, Cody. You're getting blistered in on some of the worst we've seen."

Bishop soon joined them with Bull Michaels, who asked, "Where do we go from here, folks?"

The squad discussed multiple lines of inquiry. They kept circling back to Grace's pregnancy.

Cody pushed the curls out of his eyes. "I was just thinking about how long Grace and her baby were kept alive. If it really was about the baby, I understand they didn't need Grace. But why kill the baby?"

Theo had been thinking about that, too. "Spain was clear that the baby's spina bifida is debilitating without extensive treatment. It's very likely they couldn't secure a sale."

"Human trafficking," Bull Michaels said.

Theo nodded. "People will pay a lot for a white newborn."

Bull groaned. "The Bureau will be here seconds after they catch wind of that theory. Let's keep that close, got it?"

Everyone agreed. The last thing anyone wanted was the Ohio Bureau of Criminal Investigation swooping in and taking them all off the case.

"We're talking about a brazen crime here," Bull said. "Why would the girls deliberately leave their own blood behind, let alone a partial print? It doesn't make sense."

"If Annabelle is pregnant, she's still alive," Cody said. "And if we follow the same timeline as Grace, that puts Annabelle's delivery date within the next two or three weeks."

"Maybe earlier," Theo said. "We don't know if she's getting any prenatal care or nutrition. All that stress could bring on a premature delivery."

Theo thought about Bree's prenatal care—ultrasounds, regular doctor visits, vitamins, nutrition planning, and more. Despite all that care and support, there were still complications. Theo couldn't imagine what it would be like without any care or attention throughout the pregnancy.

"That baby and mama are going to need immediate medical intervention," Bishop said. "They've proven to us they won't seek medical care with Grace's baby, but you never know who might intervene. We'll put all northeast Ohio hospitals on high alert for pregnant teens."

"We need to look for a woman," Bishop added. "Someone who helps with the birth and cares for the teens. Grace and Annabelle aren't the first girls she's dealt with."

"It's got to be more than one person," Theo said. "A partnership of some kind, so they can keep the upper hand on these girls. But the more people involved, the more vulnerable everything is to a loose thread that will unravel everything."

The team tossed around ideas for next steps. They had more questions for Annabelle's mother. Daniel was a key player, and more investigation needed to be done into his parents. No one on the team had spoken to his father other than Weston. And Sam Polanski. They really needed to talk to him.

Theo added Annabelle's cousin Ruby to the list as well. On a whim, Theo had run her through the system and found a record. Mostly petty stuff—public intoxication, drug possession. Ruby also had a juvenile record that was sealed, and Theo had petitioned for that record to be unsealed for their investigation into Annabelle's disappearance.

The team composed a statement to the press, a short comment that omitted any details linking the Brecksville case and Grace's. Reporters had already begun to make those connections on their own, but Bull Michaels wanted to hold them off as long as possible.

The team dispersed with their orders, but Theo remained. She'd been charged with delivering the clothing to evidence before running down her first lead of the day.

She reached for the baggie that held the tiny sleeper. Through the plastic sheath, Theo felt the soft edges that fit against the baby's wrists and ankles. The material had been laundered and well-worn. Little yellow ducks splashed in puddles while some held colorful umbrellas. Big red rainhats with laughing faces wore tall boots and stomped near the ducks. Theo recognized this yellow, the same shade she'd painted the baby's room. The same color Bree had chosen for the baby's towels and bedding. Soon her child would join the world, a living, breathing being that would fill clothing just like this sleeper.

Theo's cane clicked along the tiled hall toward the evidence locker. When she arrived, the phone vibrated against her hip.

"Theo, it's Weston. I've got something." He'd spent the morning contacting garages in the Brecksville and Cleveland area. "The part Annabelle needed for her Hyundai was very specific. I found mechanics I never knew existed, including one on the west end of Cleveland. City Motors."

"Did they service her car?"

"More than that. City Motors is the Cleveland branch of Castleton Motors."

Theo's mind flooded with the images of Dick Castleton's office. *We have another location in downtown Cleveland.* Castleton said Henry Nerra had occasionally filled in there.

Detective Maxwell Weston had found Sam Polanski's hideout.

CHAPTER THIRTY-SIX

Theo helped Bree's mother carry in the last of her bags to the guest bedroom. She set the duffel on top of the bed next to a stack of clean towels and linens.

"I can't thank you enough, Julie. It relieves my mind to know you'll be here for Bree if something happens while I'm at work."

Julie waved Theo's comment away with a flip of her hand. "It's my pleasure. We'll get through this, Theo. He'll be here before we know it!"

Theo gave Julie the side-eye. "He? Do you know something I don't?"

Julie gave Theo a wink. "Grandmas always know."

Theo had secretly hoped for a boy. When she imagined herself with the baby, it was always a little boy in a Dayton Dragons baseball jersey.

"I hope so," Theo said. "And let's hope the birth goes perfect."

Julie sat on the edge of the bed and patted the space next to her for Theo. "I'm not sure any birth is perfect, but I know what you mean."

"I've been meaning to ask you something," Theo said, leaning over the corner table and clicking on the bedside light.

"What's that?"

"How long has Bree been struggling with the pregnancy?"

"She didn't want to worry you. You have a lot on your plate, Theo. She thought she could handle this."

"I missed the last ultrasound and doctor's appointment." Theo rubbed her temple. "I should've been there."

Julie rested her hand on Theo's back. "Don't think of that now. Let's move forward, okay?"

Theo eventually agreed and went through Bree's daily schedule for the past week.

"I'm just the food delivery person," Theo joked. "Whatever Bree's craving, I make it happen."

Theo went on to describe Bree's sleep patterns and the difficulties she'd had staying asleep. The baby rested heavy on her bladder, and Bree had to pee almost every hour. And when Bree finally slept, Theo reviewed case interviews and fell into countless rabbit holes while searching for missing teens and the illegal market for white American babies.

"How's the case going? You look exhausted."

Theo dropped her elbows to her knees and let her head hang. "I am. We get a little closer, and then we hit a brick wall. Rinse. Repeat." Theo felt the warmth of Julie's open hand on her back. "There's a slim chance the teen from Brecksville is still alive. Her boyfriend, too. We just can't locate them."

Julie reached for her duffel bag and unzipped it. "You carry so much. The protector of everyone."

Theo shook her head. "I'm not living up to that title right now, am I? Grace and her baby are dead. Most likely Annabelle is, too."

"Have you ever considered this role may be holding you back from fully healing?"

Theo arched an eyebrow. "Role?"

"Protector. It's a lot to constantly be on guard for everyone. Others can help if you let them."

Theo fought an eye roll. Sometimes Julie sounded just like Bree. Or Bree sounded just like her mother.

"It's an act of faith, isn't it? So much of a pregnancy and a baby's birth are out of our hands. You remind me of myself when I was your age, Theo. I wanted to be in control of everything. Surprises were my night terrors."

Theo laughed. "Hard same."

"Let me take this off your shoulders, okay?" Julie said. "I'll be here for Bree and the baby when you can't. You'll be the first to know if there are any problems."

"Thank you."

"Just catch those assholes, Theo. Bring these kids home to their families once and for all."

CHAPTER THIRTY-SEVEN

The shipping container's steel door clattered open, and the bright morning sun burst through the darkness. Annabelle sat cross-legged on the mattress with a hand shielding her eyes from the blinding onslaught.

"Yoo-hoo! Good morning, love," Pearle chirped.

It had been days since Emmett closed Annabelle inside. Days since she'd heard the unknown voices. Annabelle had been waiting for Pearle. Annabelle had heard Pearle call for Tillie earlier in the morning, the dog scampering away from the outside of Annabelle's container toward the house. Annabelle had gotten up then, washed her face with what was left of the water in the last gallon jug. She hoped the water would reduce the redness. Then she let the end of her freshly braided hair hang over her shoulder like a thin rope.

"Ready for breakfast?" Pearle carried in a plate of food and a thermos of steaming coffee.

"Yes, thank you." Annabelle was more than ready to play Pearle's game. "I'm very hungry."

Pearle looked pleased with herself. "I bet. No good refusing food, you know. That baby needs those nutrients even more than you do."

Pearle stepped in and overturned a milk crate. She set on top the steaming plate of fresh eggs, sizzling bacon, and toast with jam.

The smell of the fresh coffee made Annabelle's mouth water. She scooted across the mattress and sat on its edge, pulling the milk crate closer.

"I'd like to join you, Annabelle," Pearle said. "We have a few things to discuss."

Annabelle almost laughed out loud. She hadn't realized she had any choice in the matter. But Pearle waited for her approving nod before sitting in the oversized recliner.

"Eat, honey," Pearle said, pulling the chair around so that she faced Annabelle. Her long silver hair had been recently washed, the ends still wet and shampoo fragrant. She'd left her work boots behind for a pair of worn sneakers, black Converse that had grayed over time.

Annabelle forked a bite of avocado and egg. Hunger had been pulling at her the last day. The baby had kicked her hard in the ribs throughout the night to show he was hungry, too.

"That's it." Pearle grinned. "I remember when I was pregnant with Emmett. I couldn't get enough avocados to save my life. He loved them. As soon as I ate one, he'd calm down and settle in. You know how they do that? Nestle in under the ribs?"

Annabelle had felt that, too.

"There's nothing more important than a healthy baby," Pearle said. "And it's my job to make sure you get what you need with nothing synthetic or processed." She wagged a finger at Annabelle. "No junk and none of that fake crap they call medication."

Annabelle swallowed her food. It had been days since she'd taken the last of the lupus medication. She knew it was already out of her system, and it was only a matter of days before the effects hit her hard.

Because Pearle seemed to be in pleasant spirits, Annabelle took a chance between bites. She had so many questions. "What is the New Nation? Can you tell me more about where my child is going?"

Pearle winced as she crossed one knee over the other. It took Annabelle a moment to realize it was the expression *my child* that got to her.

"You've been chosen, Annabelle. That's a privilege not too many mothers can say they've had."

"Chosen for what?"

"To deliver a baby that will help make the New Nation. We are building something new. Something this world has never seen. It all starts at birth, raising them up right. We are a people of strong conviction and morality. You'll see."

"Where is this New Nation?" Annabelle asked. "How many are there?"

Pearle's face broke into a wide grin. "We're growing, Annabelle. We're a people who hearken back to the start of this country. We work hard for what we have, and we won't let anyone take away our land or our rights. We cannot be destroyed."

Annabelle didn't understand. She'd been promised money and a fresh start anywhere she chose. Whatever this New Nation was, it didn't sound like anything Annabelle wanted to be a part of. "I'll be happy with my fresh start, Pearle. I've already decided where to go."

"Honey, the New Nation is your fresh start." Pearle's smile grew bigger. "We're *all* starting over. Don't you see?"

Annabelle knew better than to argue. She didn't trust Pearle and how fast she could go from sweet to a full-on rage. Annabelle pushed her empty plate away and said, "Tell me more."

Pearle talked with a gleam in her eye as if she was describing the love of her life. No electronics, no influences from the outside, she told Annabelle. "We are looking for purity in bloodline, action, and thought," she said. "We demand a place where we control the narrative. We're growing every day. You and the baby are the latest, but more are coming. So many more are coming."

Annabelle had heard this kind of talk from Ruby when she'd argued with Annabelle's mother and Gran. Annabelle took a breath of the fresh air and tried to remain calm.

"We aren't the enemy, dear," Pearle said. "It's time everyone stopped behaving that way."

"But you've never asked about the baby's father," Annabelle pointed out. "You don't even know anything about him, let alone his race."

Pearle gave her that sickening sweet smile again, the one that screamed, *Silly little girl*. "We know Daniel. He's been vetted."

Annabelle's chin almost hit the floor.

"Yes, we wouldn't have gotten involved with you if we weren't sure."

"But how do you know him? How did you vet him?"

Pearle smiled that creepy grin again. "Your car, Annabelle. Don't you see? For weeks before you came here, we knew everywhere you'd gone."

Annabelle's stomach rolled. Of course, the car place. They'd placed a tracker along with that new wheel and tire. Something else made Annabelle's stomach roll. It had been at least forty-eight hours since she'd left a message for Daniel. She hadn't heard back from him. A terrifying possibility occurred to her. What if Daniel was in on the entire thing?

Annabelle did her best to hide her growing terror. "There've been others. Pregnant girls like me. Where are they now? Where is Grace?"

"Darling," Pearle said, clearing away the empty plate and coffee mug. "I've got work to attend to, and you have a manifesto to read." She reached into the bag where the food had come from and pulled out a navy-blue binder. She brushed her fingertips across the cover. "Once you learn more about the New Nation, you'll understand."

Annabelle took the binder and opened it. The first page featured an image of an enlarged front door with a colorful welcome mat. *Welcome home. The New Nation has been waiting for you.*

As Pearle gathered the empty plates and moved to the opening of the container, Annabelle called out to her. "Leave the door open, please? I need the sunshine and the light. I want to give this reading my full attention."

Pearle considered Annabelle. "I can leave the door open, but I must secure you, Annabelle. No running away on me, now." She waved a hand over her shoulder, and Emmett brought a chain in from the four-wheeler.

"Clamp her ankle."

"No, Pearle! You can trust me. I won't leave."

Pearle grinned. "I do trust you, Annabelle. It's the only reason I'm entertaining this idea of leaving the door open."

Emmett gripped her ankle too hard, yanking her until he had the metal clamp secured around her ankle. He took the other end and clamped it to a ring on the wall.

"One chance." Pearle held up her long pointer finger. "One chance to keep your mouth shut and enjoy the fresh air. Don't blow it."

CHAPTER THIRTY-EIGHT

Sam Polanski sat with his back to the wall. He folded his long fingers over his belly and straightened his legs, crossing his feet at the ankles. His long slim frame faced the mirrored window of the interrogation room.

Theo, Weston, and Cody stood on the opposite side of the glass, watching him.

"We have nothing to hold him," Cody said.

"He knows that," Theo said. "He can walk anytime, but he hasn't. He's toying with us."

It had taken Weston a few hours to determine whether Polanski was inside the auto shop. After sending in a plainclothes officer to ask specific questions about mufflers, Polanski showed up to help. Weston and the officer convinced Polanski to come in for questioning without much of an argument. Theo and Cody were already on their way to Brecksville PD in separate cars, but Polanski had to wait about two hours for them to arrive. His mood had soured.

"Let me have another go at him," Theo said. "I'll hit harder this time."

Sam Polanski eyed the mirrored window as if he could hear them. He stared directly back at himself, unflinching.

Weston and Cody entered the room first, offering Sam a cup of coffee.

"Not again." He wrapped his fist around the small cup. "Where's your third stooge? How long is this going to take?"

Weston shrugged. "You have important business at the garage to get back to?"

"We're always busy this time of day. The guys need me."

Theo watched Sam's steadiness through the window as she reviewed her plan. Minutes later, she pushed through the door and into the interrogation room.

"And she's here," Sam said. His dark greasy hair was pulled back in a pathetically thin tail.

Theo took a seat directly across from Sam and set down the pile of folders she'd carried in.

"Uh-oh." Sam playacted fear. "Are you arresting me?"

"That depends," Theo said.

"On what?"

Theo pulled two photographs from the back of her notebook and set them on the table. One featured Grace holding her baby exactly as they were found in Carillon Park. The other was a closeup of the baby's face. "Whether or not you start talking."

Sam bit his lower lip and looked away from the photos. "We've been through this. I had nothing to do with that girl or her baby."

"We have video of Annabelle in the Cleveland garage." She slapped another photo before him. It had come from the security footage at City Motors. "And Grace?" Theo tapped her finger hard a few times on top of a photo. "She came through the garage, too."

Sam looked at his hands. "A lot of girls come through there."

"Apparently you have a way with women." Theo grinned at Weston to jump in. "I don't really see it, but…"

Weston caught the pass. "He's a regular Casanova with women in two cities." Weston reached for a folder and produced more photographs. "They really fall for you. In a way, I'm jealous," Weston said.

"I guess you talked to Mary."

"We did," Theo said. "Rose, too. You've caused these women a lot of hurt, Sam."

He barked out a laugh and kicked back in his chair, leaning on the back two legs. "I'm sure they were more than happy to dish dirt on me."

"We also talked to your mother," Theo added.

Sam winced at the mention of his mother, and Theo marveled at finding a tender spot she could manipulate. "How does it feel, leaving your mother to fend off the angry neighbors alone?"

"She's a tough old bird."

"I believe that. Still, she needs you."

Cody's phone vibrated. He reached for it and excused himself. Theo frowned and tried to stay focused.

Sam groaned and crossed his arms over his chest. "How many times are we gonna do this? I told you, I don't know anything."

"We have a source that says otherwise." Theo held the silence, studying Sam's every movement.

"What are you talking about?"

"You have a fan," Theo said. "Someone who's been following you." She slid a photograph of the entrance to Woodland. "This witness can place you with Grace inside the cemetery before her death."

"I don't believe you." He sat up in his chair, straightened his shoulders.

"It's true. This witness says you met with Grace a few times and offered to help her."

"Who is this person? Mary? What did she accuse me of this time?"

No one responded.

Sam balled his hands into fists and let them go. He turned his head to the left until it gave a pop and then turned it the other way. "Bullshit. You're just trying to get at me."

"Am I?" Theo asked.

"Look, I'm no pervert, okay?"

Theo nodded. This line of questioning had gotten to him. "Perhaps you left that business to Henry Nerra."

"I'm asking you again. Am I under arrest?"

After a moment, Theo shook her head.

Sam pushed the chair back with his knees so hard, it fell over. He opened the door and stopped inside the doorway. "We're strong, you know. Our family. Our Nation. And we're only getting stronger."

CHAPTER THIRTY-NINE

The screen door slammed. Pearle's boots clomped along the back porch.

Tillie jumped up, a whine on her lips.

"*Annabelle!*"

Annabelle jumped, her heartbeat slamming inside her ears. Whatever was going on, it couldn't be good.

Tillie slid out the open door of the container and disappeared into the dense woods. Night had fallen, and there'd been no sign of Daniel. A hard reality set in for Annabelle. Daniel didn't care what happened to her and the baby. She imagined he'd felt an enormous relief with her gone, his problems solved. And Ruby, was it possible she was celebrating Annabelle's absence, too?

Pearle's steps were closer now, the tall grass swishing against her boots near the container. Annabelle stood up to greet her captor, and her chained ankle felt like it could give out beneath her. She gripped the wall as the chain clanked against the container.

The locks keyed open. The door rolled up. Pearle stood at the opening with her hands on her hips. Her white-silver hair was pulled away from her face in a severe ponytail. It was only then that Annabelle realized she'd never seen Pearle without makeup before. Pearle's sun-weathered and mottled skin surprised her.

"Where's the phone, Annabelle?"

"I...I don't know what you mean."

Pearle showed her teeth. "I trusted you." Pearle opened her fisted hand. In the dim glow she saw the keychain she knew so well. The Jeep logo keychain.

Daniel.

Emmett stepped in beside his mother.

"Toss everything," she directed him.

"Pearle, no! Don't hurt Daniel."

Pearle stepped closer to Annabelle, so close Annabelle could feel her breath on her forehead. "I never took you for a fool, Annabelle. If it wasn't for the baby, I'd kill you now."

Annabelle's blood ran cold. She thought about the voices she'd heard but didn't recognize. Then it hit her. The New Nation. Pearle had called in members to search for Daniel.

Emmett tore through her things as bile roiled in her stomach. He ripped the sheets and blanket off the bed and tossed the mattress. He kicked his heavy work boot along the container's seams, the corners where the metal slabs met. His thick paw-like hands felt along every crevice until he found her stash.

Emmett held out the empty pill baggie and the burner. Pearle took them both, rubbing the empty baggie between her fingers.

"They were just prenatal vitamins, I swear."

The look on Pearle's face shut Annabelle up.

"What did you think, Annabelle? Daniel would show up and whisk you and the baby away? That he actually *wanted* you?"

"Where is he?" Annabelle tried to sound demanding, but her voice trembled. "Where's Daniel?"

Pearle's eyes blazed against her flushed cheeks. "You made promises to The Handler. You made promises to me."

"Toothbrush," Emmett called out from behind the stack of books. He was almost through the entire area.

"Leave it," Pearle said. "We don't want the oral hygiene to suffer."

Annabelle heard the sarcasm under the anger. Emmett walked out of the container, and Pearle followed. She turned back to face Annabelle.

"You're not leaving this container until the baby is born. I told you, Annabelle. One chance. You blew it."

Emmett and Pearle slammed shut the container door, leaving Annabelle standing in the middle until her knees buckled.

Daniel.

Annabelle grinned and held her stomach.

He'd come for her after all.

Annabelle pushed a clump of thick hair behind her shoulders and groaned. What she wouldn't do to be free of the clamp and its chain. She longed to be with her mother at home in Brecksville. She dreamed of standing in a long hot shower until the water tank ran dry.

Annabelle had been digging at the metal around her ankle and the lock all day. She'd even managed to scrape down the end of the plastic toothbrush to a rounded point. If she could just get it a little smaller, she thought, she could pop the lock on the clamp.

How could I have been so stupid, she continually asked herself and the baby. *How could I have trusted her?* These questions scrolled through her mind.

Annabelle tried once more, pushing the toothbrush between her bloody skin and the clamp. Using her ankle as leverage, she pushed. The plastic snapped in half, but the cuff remained. She threw the plastic end left in her hand, letting it clatter against the metal wall. She collapsed onto the container's floor, flat-backed and defeated.

The puffy scar on her palm itched, and Annabelle fisted her left hand. She'd been picking at the scar's edges in the dark of the storage container, prying the skin open. She liked the warmth of her own blood against her skin. She liked the bite of dirty blood on her tongue. It made her feel real. Alive, despite her circumstances.

Cutting her palm and leaving the bloody handprint had been the thing that had scared Annabelle most about her deal with The Handler.

"We need everyone to know you were there," Pearle had said. "Physical evidence that proves you've passed from one world into another."

Ruby had explained it another way, one that made the most sense to Annabelle. "Think of it as a blood promise. Before that promise, there's a *you* and a *them*. After, there's only an *us*. Your baby becomes part of the family."

Annabelle desperately wanted a large family for her child. A village to help raise her infant.

The day she left home, she'd followed all of Pearle's directions. She'd packed a change of clothes and the burner phone they provided, leaving everything else behind. She'd dropped a glass into the sink the day before and kept one of the sharpest shards. She brought that with her, the edges protected inside a hand towel. When the message came through the burner, Annabelle drove to the Brecksville Reserve and made sure to park in front of the security camera.

On a side path, Annabelle waited for the final signal. In the distance, she heard the voices and laughter of children in one of the park's playgrounds.

The burner buzzed with a message. *GO*

Annabelle held the burner in her hand for a few minutes, looking at the two letters on her screen. Two letters that she could choose to ignore. It wasn't too late. She could pay the money back and have Ruby talk to the Handler. Ruby always knew what to do.

GO

Annabelle's stomach bubbled and kicked up her heartburn. The baby.

She couldn't turn back, not really.

Annabelle unwrapped the towel, the edges of the glass shining in the late afternoon sun. She held the sharpest side against the palm of her hand. Pushing. Harder. Then pulling back. A trickle of blood filled in the white line she'd cut, that space where her skin separated. It wasn't deep enough.

Annabelle took a deep breath and closed her eyes. This time she thought about Daniel. How he'd walked away from her in this park. How he'd denied the baby was his and wanted her to abort it. How he'd looked at her in the hallway at school that very morning, his eyes glassy and distant. No flash of recognition, as if he'd never seen her before.

The tip of the glass shard sank into her palm. Deeper, a little deeper. She ground her teeth and pulled the glass as hard and fast as she could, then fisted her hand. Warm blood rushed between her fingers, and she kept her hand fisted until she found the perfect spot on a path, a common area that led to multiple paths in the park. When she knelt and unfurled her hand, the amount of blood alarmed her. It ran down along her wrist, and she quickly smacked her open palm against the cement. Pearle had been clear: no dripping. Annabelle pulled her hand back and wrapped it tight inside the towel. By the time she'd gotten back to her car, blood was seeping through the thick towel.

Thinking back on it all, Annabelle saw that cut, that handprint she'd left in the park, as the moment of no return. She'd left her mark, her visual claim of giving herself and her baby to The Handler by way of Pearle, a bloody promise for the world to see. Now Annabelle saw that scar as representation of everything she'd given up.

In the beginning, it all sounded so independent...so free. God, she felt so stupid.

A branch snapped outside the container. Annabelle froze. She fixed her attention, listening for the sound of Tillie's panting or her paws pattering along the path. Instead, she heard a sliding, like someone's foot losing purchase.

Annabelle wrapped her arms around her belly. She buried her face between her knees. Someone grabbed a lock on the container. Metal scraped on metal. The snap of the lock released. Then the second lock.

The accordion door slowly rolled up to the night's sky. Annabelle saw Air Jordans, jeans covered in mud, and a T-shirt torn at the shoulder. With his arms stretched overhead, he stood there, almost like a dream.

Daniel.

Their eyes met but neither moved. He looked pale. Thin. Drawn. He dropped his arms to his sides and stepped toward her.

Annabelle jumped to her feet and pulled Daniel into a fierce hug. She reached up and ran her hands along his jawline. A growth of beard. The smell of home. Daniel felt like a whole world of hope inside her arms.

CHAPTER FORTY

Daniel knelt beside Annabelle. He'd used the point of his pocketknife to pop the locks on the container, and he used it now to pick at the locked clamp around Annabelle's ankle. "You've been working hard on this," he said, flipping the lock over in his hands.

"I only had a toothbrush." Annabelle still couldn't believe he was there. "Didn't work."

Daniel smiled at her then, a smile she'd never seen from him. He saw her. For what felt like the first time, he really saw her.

After her initial shock at seeing Daniel, she panicked. She worried Pearle or Emmett would soon follow, as if Daniel had somehow broken free of their captivity.

"They never found me," he said. "I've been looking for you and mostly walking in circles to avoid the voices in the woods. I can't find shit without my GPS."

"But Pearle has your Jeep keys."

Daniel shrugged. "I dropped them two nights ago along with the printed map you insisted I bring with me. I did what you said and tossed my phone out the window about a half hour before I exited the highway. I didn't have any kind of light, and I couldn't find the keys."

Annabelle thought back on her confrontation with Pearle. *She'd* been the one to say Daniel's name. Pearle didn't know he'd been on her property.

"How are we going to get out of here without your keys?"

"There's a spare in one of those magnetic boxes under my Jeep."

Now, as Daniel worked on the stubborn lock, it felt like Pearle and Emmett had vanished. The boat wasn't at the dock, and Pearle was nowhere to be found.

A wet tongue licked Annabelle's hand. "Tillie!" she whispered and rubbed the dog behind her ears. "I missed you."

The dog leaned against Annabelle, settling into the space along her shins. Tillie wasn't sure about Daniel, and her eyes followed his every movement.

"He's a friend," Annabelle whispered to the dog. "He's safe."

Daniel worked fast with the pocketknife and used the blade's blunt edge inside the lock. It finally clicked, but it only released the chain from the wall and not the heavy clamp around her ankle. He tried the second lock, but it wouldn't budge.

"Sorry. You might have to live with this until we get out of here."

Annabelle nodded. "Where are we going, Daniel? We're in the middle of nowhere."

He leaned in, took her thin hand in his. "Don't worry. We'll get to the Jeep and just drive. Anywhere. First house we see, first gas station. Whatever. We'll face it together."

Annabelle patted her thigh, and Tillie rubbed her big wet nose against Annabelle's hand. She sank her hand into the dog's fur and worried about the darkness. How were they ever going to make their way out in the thick blackness of night?

Tillie licked her fingers, a reassuring gesture. It was then Annabelle made the dog a promise—she'd come back for Tillie. She'd save her from Pearle and Emmett, too.

For a moment, Annabelle's eyes met Daniel's.

"Why did you come for me?"

Daniel looked away, rubbed the back of his sweaty neck with his hand. "You called. I knew you were in trouble."

Trouble. Annabelle instinctively understood. "They've threatened you."

"They said they'd kill you and my mom if I went to the police."

Annabelle had heard those same threats. It was why she used the burner to call Ruby and Daniel instead of 911. The thought of her mother or Ruby dying because of her was unthinkable.

"Someone slashed all my tires two weeks ago. The Jeep was parked at the curb in front of my house all night. I came out in the morning to find them flat. I knew then they'd never go away until they had our baby. I had to do something."

Annabelle took a breath. She heard what he was saying *under* his words. Daniel hadn't come for her out of an undying love or to save her and whisk her away to a happily ever after. He'd come because he was terrified that if something happened to Annabelle, it would fall back on him. People would find out about the baby. They'd find out he'd been with her. He'd always wanted to keep Annabelle hidden from his friends and family. Daniel had come to Pearle's land because he wanted to keep their story hidden.

Daniel's honey-brown eyes, usually so calm, were now wide and dark with fear. "You ready?"

"Yeah." Annabelle gave Tillie a good rub behind her ears and kissed her between the eyes.

She gripped Daniel's hand and stepped out of the container. Her bare toes dug into the cool earth. She decided to leave the unicorn slippers behind. They were filthy, and the soles always folded under her feet. She'd never be able to run in them. A squirrel scattered up a nearby tree.

Daniel took the lead, and her footsteps followed in the darkness. If they could just make their way to the Charles Mill Lake Park's main entrance.

Annabelle used her other hand to support the baby. Her mind whirred in circles with worry. She wanted to leave, more than anything, but what about The Handler? She'd broken the contract, the one that she'd signed in her own blood. The Handler would find them. Then he'd kill her mother. Ruby, too.

If Annabelle could just get home, her mother would know what to do. Annabelle felt certain of that.

Annabelle's toe slammed into the side of a rock. Pain ricocheted up her shin. She kept going, limping along as Daniel picked up the speed. Her eyes had adjusted to the dark, and she looked for the rays of moonlight to guide her way. Branches and undergrowth swiped against her bare legs as Daniel led them deeper into the forest.

"These woods are like a fun house," she whispered, after they'd been walking for at least forty-five minutes. "Where are we?"

"How's your foot? It can't be too much farther." Daniel stopped so she could catch her breath. He turned around, surveying the area around them. "Stay here a minute. I think the state route is only a few feet away. Let me check, and I'll call you to me."

She watched Daniel vanish into the woods. She was grateful for the moment to collect her strength. The baby felt like the weight of a large bowling ball inside her stomach, squeezing against her lungs and bladder. She had to pee.

The flash of a light.

"Daniel?"

She walked to her right, pushing through the undergrowth and stepped around a mammoth tree. She tripped on a vine. Recovering, she turned around. Annabelle froze in her tracks. Her breath caught in her throat. Hot urine streamed down the inside of her leg.

Emmett's hulking figure stood there, and he had Daniel's neck inside the crook of his enormous arm. The gleam of a knife blade shone in the darkness.

"Move, and I kill him." The words spittled from Emmett's mouth.

A shrill bark cut through the humid air, and Tillie charged. Her teeth sank into Emmett's leg. Daniel fought, breaking free from the meaty arm around his neck.

"Go, Annabelle!"

She ran, his breath on her shoulder. For all she knew, they were running in circles, but if they could find a place to hide…

Lights. The swipe of headlights through trees. Emmett and Pearle were on the four-wheeler, zooming through the trees and headed directly at them.

"Annabelle!" Daniel's scream came out in a choked holler. "*Run!*"

Annabelle almost did. She felt herself gearing up for the run of her life. She even stepped off with her right foot until she heard the grille of the four-wheeler ram into Daniel. She heard his sharp exhale and then his body crumple to the ground.

Emmett jumped out and loaded Daniel into the bed of the vehicle. Pearle revved the engine with her eyes on Annabelle. A shotgun was aimed at her chest.

"Get in the vehicle," Pearle demanded.

Annabelle felt her head nod, but her body felt like it was a mile away. Numb and frozen, her mind split from her body, allowing her to float above it all. She watched the terror unfold below as she slowly walked toward the four-wheeler.

"Annabelle," Daniel called to her, his voice garbled. "Save the baby."

Annabelle's mind screamed, *Stop moving!*

Her body didn't listen.

Days had passed since Pearle had slit Daniel's throat from ear to ear. Annabelle had watched in horror as Pearle pulled the knife's blade over his pale skin and blood poured from the yawning wound. Daniel's mouth gaped like a fish. He reached for Annabelle, falling forward into her.

Pearle reached up for the accordion door. "Look what you made me do, Annabelle. Shame on you."

She slammed the door and locked Daniel and Annabelle inside the darkness.

The first night of lockdown with Daniel, Annabelle's heart rate ratcheted up. The walls of the storage container felt like they were closing in, inch by inch, and sucking out all the air. She pressed the palms of her hands against the container's locked opening. She shook it with all her might and screamed until she had no voice.

Endless nights followed and time became distorted. During the day, sunlight filtered in through the two ventilation openings at the top of the container. Most days, the baby kicked against her hard drum of a belly. She pressed her shaking hands against her stomach, splaying her fingers wide, palming her baby while she hummed a lullaby.

At night, Annabelle rested beside Daniel's body. She curled herself against the soft carpeted floor of the shipping container and his hard back. The cool thickness of his blood covered her hands, her clothes, her baby belly. She spooned against him in the dark, sometimes humming, sometimes crying, sometimes talking to him about the baby, all along imagining Daniel would soon wake from his deep sleep.

"Take us with you," Annabelle finally begged him after days in the dark. She was terrified of what might come, and she thought a lot about Gran. It calmed Annabelle to think of seeing her again.

In the stifling heat, Annabelle remembered her promise to the baby, the one she'd given her at the Brecksville Reserve. Her memory flashed back so fast and clear, she imagined it as a sign from Daniel. Maybe it was his way of saying she must stay the course for the baby.

Annabelle denied the hard facts of her situation. Her mind felt as though it could disintegrate at any moment. Yet, facts were facts.

Daniel was dead.

She was dying.

And the baby had gone still.

CHAPTER FORTY-ONE

Theo's eyes burned in her computer monitor's glare. She'd been in the department, running searches through databases for hours on missing pregnant teens in the United States. She'd also been curious about the phrasing Sam Polanski had used on his way out of the interview. *We're strong. Our family. Our nation.*

It struck Theo because she'd seen something similar in Annabelle's records, hadn't she?

After digging through the phone records, Theo finally found it. A text exchange between Annabelle and a prepaid phone. There were references to the New Nation and The Handler. There was also discussion about payment and how The Handler kept a portion of the proceeds. Could this have been the sale of Annabelle's baby?

Homeland Security had been warning all state and local police forces of startup militia groups, particularly in the Midwest. Most were tiny compounds that comprised family and extended family members. All worked to extend their stockpile of weapons. Homeland Security warned about the possibility of these groups unifying for an attack. Sam Polanski's words on the way out of his interview reminded Theo of the way the militias gained loyalty. They liked to focus on the idea of family and taking care of each other. The righteous, fending for themselves as a solid community against the cruelty of the world.

Theo found a few references to a small alt-right militia with Ohio roots. The New Nation, they called themselves. Homeland Security reported that they were actively recruiting members throughout the

Midwest, but particularly in the southern counties of Ohio and in the northeast area of the state.

While the location fit with both Annabelle's and Grace's cases, the question remained: What would a private militia want with pregnant teens from suburban Ohio? Theo couldn't make sense of it but decided to send the information to her contact at Homeland Security.

Cody Michaels pushed through the squad room door. "You been here all night?" he asked Theo.

"Couldn't sleep. What's up?"

"A few things." He sat down in a roller chair beside her and completed a few spins for the fun of it. "One of Weston's guys was able to trace the sale of the phone Daniel received calls from. It's taken a while to get through it all, but the prepaid phone was purchased at a fuel and convenience mart near Mansfield. Right off the highway. It's the main exit for a large park called Charles Mill Lake."

"Mansfield? That's not too far from where Daniel's phone last pinged, right?"

Cody nodded. "Weston called the store, but they don't save in-store security camera footage this long. The person who would have sold the phone wasn't in, but we should be able to question her soon."

Theo clicked the end of her pen cap. Her knee bounced under her desk.

"Daniel's mother reported she'd bought him a prepaid credit card for his birthday, remember? But the team is having a hard time locating any individual purchases with it."

This was how Daniel was able to access cash without withdrawing anything from his savings account.

Cody's and Theo's phones buzzed simultaneously, and Theo checked the incoming text from Bull Michaels: *My office 15 minutes.*

A buzz sounded when Theo pushed through the convenience mart door. A fast-food restaurant attached to the back of the store was frying chicken. The entire place smelled like french fries.

Theo approached the register. "Hi, Vera. I'm Theo, a detective with the Dayton Police Department." She pulled back the edge of her jacket so the cashier could see her badge. "I talked to your boss earlier today about a prepaid phone you sold a few weeks ago."

"He told me." She analyzed Theo through dark blue tinted glasses. "Can we do this outside? I need a smoke."

Theo agreed after she checked her phone. She was on borrowed time. Bull Michaels had dispatched her and Cody to the Brecksville PD five hours ago to be a part of the new task force formed by the Ohio Bureau of Criminal Investigation. Theo had hoped for a few more days without someone else telling her how to do her job. So she decided to go to the convenience mart before checking in with the new task force. Technically, she didn't have any orders from the task force yet. The cashier could have waited, but Theo wanted to question her alone. Cody agreed to cover for her until she arrived at the Brecksville PD.

Behind the building, a steel picnic table sat near the back bay. Vera sat down and lit a cigarette.

"I remember her." Vera blew out a stream of smoke.

"Was she alone?" Theo stood, her hands on her hips, adjusting the weight of her body on her feet. She'd left her cane in the car, something she'd been doing a lot of in the last two weeks. Bree worried Theo was pushing herself too much, but Theo felt confident and strong.

Vera nodded. "She had questions about how the prepaid phones work."

"What kinds of questions?"

"She was kind of jumpy. Anxious. She wanted to know if the phones could be traced."

Theo scribbled down a few notes. Her phone rang with a number she didn't recognize. Theo pushed it on to voice mail. "Jumpy—how? Fearful? Anxious?"

"She wasn't so nervous that I was worried about her safety. I look for people in danger, and she wasn't like that."

"She gave you no signals of distress?"

"Nope."

Theo wrote some more in her notebook. Vera's account of the sale confirmed what she'd assumed. Annabelle had gone to an agreed location of her own free will. When she met Vera, Annabelle didn't know she was in trouble. But she must have had an inkling. Otherwise, she never would have purchased the phone or cared about how it could be traced.

"We're having a lot of trouble tracing that number, which is why it's so important for me to talk with you. You're the last known person to see Annabelle before she disappeared."

Vera looked down at her knees. She rubbed her thumb over the bony part of her kneecap.

"You think she's dead."

"I didn't say that." Theo leaned her elbows on her knees. "We need to find her before it's too late."

Vera continued to trace the edge of her knee. The late afternoon heat was oppressive, and humidity blanketed them. It was difficult for Theo to take a full breath, and she couldn't imagine trying to smoke in that muck.

"Was there anything that made this girl stand out? Made her different from the average customer?"

Vera thought a moment. Her glasses were slipping down her nose. "She was nice."

"How so?"

"She smiled. She asked me how my day was going. She told me to have a good night. That kind of thing."

Theo thought about Annabelle's schooling and the work her mother had done to keep her in those schools. Annabelle had clearly learned to do the suburban friendly well.

"I take it you don't usually get that level of polite."

Vera laughed. "Not off the highway. We get people in a big hurry, you know? They want to get back to the road or out on the lake. We get a lot of creepers."

Theo arched an eyebrow.

"The ones who are too friendly. The ones who hang around for a few hours." Vera stubbed out her cigarette. She twisted her head to the right until there was an audible pop, then the left. She leaned back until her midback rested against the edge of the table. "Look, I usually don't talk to police."

"I understand."

Vera pulled a folded piece of notebook paper from her work smock. She handed it to Theo. "She needed directions. I drew her a map a lot like this one."

Theo unfolded the crude map. It showed a long line for State Route 707 and the water labeled *Charles*.

"I grew up around here, and I pointed her in the right direction."

"Do you remember the house number?"

"No. Most of the properties on that side of the bridge are hidden, but this *X* marks the area. The yard backs into the Charles."

Theo thanked her and pocketed the map. "Do you know anything about who lives there?"

Vera shook her head. "They get traffic, I can tell you that. It's quiet out this way, and most folks stay to themselves. I've seen a fair number of vehicles going in and out of that area."

Theo thanked her again and walked toward the parking lot.

Vera called after her, "I hope you find her."

"Me, too."

❖

Theo let the car's air conditioner blast against her. She wiped her brow with the back of her hand. Cody had already texted that the team was waiting for her. She threw the car in reverse when her phone beeped again. Another voice mail. Theo let the message from her contact in the county prosecutor's office play through the car's speakers.

The judge has released Ruby Jackson's juvenile record. I'm emailing the documents, Theo, but it pertains to an arrest seven years ago with a defendant who served time. Samuel Polanski of Montgomery County, Ohio.

Theo slammed the car into park. She played the message again while opening her email. They'd sent her two documents. One featured citation information for Sam Polanski, Ruby, and Tawnia Jackson, her mother. The second was an arrest record for disorderly conduct and destruction of property in Dayton. Both Polanski and Ruby had been arrested outside a free women's clinic. The same free clinic Grace Summers used.

Chapter Forty-two

*D*aniella Rose.
Annabelle held her baby tight against her chest. Annabelle's thin breaths rattled with congestion. She said the baby's name over and over, loving the way it felt on her tongue and in her heart. Annabelle felt the baby's warm cheeks and her blanket of fine soft hair. It didn't matter what had happened during the birth. Daniella Rose was so perfect, so tiny, and so incredibly *hers*.

No one had delivered food or water for days, and Annabelle had run through her supply. Pearle and Emmett had slammed the door shut after they inspected the baby.

Leave them both, Pearle had said. Emmett handed the crying newborn back to Annabelle before following his mother's orders.

Annabelle had then fallen into sleep, the exhaustion of the birth settling in for days. The baby mewed and suckled against her chest, her tiny movements waking Annabelle every so often. The container was stifling, even with the vent flaps open, and darkness enveloped them at night.

Sometime after the birth, Annabelle fumbled around with her fingertips. She felt the deep ridge in Daniella Rose's upper lip that connected to her nose. The more she touched the hole that ran like a valley in her baby's lip, she remembered a boy at her elementary school with a bright red scar in the same place. She remembered the way he held his hand over his mouth as he sat in class.

Cleft lip and possibly palette.

Her baby wasn't what Pearle wanted after all.

Pearle had left them both for dead.

Annabelle tried to ration what was left of the water and food, slicing her amounts smaller and smaller until there was none. The baby had been drinking her milk, but Annabelle's body felt depleted and weak.

Once Annabelle realized she was pregnant, she'd spent hours researching how to care for her own body during and after the pregnancy. She'd read site after site, detailing how a mother's placenta and afterbirth were filled with nutrients and the life force needed to be a new mother. There were recipes for placenta smoothies and soups. The thought of eating something that had come out of her had made Annabelle gag and turn away from the laptop. The thought still turned her stomach.

Four days later, Annabelle's tongue was swollen and dry. It felt like a foreign object in her mouth, so large and cracked. Her nipples had run dry. The baby had grown frightfully still and quiet against her. There were only the shallow breaths, letting Annabelle know the baby was still alive. She whispered into the soft edges of her ear: *Don't leave me, baby girl. You have Gran's blood and strength. Stay with me, baby girl.* A soft sound escaped the baby, much like the mewling of a kitten.

Despite everything, Annabelle believed there was still a chance. She thought Pearle would change her mind and take pity on the baby. She though Pearle would do the right thing and set them free. Annabelle believed this until she heard tires crunching on the gravel drive, followed by the sounds of vehicle doors opening and closing. More voices. Pearle's stood out, the one directing everyone else. But there was another voice. A strong one that Annabelle would know anywhere. Ruby's.

Annabelle's heart leaped. Ruby had come to save her and the baby! She'd finally found them, and she'd come to take them home. The longer Annabelle listened, though, the more she finally understood. Ruby had known where she'd been all along.

We're not coming back. This exodus is final.

We'll make do with what we have.

The New Nation awaits.

Then Annabelle heard someone refer to her cousin The Handler.

No no no no.

Her cousin, Ruby? The kingpin of this whole operation? It didn't make sense.

Yet it did.

Ruby had been the one to do all the research on the chances of a mother with lupus passing the disease on to her baby. She'd been the one to crunch those numbers, knowing that Annabelle had had regular care from specialists and managed her own disease quite well.

I don't think the baby will have it, Ruby had told her. *Look at how lupus jumped a generation with our mothers and landed with you. It will jump your baby's generation, too.*

Everything fit in place now. This was how Ruby had known about the payment other mothers had received. This was how Ruby knew exactly who to set Annabelle up with and why she'd pushed so hard for Pearle. Annabelle never really had any control over her decisions. Ruby held all the power.

Annabelle stared at the ceiling and remembered some of Ruby's tirades about politics and the liberal agenda. Annabelle and Rose had explained away her cousin's beliefs as something she'd learned from her own mother. When Ruby started in about why she should be able to carry a gun in her own car or carry a weapon inside a grocery store, Annabelle ignored her. She also ignored Ruby's talk about the government spying on its citizens and how the United States would soon become a place where freedom was a way of the past. Annabelle had chosen to believe it didn't matter that her cousin thought so differently from her. After all, they lived in Ohio, a stronghold of the Republican party.

Annabelle's mother, though, had been the voice of opposition to Ruby. Rose had been the one to tell Ruby everyone deserved rights and protections, and we all had an obligation to help those who needed it most.

"You're wrong, Auntie Rose," Annabelle remembered her cousin saying to her mother. "We aren't a dumping ground, you know."

"It's all those differences that make us stronger. Can't you see that, Ruby? And those weighing us down? It's us, you know. Your own great-grandmother was an immigrant from Italy. It's in *your* blood."

The arguments continued, particularly about the Second Amendment and the militia Tawny was involved with, but Annabelle tuned them out. At the time, their chatter didn't matter. Now it was everything. Ruby managed to pull Annabelle into the New Nation with nothing more than the promise of money for her baby and a fresh start. Her face burned with the shame of it, the horror of what she'd agreed to.

The scar on her palm burned, and Annabelle understood why that cut and bloody palmprint had been so important to The Handler. Cutting and blood were important to Ruby—she'd had a taste for them since she was a teen. Ruby's arms and stomach held the scars to prove it.

Annabelle tried to sit up, to bang her fists on the side of the container. Her body felt like it weighed hundreds of pounds. Her muscles screamed with pain. But she needed to get Ruby's attention. If she could just look her cousin in the eyes, she and the baby would have a chance at life. Her favorite cousin who used to love to braid hair and eat McDonald's Happy Meals on Saturdays couldn't really be gone. Could she?

Hours later, the temperature in the storage container had cooled. The sun had gone down for the day, and most of the noise had settled down. Annabelle closed her eyes and listened to the tires crunch out of the driveway. Horns beeped and someone yelled about Annabelle's car.

"Leave it under the cover."

Another voice said, "She'll die here, anyway."

Then Annabelle heard a familiar voice. "I want it! I fixed that damn car."

Sam. The guy from the auto repair shop.

Then it hit her. She understood why the other girls hadn't left bloody handprints. Ruby was new at her position as The Handler. Her first girl was Grace Summers. Ruby had always had a flare for the dramatic, and a bloody handprint at the scene brought out a level of fear in people that Ruby reveled in. This begged the question: What happened to the previous Handler?

And Tillie. Where was Tillie? Her heart ached at the thought of what might have happened to that sweet girl.

Eventually, she opened her eyes. They'd all left her with nothing but country silence. That strange sensation filled Annabelle again, that split between her body and mind. She was a million miles away from her body but could still feel the baby against her bare skin.

Daniella Rose stirred. Although listless and obviously uncomfortable, she fought against Annabelle's arms, and a cry came out, stifled against Annabelle's breast.

"It's okay, baby." She offered her nipple for comfort, but there was no more milk.

The baby howled and pushed against her chest with tiny fists.

Suddenly Daniella Rose went stiff like a plank. Her little legs were rigid against Annabelle's thighs, her neck and head arched back against Annabelle's arm.

"Daniella Rose?"

Something wet spilled over Annabelle's arm. The baby seized.

"Daniella Rose!"

CHAPTER FORTY-THREE

Theo made her way on foot through the silent forest. Then a sound, possibly a muffled voice. She stopped in her tracks. The trees and underbrush were so thick, it was difficult to determine where the sound came from.

The gravel drive leading into the property had been no bigger than a slip inside the forested area. Theo had finally found it after searching along the state route in the area Vera had described. A lonely black mailbox marked the entrance. Fresh tire tracks lined the dirt and gravel.

The hot summer evening settled in, the humidity so thick it was hard to breathe. Theo had pulled her car onto the shoulder of the state route and then angled the front end closer to the tree line. She didn't want the car to stand out along the side of the road, but she also needed the vehicle poised to roll out fast.

Theo took everything with her except her cane— it would only slow her down. She double-checked her belt for her badge, cuffs, and weapon with two extra rounds. She tested the radio attached to her shoulder through a private line with Cody.

"Where are you?" Cody asked.

"Pit stop. Checking out the property."

"Theo…"

"Annabelle asked for directions to this place. I'll be at the station soon."

"Address?"

"SR 707. Black mailbox. No markings. Last address I saw was 1587."

"Hold back, Theo. I'm on my way."

Theo didn't wait. She'd already broken the chain of command and ignored orders from Bull Michaels. The only thing that mattered now was finding Annabelle and her baby.

The house before her showed no signs of life in the oppressive heat. A porch light beamed above the front door. A dim interior light shone through a side window.

Theo heard it again, a faint voice calling out. It could have been an echo from across the lake. Sound moved funny in rural areas, particularly around water. Theo tried to gather her bearings. A dog barked. A distant motor sputtered.

Theo's feet whisked along the grass surrounding the house. Bugs whapped against the front porch light. Theo walked around the side of the house searching for any flash of movement. Nothing. She circled the house, clearing it.

A footpath led Theo into the darkened wood, a tree line so thick the house disappeared behind her. She flipped on her flashlight as water softly lapped against the nearby shore. The path led to a clearing. Theo blinked, taking a minute to make sense of what she'd found. The beam of her flashlight showed a large moving and storage container nestled into the woods before her. Painted dark green, it blended perfectly into its surroundings.

Theo moved toward the container's closed door. Her light beam landed on the silver shine of an open padlock. She lifted the lock from the rings and slid open the door.

A burlap covering dominated the center of the container, big and solid like a sleeping elephant. A dirty single mattress was pushed up against the side wall of the container. An empty bucket sat near the opening of the container along with some empty water jugs and a torn yellow blanket.

Stepping closer, Theo grabbed the edge of the burlap and lifted. Tires. The bumper without a license plate. Theo recognized the make and color of the car as Annabelle Jackson's.

Theo pivoted when something caught her eye. The flashlight beam swung along the corrugated metal flooring. Something dark. Possibly spilled paint. She knelt. Dried blood.

She reached for her radio, pressing the emergency button, which signaled immediate assistance was needed.

"Daniella Rose!"

The disorienting scream sent a chill up Theo's spine.

Adrenaline pumped through her veins. Gun drawn, she sidestepped toward a second container. Despite her heightened state, Theo's breathing calmed. Her head cleared, and she was so focused she could have heard a cricket sing from yards away. Her body felt strong. She transitioned into another version of herself, the one that had been trained to handle any crisis.

The beam of light grazed over the closed accordion door. This time, the padlock was closed. Fresh boot prints surrounded the container's opening. The high grass along its sides had been stamped down. Theo shone her light over the container, searching for any opening that might give her a look inside.

A boom came from the side of the container. Theo jumped back with the sudden sound.

Then four quick bangs. It sounded like someone was throwing their fists against the side of the container.

"Police! Show yourself."

"Help! My baby needs help!"

It had to be Annabelle Jackson.

"Help!" the muffled voice called again.

Theo's first thought was to shoot the padlock, but she couldn't risk the sound drawing attention to their location. Not far from the container, she found a sharp-edged rock. She bashed it against the padlock until it fell away.

Theo drew her gun, readying herself for whatever might come. She rolled the door open and wasn't prepared for the odor that hit her like a brick wall. The air was thick with the stench of death, blood, and excrement. She fought against her gag reflex.

A young woman stood near the entrance of the storage container. She held a limp baby in her arms. Long dirty hair hung over her face in matted clumps. Sickly pale, her dirty arms and legs were reedy as a scarecrow's. She wore nothing but an oversized button-up shirt, stained and torn. Dirt and blood caked her bony legs and feet. Annabelle Jackson, alive.

"My baby." Annabelle's gaze met Theo's. "Isn't she beautiful?"

Theo kept her weapon trained on Annabelle as she shone the light throughout the container. A bed. A chair. Empty buckets strewn throughout.

"Are you alone? Who locked you in here?"

Annabelle smiled. "It's just me and Daniella Rose." She swayed on her feet as if she might fall over.

The baby didn't move. She didn't make a sound.

Theo holstered her weapon, entered the container, and reached for the bundle in Annabelle's arms. The flashlight beam spun frantically.

"What's happening with the baby, Annabelle?"

Annabelle giggled, a high-pitched sound that echoed throughout the container.

Theo set the baby on the floor and unwrapped the small bundle. She placed her fingertips against the baby's pale sweaty skin. A pulse. Light and quick as a rabbit, but a pulse.

Theo gripped her radio. "Medical intervention needed now!"

"She's hungry," Annabelle said in a sing-song voice.

"Keep her warm and dry," the operator advised. "Support is en route."

Theo followed the medic's directions. "Help is on the way," Theo told Annabelle. She tried to soothe Annabelle as she checked the baby's body for open wounds. Annabelle seemed to be dissociating, and really, who could blame her.

Annabelle giggled again as tears streamed down her face. "No one will find us out here."

"They will," Theo told her, rubbing the baby's back. "A backup team shouldn't be more than a few minutes out. You're safe now."

She laughed again. "There's no such thing as safe."

The rumbling of a motor grew louder before it shut off.

Annabelle's laughter grew into hysterics. "It's Emmett. He'll kill us and dump us off the boat."

A boat. Even though she'd seen the water, Theo hadn't considered a boat as a means of transportation to and from the property.

A distant wail of a siren. "Hear that? Help is on the way, Annabelle. They won't leave us stranded."

Despite her words, Theo's own anxiety rocketed. How many people were on that boat? If they were a part of the New Nation, everyone would be armed. Backup was at least ten minutes out, given the density of the woods around them.

In a split-second decision, Theo handed the baby to Annabelle. Then she stepped out of the container, yanking the door closed behind her.

CHAPTER FORTY-FOUR

Theo needed eyes on what was coming for them. Hiding not far from the water's edge, she watched as a figure built like a linebacker—she guessed this was Emmett—jumped to shore, his weight dangerously rocking the pontoon behind him. A shotgun swung from his shoulder. Water lapped against the sides of the boat.

The baby howled.

Emmett lumbered through the woods toward the house. His bright headlamp arced a beam of light not far from Theo. She heard the swish of liquid inside a container.

"I'll shut that damn baby up," Emmett grumbled as he neared the house.

A second beam of light near the house. Someone else was there.

Theo sidestepped closer to the house. She watched from the woods as the light beams bobbed and weaved around the house. She realized what they were doing the second before it happened.

PVOOM!

The farmhouse ignited in flames.

In the glow of the fire, Theo recognized the second person. She'd last seen him in the Brecksville PD interrogation room. Sam Polanski tossed containers into the fire. Emmett had tossed one container and grabbed another from somewhere. Soon a second structure—a shed?—went up in flames, too.

Emmett led Sam toward the footpath, and she knew where they were headed. Theo pivoted and headed through the thick trees as the fire grew behind her.

She watched in horror as Sam and Emmett positioned themselves in front of the shipping containers. Emmett stood before the one that held Annabelle and the baby.

"Emmett!" Annabelle called out. "Emmett, help!"

Theo stood behind him, out of his line of sight.

"What the Almighty?" Emmett held the open lock in his hand. He looked around, the bright light from his headlamp swinging through the branches. He reached down for the handle and pulled open the door.

In the bright light of Emmett's headlamp, Annabelle stood tall at the lip of the container. Her arms rested at her sides, the baby nowhere in sight. Annabelle's cheeks blazed, and her light-colored eyes shone. Emmett froze before her, before a young woman who was strong but who had been pushed, Theo feared, to the very edge of sanity.

PVOOM!

The other container went up in flames.

Theo used the noise of the flames as cover. She charged Emmett from behind, her shoulders ramming into his thick body. She took him by surprise, and he swayed forward, falling into Annabelle.

Leaping on top of Emmett, Theo reached for his weapon. He rolled away from her, tangled in Annabelle's long legs. He kicked back his boot, catching the edge of Theo's shoulder. She tumbled to the side.

Emmett's headlamp and Theo's flashlight beams ricocheted throughout the container. When Emmett emerged in the light again, he held Annabelle's back tight against his chest, a pistol against her temple. "Get back," he shouted at Theo, "or I'll shoot."

Theo complied, standing with her hands in the air. She stepped back farther, edging closer to the opening of the container. The baby howled from where Annabelle had tucked her away, somewhere in the steel container. Theo backed into Sam's arms and a pistol pointed at her own head. "We meet again, Detective." He maneuvered her so that she was facing Annabelle.

"Don't do this," Theo told Sam. "You'll never get away with it."

Emmett laughed. "Shut her up, Sam, will you?" He turned back to Annabelle. "I told Mama you were trouble from the start. I shoulda dealt with you the day you showed up on our doorstep."

Annabelle tried to push away from Emmett. She pulled down on his thick forearm, but he only gripped her harder, choking off her air supply. Annabelle cried out when he smacked the gun against the side of her head and held his tight grip on her neck.

Sirens were closing in, and their bright headlights were making their way through the woods.

"We shoulda tossed that thing into the lake the minute it was born," Emmett said.

There was something about the way he spoke, the pitch of fury mixed with despair in his voice that took Theo back to Castleton Motors. She'd felt this way then, hadn't she? Overwhelmed by the shooter's weapon and his position in the room. The stink of fear, from Cody and Castleton. She could smell that same stink now on herself. She froze, staring at the scene before her, helpless to move. She heard Emmett spouting off his hate as if he was speaking to her through a tunnel, fuzzy and distant.

"The New Nation has already begun. There's nothing you can do to stop it," Emmett told them all. "It's time to rise up." He cocked the pistol.

Annabelle's eyes pled with Theo. Tears rolled down her red cheeks.

Suddenly the baby stopped crying. The jolt of the silence brought Theo back to herself, and she felt herself slip back into her body, one limb at a time. She held Annabelle's gaze: *We're in this together.*

Then, almost as if they had planned it, Annabelle tossed her head back, smacking Emmett's chin with the crown of her head. She fought hard, kicking his legs and biting his arm. Theo elbowed Sam, turned, and smashed his nose with the heel of her palm. He dropped his gun and turned away screaming as blood spurted through his fingers. Theo lunged for the gun, beating him to it. When he reached for her, Theo launched a roundhouse kick, slamming Sam's knee out from under him. Bones crunched, and Sam writhed on the ground.

Annabelle tore at Emmett's hair and scratched at his face and arms. She kicked him with her bare feet, but he refused to let her go.

For one terrifying second, Theo felt like her feet were cemented to the ground. Flashes of the shooting at Castleton Motors replayed in her mind: the way Cody froze, the sound of Dick Castleton's body hitting the floor, the searing pain of the bullet tearing through her own body.

Theo lunged, and her body mass was sufficient to push both Emmett and Annabelle down. Emmett collapsed on his back. Annabelle drove her fist into his face. Again. Emmett howled but refused to drop the weapon.

Theo's bullet blasted inside the container, the boom of it deafening.

Annabelle rolled away until she lay over her baby, protecting her.

Theo snapped the cuffs on Emmett's beefy right wrist. He yanked his left away before she could capture it.

"Drop the weapon now!"

Theo knew that voice.

"It's over," Cody yelled. "You're surrounded. Sam is in custody. Hands above your head."

Emmett let Theo move away from him, but he refused to let go of the pistol. He didn't raise his hands. As more light spilled into the container, Theo saw what Annabelle had done. She'd stabbed Emmett in the eye with the long end of a toothbrush. The plastic edge still hung from his eye socket.

Officers and paramedics made their way to the container. Theo thought about how Emmett must feel, the very agency he feared most surrounding him at gunpoint. His entire world had crumbled.

Emmett held the gun under his chin.

"No, Emmett!" Theo aimed her gun at his chest. "Don't do this."

Emmett refused to drop his weapon as blood seeped from his eye.

"Emmett, please." She understood he meant to die in that container one way or another. "Your mother's lies aren't worth dying for."

He turned the gun on Theo.

Officers had the outside of the container surrounded, but most couldn't see what was going on inside. Cody had him in his sights, but Theo felt his hesitation. She wondered if he was thinking of Henry Nerra.

Emmett aimed at Theo's chest. She saw his trigger finger tense. Theo fired twice, the double tap landing squarely in Emmett's chest. He collapsed on top of Annabelle and the baby, his blood spreading over them.

Then Cody was there, helping her pull Emmett away. Other officers helped Annabelle and the baby out of the container toward waiting paramedics.

After Cody checked for Emmett's pulse, he helped Theo to her feet. "Can you walk?"

Theo's legs collapsed beneath her. Adrenaline had gotten her through the last few hours. Now reality set in. Cody wrapped a strong arm around her, and she leaned in to him, letting him carry her weight.

Just like that, Theo fell back in time. She was inside Dick Castleton's office and in the competent hands of a rescue worker. A blood pressure cuff pumped against her arm, and a penlight checked her pupils. The paramedic worked fast, and the IV was in Theo's arm and a stretcher beside her in seconds.

Bree.

Bree sat beside her in the ambulance after Theo had been loaded for transport. Or, rather, her hallucination of Bree, who was home in bed. There must have been good drugs in that IV, Theo thought absently, deciding to enjoy Bree's company, real or not.

"You okay, love?" Bree spread the blanket over her as the emergency vehicle pulled away and into Dayton traffic.

"It's not supposed to be this way."

Bree tucked the edges of the blanket around Theo and sat down next to her. She brushed the hair away from Theo's eyes, her fingertips lingering.

"I'm not supposed to get hurt." Tears seeped from the corners of her eyes, rolling back into her ears.

Bree took her hand. "Ah, Theo. You. Are. Human. Made of flesh and blood just like the rest of us."

"Everything's falling apart."

"Not everything," Bree said, while her other hand rubbed her baby bump. "I'm still here. Baby, too. We love you, broken bones and all."

CHAPTER FORTY-FIVE

Annabelle relished the quiet as she wrapped herself in the cool hospital sheets. Her room felt safe, especially with the security guard stationed outside her door.

Her body ached. Her feet screamed. A nurse had rolled up the sheet and blanket to her ankles, leaving Annabelle's bare feet to hang over the edge of the bed. The slightest pressure, even from the thin bedsheet, made Annabelle groan in pain. Stitches across the soles of her feet closed the deep lacerations from her race through the woods with Daniel. Deep bruising and cuts from the ankle clamp kept her right foot swollen to twice its size and throbbing with every heartbeat.

It had been five days since Theo and Cody had found her and the baby in the container. The memory of that night came and went for Annabelle like the flicker of those LED lights in the container, losing battery juice. But nights...those were the worst. Images of Daniel, the container, Emmett, Pearle, and the birth flashed across her mind. It was like her brain had taken second-by-second photos of everything and saved those terrifying images for when she closed her eyes. It was one of the ways her sensitivities had worked against her. The doctors explained the PTSD would linger. It would be something she'd have to work through, and she had already met her new psychologist.

The baby mewled. Her tiny arms tried to battle the blanket the nurse had swaddled her in.

Annabelle held Daniella Rose close to her chest. She felt like a warm ball against Annabelle's neck. Too weak and ill to produce her own milk for the baby, it relieved her to know the doctors were now caring for Daniella Rose's nutrition.

"Shh," Annabelle whispered into the baby's fine, soft hair. "We're safe now."

Daniella Rose had shocked everyone with such a quick recovery. Once doctors had her electrolytes and nutrition stabilized, color returned to her tiny body, and she gained weight. The doctors expected her to be thriving soon. They promised Annabelle they'd begin consultation with a surgeon for her cleft lip within a few weeks.

"There's a good chance your baby will make a full recovery," a doctor told Annabelle. "She wants to live. She clung to life. Daniella Rose is a fighter."

"I know it's silly, but…" Annabelle rubbed her brow.

"Please. Ask away."

Annabelle looked up at the doctor and tried not to cry. "Will she remember this? Any of it? I don't know if I can bear it if she does."

The doctor reached for Annabelle's hand and squeezed it. "We don't know exactly how memory works, but there isn't much evidence to support children under two years of age retaining memories." The doctor gave her a concerned look. "You, on the other hand, will remember. You must take care of yourself, Annabelle."

Annabelle agreed as she watched the doctor go. She knew her recovery would be slow and painful. The baby's birth and its aftermath had thrown her into the worst lupus flare she'd ever experienced. Her lungs gurgled with fluid. Her body had come very close to completely shutting down. Dehydration left her internal systems flailing. Her kidneys took the brunt of it all. Her doctors had so far been able to restore function in the left kidney, but her right was still tenuous. With the disease more active in her body than it had ever been, her joints swelled. The doctors had started her on steroids to reduce the inflammation in her lungs and joints, but she still had the remnants of the rash over her face, neck, and chest.

A light rap of knuckles sounded against Annabelle's hospital door.

Rose Jackson carried in an insulated cup full of something steaming. "Hi. I brought your favorite."

"Chicken and stars?"

"Of course!"

She placed the steaming soup on the small bedside table along with a bottle of water and packets of crackers.

"Hydrate, hydrate," she reminded Annabelle. "I'll take the sweet baby girl, so you can eat."

Annabelle handed Daniella Rose to her mother, but the tingling of the baby's light weight lingered against her bare forearms. She'd come so close to losing her baby. Another few hours in that container, and both she and the baby would have died.

Rose filled her in on Tillie, who would be coming to live with them as soon as Annabelle was released from the hospital. "The vet gave her a clean bill of health. She's been spayed and chipped. The sweet girl's doing well."

Annabelle couldn't imagine losing Tillie. While her memories of the time spent in the locked container flickered, Tillie was the one constant. Annabelle felt certain she and Daniella Rose would have died early on without the presence of that dog.

Annabelle stirred the thin soup with a white plastic spoon. "Mom?"

"Hmm?" Rose rocked the quiet bundle in her arms.

"Are you ever going to tell me what really happened? With Aunt Tawny?"

Rose avoided her daughter's gaze. "What do you mean?"

"You know what I mean. The New Nation. All that."

"Oh, Annabelle. We've just found each other again. Let's give it a minute, okay?"

Annabelle watched as her mother rubbed the side of her finger over Daniella Rose's warm cheek. Her mother was good at keeping secrets, and these kinds of revelations were hard for her. Still, Annabelle wanted the truth. She needed it to make sense of what had happened to her with Pearle.

"I just want to know the story, Mom. Please."

Rose nodded before leaning back in her chair. While Annabelle finished up her soup and crackers, Daniella Rose eventually quieted into sleep inside her grandmother's arms.

"Your aunt Tawny always struggled," Rose finally said. "When our dad died, she went off the rails."

Annabelle listened carefully as her mother recounted the past of an aunt she'd never known. She'd always been curious about Tawnia, who was almost eight years younger than Annabelle's mother. Rose always said Tawny had been coddled and sheltered from the world by their mother and father. The baby of the family, Tawny always got what she wanted, and what she always wanted most was attention. "When she fell and broke her back in middle school at cheerleader practice, she had just the excuse to be coddled once again."

To be fair, her mom pointed out that Tawny's injury had been severe. And while she healed well, the injury always caused her pain. Tawny spent weeks in bed at a time while their parents waited on her.

By high school, Tawny was doing better. Nights were difficult because of the pain, and she couldn't sleep without daily painkillers.

"Tawny liked that med way too much," Rose said. "She wanted to feel numb all the time. When the doctors refused to prescribe her higher doses, she found that kind of numbness with street drugs. She was hooked on heroin by the time she was twenty."

Annabelle thought of her cousin Ruby. She'd grown up watching her mother use.

"There were rumors Tawny prostituted for drug money, but Gran never knew for sure."

"Sounds like Ruby," Annabelle said.

"Gran didn't know how to help my sister. She worried endlessly, particularly after Ruby was born," Rose said. "Then Tawny just sort of vanished away from us, you know?"

The soup warmed Annabelle, a ball of comfort that moved down her throat and chest and settled in her belly. This quiet talk, this family talk, was comforting, too. It reminded Annabelle of her grandmother.

"We heard Tawny joined some kind of a co-op and lived with a group of people near Cleveland. Tawny first told us it was a sobriety group sponsored by a local church. Later, Mom heard it was more like a cult. The only thing we really knew about it was they promised to change Tawny's life forever."

"Mmm. I know that promise." Annabelle twisted open the pack of saltine crackers.

"That's exactly how they sold themselves twenty years ago, too. It was all about this new state of mind for the entire country. They preached about living off the land and boycotting medications and processed food." Her mom shook her head. "We didn't learn until after Tawny died how severe her drug abuse had become. The New Nation," Rose said, disgusted. "What a pack of lies."

Annabelle had known her aunt had vanished, and her cousin lived with Gran. But there was so much she didn't know.

"The New Nation wanted Ruby," Rose explained. "She was a white child and healthy. They needed her to build what they called their new world. I couldn't let that happen to my niece, so I petitioned for custody."

"Why couldn't she stay with Gran?"

"Mom never had legal custody of Ruby. We always worried Tawny would take her at any minute. I wanted it to be legal. I hoped that would help Ruby feel secure and safe."

Annabelle remembered how angry Ruby had been when she'd first come to stay with them. Ruby said she missed Tawny, even though she'd spent very little time with her mother. Ruby's emotions exploded—she'd launch into a full rage one minute and then silently sulk in corners of the house the next. She sliced her arms with broken disposable razors, pulling out the blades, all the while plotting ways to go back to her mother. Back to the New Nation.

The court sided with Annabelle's mom. Ruby, they'd said, needed a stable and healthy home. Ruby bucked everything about living with them. And when Tawny was found dead only a few months later, Ruby never forgave her aunt. The death was officially ruled an overdose, but Ruby never believed it.

"I thought I was doing the right thing," her mom said, reminding Annabelle of how Ruby would leave their home for long periods with no word.

Annabelle understood. "Ruby never really left the organization."

Her mom shifted the baby into her lap. Daniella Rose fit like a football against her thigh. "I wanted to give you the best life possible, A-Bird. I only wanted to keep you safe."

Annabelle didn't ask the question because she already knew in her gut. This was the reason her mother was always working. It wasn't for rent or her tuition as Annabelle had always been told. It was for her safety.

"And then I went and got pregnant," Annabelle said.

Her mother smiled. "It happens—I know."

Like her mother and her aunt, Annabelle had continued the family pattern of teenage pregnancy. A never-ending family cycle. Now Annabelle wanted her own daughter to obliterate that family legacy.

For the first time, Annabelle understood why she'd chosen to keep the baby and go to Pearle's. It wasn't really about Daniel or her mother or even Daniella Rose. It had been about filling a gaping hole of loneliness. She'd fallen for Pearle's kindness, hook, line, and sinker. Annabelle believed she needed a mentor to guide her on to the next stage of her life. She'd been looking for someone to call her home. And all this time that person had been right beside her.

"I hate Ruby," Annabelle said, the anger burning her cheeks. "I hate her for pulling me into this."

"You don't mean that. She's been looking for a place to land for a long time. A place to feel loved and important."

"She had that. With *us*."

Her mom shook her head and held her swaddled granddaughter closer to her chest. "Sometimes it's too hard to see what we already have."

Annabelle reached for her mother's hand then, careful not to get hers tangled in the monitor wires. At first, her mother didn't respond. Annabelle insisted, though, wrapping her fingers around her mother's wrist. Her mom relented, and they clasped hands, suspended between the hospital bed and the chair, a bridge.

She recognized the cool leathery feel of the back of Rose's hand, the part where sun and wind and winter beat against the sensitive skin. But it was the inside of the palm that told her mother's true story. Annabelle's fingertips grazed over those patches of callus from hard work. She felt the raised and thick areas of scarred flesh from steaming dishes at the restaurant, cleaning supplies eating away at the soft skin, hot plates and drinks burning the fine pads of her fingers. Annabelle's fingers felt the plump blue veins that began somewhere in her mother's forearm and roped down around her wrists, over the back of the hands, and along the base of her fingers. *Gran's hands.*

Annabelle couldn't remember when she'd last held her mother's hand, and it felt so familiar and so foreign all at once. This hadn't been the apology Annabelle hoped to hear from her mother, but Annabelle knew she meant it. She wound her thin fingers through her mother's, warm skin with the hard edges of bone. Both held on tight.

CHAPTER FORTY-SIX

Theo balanced two large coffees in her hand and pushed through Bree's hospital door. Corbin Henry was two days old and the most perfect human she'd ever seen.

Theo set the cups on the bedside table as Bree stirred awake. She held the swaddled baby against her upper chest.

"He's sound asleep," Bree said. "Feeling better?"

Theo nodded and sipped her coffee. She'd gone home for a nap and a shower. She rested her palm against Bree's forehead and let her hand fall to Bree's cheek. "You look exhausted. Let me take him so you can sleep."

Bree sniffed and rubbed her bloodshot eyes. She handed the baby to Theo. "Thank you."

Theo shrugged. "For what? You've done all the work here, Mama."

Tears filled her eyes. "Thank you for being here with me. I'm so happy," she said, crying. "And I'm so full of hormones right now."

Theo handed her a tissue and sat down on the edge of the bed with the baby in the crook of her arm. She rubbed Bree's knee while she sniffled until she eventually drifted into sleep.

The hospital room had a rocking chair in the corner, and Theo settled into it with the baby and her coffee. As she gently glided with the newborn, Theo couldn't help but think of Ruby. Out of the entire New Nation group, Ruby struck Theo as the most heinous. She'd targeted her own cousin for this group, knowing full well Annabelle would most likely be killed after giving birth. She was willing to give up what little family she had for a private militia that stole her own mother from her.

During the interrogations, it came out that Ruby had gotten the job as The Handler based solely on her ruthlessness. Everyone said they knew Ruby was involved with pushing out the previous Handler. Then the guy simply disappeared. He left no word. Vanished. The consensus of the group and law enforcement was Ruby had killed him for one of the highest positions in the organization. If they hadn't caught her, Theo imagined Ruby would have become the most dangerous leader the New Nation had ever seen.

Corbin was fast asleep inside Theo's arms. His dark eyelashes splayed across his pink cheeks. There was a hint of a smile on his tiny puckered lips.

"Okay, little guy. It's just us."

Theo pushed the rocker back slowly and then forward, keeping the movement as gentle and consistent as possible. The edges of the blanket cradled Corbin's head like a fur-lined hat, and Theo couldn't help but reach in and touch the soft curl of his warm ear. Absolute perfection.

Lullabies had been playing all afternoon in Bree's room at a low volume. The sweet music was like an undercurrent, a consistent whisper beneath their breaths. As Theo's own heartbeat slowed and her breathing became rhythmic, she recognized the tune: "Amazing Grace." It had been a few years since she'd heard the full hymn, and the soothing notes brought tears to her eyes. She watched the tips of Corbin's nostrils flare as he took each whispery breath.

"Here we are, little Corbin," Theo whispered. "I never thought I'd have a child. But your mama, she believed in our family. She brought us all together."

Corbin had a thin cap of dark hair, and Theo rested her forehead against him. That fresh baby smell, Theo couldn't get enough of it.

"I'm not sure I'll be a good parent, Corbin, but I promise to be the best T you'll ever have."

As the late evening light filtering through the blinds slowly faded, Theo held the baby closer. She rocked and rocked, whispering promises into Corbin's warm ear.

CHAPTER FORTY-SEVEN

Theo greeted Mary Summers at the station doors. She'd waited a long time for answers about Grace. Time and again her patience had been rewarded with heartbreak. Theo put Mary in touch with other parents who had lost their children and grandchildren to the New Nation. It helped to know there were others, even if it was a club no mother wanted to be part of.

"I'm glad to see you, Detective," Mary told Theo. "That shooting near Mansfield sounded awful. I worried the minute I heard your name associated with it."

Theo smiled and pushed open a conference room door for Mary. "Thank you, I'm happy to be back."

Theo knew she was lucky to be alive. She also understood how lucky she was to have Bull Michaels stand behind her actions. She'd broken protocol in the rescue of Annabelle and her baby. Theo had ignored direct orders from her superior. She'd entered a potential crime scene without backup. Theo had a lot to live up to, and a lot to be grateful for.

Theo had been reevaluated and discharged to duty by her orthopedic surgeon. She'd pushed herself hard that night in those woods, and her body paid for it. She'd spent a long week icing and resting her hip before going back to physical therapy. No one could deny her ability to move and do all the activities needed for her job. With time, the surgeon hoped more strength would return to her leg. *No guarantees.* That phrase regularly pulled at the back of Theo's mind. She'd spent her whole life taking her athleticism for granted. She'd never imagined her body might someday not respond the way she expected it to.

"You've proven your skill and dogged investigation skills, Theo. You might be a little under par in terms of physical fitness, but nothing that shows you aren't capable of doing your job well," Bull had said. "Your team needs you back at your own desk. I need you back, too."

Bishop, Cody, and Bull Michaels welcomed Mary Summers and Theo into the conference room with fresh coffee and bagels. Mary's anxiety permeated the air, and no one touched the food.

"Thank you for meeting with us," Bull began. "We have some information about your daughter's case."

Mary braided her fingers in her lap and held her palms together. "You know who the baby's father is." It was a statement more than a question. Apparently she'd been waiting a long time for this answer.

Bull gave Theo a slight nod.

"The DNA came back, Mary. I'm so sorry, but the baby was Sam Polanski's."

Mary inhaled sharply, followed by, "That bastard."

Theo gave her a minute to digest it. This had been Mary's fear all along. The great guy who'd swooped into Mary's life and supported her so well had also taken advantage of her daughter.

Mary popped a knuckle and looked Theo in the eyes. "Deep inside, I knew it was him. I've been going over the little things, you know? The day-to-day stuff between the two of them. There was tension, but I assumed it was because she didn't want me with him."

"I'm sorry, Mary," Theo said. "I can't imagine how hard this is to hear."

Mary thanked her. "The New Nation. Sam was a big part of that, wasn't he?"

"Yes. We're hoping it will fall apart now that Ruby, Sam, and Pearle are in custody," Bishop said. "There's been a lot of damage to their hierarchy, beginning with the death of Dick Castleton. It threw the organization into chaos and, frankly, made it easier for us to find them."

Homeland Security had located the compound in Northern Michigan within ninety minutes of Annabelle's rescue. Pearle and the others who fled the Ohio property for the compound in Michigan left Sam Polanski and Emmett behind to burn away their tracks, including Annabelle and the baby.

Homeland Security raided the rural property in Michigan and found forty-seven people following The Handler. Twenty-two children were found on the premises, children that had mostly come from mothers who vanished like Grace and Annabelle. Some of the mothers survived, the ones who believed in Pearle and followed her every order. They were found living with their children in the compound. All the children had been taken into Michigan's Department of Health and Human Services. Everyone was hopeful they'd be reunited with relatives.

With the arrests of Ruby, Sam, and Pearle, law enforcement was able to turn their attention to other members of the New Nation. Theo tried to ignore the media coverage, which always stoked society's fears with terrifying information about private militia groups. How many other groups like the New Nation were out there?

The upcoming trial promised to be a media field day, and Theo hoped it would send a message throughout the Midwest that these types of groups wouldn't be tolerated, at least not on her watch.

But Theo was realistic. She liked to compare these private militias to warts because they just keep coming back. Someone in the group always stepped up, and someone else always jumped in to help recruit. Theo found hope in the fact Pearle, Sam, and Ruby would likely be spending years behind bars. The New Nation would have to learn to survive without them or crumble apart. Either way, they'd been severely damaged by Theo's work. She took pride in that.

"The memorial service for Grace and the baby will be next week," Mary told the detectives. "You're welcome to come."

"We'll be there and would like to help you in any way we can," Bull said.

Mary thanked them and dried her eyes with a tissue.

"This might sound, I don't know..." Mary searched for the word. "Morbid, maybe? But could I have the clothes Grace and the baby were found in?"

Theo and Bull shared a glance. He took the lead on this one. "I'm sorry. For now, they're evidence. But once the people who killed them are brought to justice, we'll do our best."

Later, Theo watched Mary make her way to her car in the parking lot. She walked with her head down and shoulders rolled forward. She'd carried so much weight for so long. Grief, Theo knew, could settle in the heart without others around to help clear it.

CHAPTER FORTY-EIGHT

Theo's headlights sliced through the darkness and into her driveway. The fall night air brushed against her face. It had recently rained, and most of the trees had dropped their leaves. Smoke from a nearby fireplace filtered through her car's vents.

It had been a long workday, but Theo welcomed the exhaustion. The last few weeks had been filled with caring for Corbin, supporting Bree, and working. Corbin's homecoming had been a whirlwind of activity. Although Theo was exhausted, she was happier than she'd been in years.

Theo rolled her ankles a few times to circulate the blood and then stepped out of the car. She climbed the three stairs to the front door. The house was dark and quiet with a lingering smell of popcorn. Theo took that as a good sign—the baby had given Bree a few hours to herself. She kicked off her shoes and padded up the stairs as the neon blue night-lights guided her way. A sense of peace washed over her. For the first time in the last year, Detective Theodora Madsen felt like she was finally back in her own skin.

After Theo locked up her service weapon and badge, she found Bree asleep on the love seat in Corbin's room. Bree had wedged herself into the corner with a collection of pillows behind her back. Her bare feet were propped on the edge of a crate filled with children's books. Corbin was nestled in a sound sleep against Bree's chest.

Bree eventually looked up and found Theo leaning against the doorway, watching them.

"Come here," Bree whispered. She moved over and patted the empty space beside her.

Careful not to wake the baby, Theo burrowed in with them. "You're both so beautiful," she said. "The two of you curled up here together."

Bree gave her a sleepy grin. "He's beautiful, isn't he?" She stroked the back of his hand with her finger, and Corbin reflexively reached for her, closing his tiny fist over her finger.

"I love his little lashes," Theo said, "and the way his cheeks look like he's holding food inside them."

Bree laughed and leaned into Theo. "That's my boy. Squirreling away his treats for later."

A light click sounded, and the baby's Wave sound machine switched off. Theo and Bree sat together in the quiet listening to their baby breathe.

"How was your shift?"

"Nothing Cody and I couldn't handle."

It used to be she couldn't imagine working with Cody, her colleague's kid she'd watched grow up. Now she couldn't imagine working without him. Bishop had been promoted to a supervisory position in Homicide, which left Theo in need of a partner. She was happy to have Cody at her side.

Bree cleared her throat. "Corbin and I found your cane in the garage this afternoon. I've been thinking about new stages ever since."

"New stages?"

Bree smiled. "It feels like a new beginning, don't you think? For us, for you, for the baby."

Theo knew what Bree meant. She'd felt a shift, too. An opening. A brand-new light.

Theo leaned in and kissed the soft warmth of the baby's head. She breathed in the smell of Corbin, the baby clean of him, and willed herself to remember it.

"I never knew how much I needed him," Theo said, looking up at Bree. "How much I needed you."

That need scared Theo. He'd only been in her life a short time, and she couldn't imagine going one minute without knowing his whereabouts. Theo knew better than others how crime could be so random and ruthless. The world boiled over with danger, and there was a randomness to crime that left everyone feeling out of control.

But Theo had seen another side, too. She thought about Annabelle and how she must be holding her baby right now. Both safe and living with Rose Jackson. Sometimes things worked out. A rarity, for sure. But on some occasions, there was a rainbow to greet you after traveling through a tunnel of pure hell.

Bree interrupted her thoughts. "We should probably put him in his crib and get to bed ourselves."

"Probably. We might be able to get a few hours of sleep in."

Bree smiled. "That sounds glorious."

No one moved from their love knot.

"Just a few more minutes," Theo finally said, pulling Bree and the baby closer. "Let me stay here a little longer with you two."

About the Author

Meredith Doench is the author of the Luce Hansen Thriller series. *Crossed*, the first in the series, won Silver in the 2015 IndieFab Awards in the mystery genre. In 2017, *Crossed* was awarded the Mary Dasher Award for fiction from the College English Association of Ohio. The second novel in the Luce Hansen Series, *Forsaken Trust*, was published in 2017 followed by *Deadeye* in 2019. All were mystery/thriller Goldie Award finalists in their respective years from Golden Crown Literary Society. *Whereabouts Unknown*, Doench's fourth thriller and stand-alone novel, was published in 2022.

Doench's works of short fiction and nonfiction have appeared in literary journals such as *Hayden's Ferry Review*, *Women's Studies Quarterly*, and the *Tahoma Literary Review*. She was one of the founding associate prose editors of the literary journal *Camera Obscura: Journal of Literature and Photography* and currently serves on the board of Mystery Writers of America, Midwest Chapter. She is a senior lecturer of creative writing, literature, and composition at the University of Dayton in Ohio.

Books Available from Bold Strokes Books

Business of the Heart by Claire Forsythe. When a hopeless romantic meets a tough-as-nails cynic, they'll need to overcome the wounds of the past to discover that their hearts are the most important business of all. (978-1-63679-167-8)

Dying for You by Jenny Frame. Can Victorija Dred keep an age-old vow and fight the need to take blood from Daisy Macdougall? (978-1-63679-073-2)

Exclusive by Melissa Brayden. Skylar Ruiz lands the TV reporting job of a lifetime, but is she willing to sacrifice it all for the love of her longtime crush, anchorwoman Carolyn McNamara? (978-1-63679-112-8)

Her Duchess to Desire by Jane Walsh. An up-and-coming interior designer seeks to create a happily ever after with an intriguing duchess, proving that love never goes out of fashion. (978-1-63679-065-7)

Murder on Monte Vista by David S. Pederson. Private Detective Mason Adler's angst at turning fifty is forgotten when his "birthday present," the handsome, young Henry Bowtrickle, turns up dead, and it's up to Mason to figure out who did it, and why. (978-1-63679-124-1)

Take Her Down by Lauren Emily Whalen. Stakes are cutthroat, scheming is creative, and loyalty is ever-changing in this queer, female-driven YA retelling of Shakespeare's Julius Caesar. (978-1-63679-089-3)

The Game by Jan Gayle. Ryan Gibbs is a talented golfer, but her guilt means she may never leave her small town, even if Katherine Reese tempts her with competition and passion. (978-1-63679-126-5)

Whereabouts Unknown by Meredith Doench. While homicide detective Theodora Madsen recovers from a potentially career-ending injury, she scrambles to solve the cases of two missing sixteen-year-old girls from Ohio. (978-1-63555-647-6)

Boy at the Window by Lauren Melissa Ellzey. Daniel Kim struggles to hold onto reality while haunted by both his very-present past and his never-present parents. Jiwon Yoon may be the only one who can break Daniel free. (978-1-63679-092-3)

Deadly Secrets by VK Powell. Corporate criminals want whistleblower Jana Elliott permanently silenced, but Rafe Silva will risk everything to keep the woman she loves safe. (978-1-63679-087-9)

Enchanted Autumn by Ursula Klein. When Elizabeth comes to Salem, Massachusetts, to study the witch trials, she never expects to find love—or an actual witch…and Hazel might just turn out to be both. (978-1-63679-104-3)

Escorted by Renee Roman. When fantasy meets reality, will escort Ryan Lewis be able to walk away from a chance at forever with her new client Dani? (978-1-63679-039-8)

Her Heart's Desire by Anne Shade. Two women. One choice. Will Eve and Lynette be able to overcome their doubts and fears to embrace their deepest desire? (978-1-63679-102-9)

My Secret Valentine by Julie Cannon, Erin Dutton, & Anne Shade. Winning the heart of your secret Valentine? These award-winning authors agree, there is no better way to fall in love. (978-1-63679-071-8)

Perilous Obsession by Carsen Taite. When reporter Macy Moran becomes consumed with solving a cold case, will her quest for the truth bring her closer to Detective Beck Ramsey or will her obsession with finding a murderer rob her of a chance at true love? (978-1-63679-009-1)

Reading Her by Amanda Radley. Lauren and Allegra learn love and happiness are right where they least expect it. There's just one problem: Lauren has a secret she cannot tell anyone, and Allegra knows she's hiding something. (978-1-63679-075-6)

The Willing by Lyn Hemphill. Kitty Wilson doesn't know how, but she can bring people back from the dead as long as someone is willing to take their place and keep the universe in balance. (978-1-63679-083-1)

Three Left Turns to Nowhere by Nathan Burgoine, J. Marshall Freeman, & Jeffrey Ricker. Three strangers heading to a convention in Toronto are stranded in rural Ontario, where a small town with a subtle kind of magic leads each to discover what he's been searching for. (978-1-63679-050-3)

Watching Over Her by Ronica Black. As they face the snowstorm of the century, and the looming threat of a stalker, Riley and Zoey just might find love in the most unexpected of places. (978-1-63679-100-5)

#shedeservedit by Greg Herren. When his gay best friend, and high school football star, is murdered, Alex Wheeler is a suspect and must find the truth to clear himself. (978-1-63555-996-5)

Always by Kris Bryant. When a pushy American private investigator shows up demanding to meet the woman in Camila's artwork, instead of introducing her to her great-grandmother, Camila decides to lead her on a wild goose chase all over Italy. (978-1-63679-027-5)

Exes and O's by Joy Argento. Ali and Madison really only have one thing in common. The girl who broke their heart may be the only one who can put it back together. (978-1-63679-017-6)

One Verse Multi by Sander Santiago. Life was good: promotion, friends, falling in love, discovering that the multi-verse is on a fast track to collision—wait, what? Good thing Martin King works for a company that can fix the problem, right...um...right? (978-1-63679-069-5)

Paris Rules by Jaime Maddox. Carly Becker has been searching for the perfect woman all her life, but no one ever seems to be just right until Paige Waterford checks all her boxes, except the most important one—she's married. (978-1-63679-077-0)

Shadow Dancers by Suzie Clarke. In this third and final book in the Moon Shadow series, Rachel must find a way to become the hunter and not the hunted, and this time she will meet Ehsee Yumiko head-on. (978-1-63555-829-6)

The Kiss by C.A. Popovich. When her wife refuses their divorce and begins to stalk her, threatening her life, Kate realizes to protect her new love, Leslie, she has to let her go, even if it breaks her heart. (978-1-63679-079-4)

The Wedding Setup by Charlotte Greene. When Ryann, a big-time New York executive, goes to Colorado to help out with her best friend's wedding, she never expects to fall for the maid of honor. (978-1-63679-033-6)

Velocity by Gun Brooke. Holly and Claire work toward an uncertain future preparing for an alien space mission, and only one thing is for certain, they will have to risk their lives, and their hearts, to discover the truth. (978-1-63555-983-5)

Wildflower Words by Sam Ledel. Lida Jones treks West with her father in search of a better life on the rapidly developing American frontier, but finds home when she meets Hazel Thompson. (978-1-63679-055-8)

A Fairer Tomorrow by Kathleen Knowles. For Maddie Weeks and Gerry Stern, the Second World War brought them together, but the end of the war might rip them apart. (978-1-63555-874-6)

Holiday Hearts by Diana Day-Admire and Lyn Cole. Opposites attract during Christmastime chaos in Kansas City. (978-1-63679-128-9)

Changing Majors by Ana Hartnett Reichardt. Beyond a love, beyond a coming-out, Bailey Sullivan discovers what lies beyond the shame and self-doubt imposed on her by traditional Southern ideals. (978-1-63679-081-7)

Fresh Grave in Grand Canyon by Lee Patton. The age-old Grand Canyon becomes more and more ominous as a group of volunteers fight to survive alone in nature and uncover a murderer among them. (978-1-63679-047-3)

Highland Whirl by Anna Larner. Opposites attract in the Scottish Highlands, when feisty Alice Campbell falls for city-girl-about-town Roxanne Barns. (978-1-63555-892-0)

Humbug by Amanda Radley. With the corporate Christmas party in jeopardy, CEO Rosalind Caldwell hires Christmas Girl Ellie Pearce as her personal assistant. The only problem is, Ellie isn't a PA, has never planned a party, and develops a ridiculous crush on her totally intimidating new boss. (978-1-63555-965-1)

On the Rocks by Georgia Beers. Schoolteacher Vanessa Martini makes no apologies for her dating checklist, and newly single mom Grace Chapman ticks all Vanessa's Do Not Date boxes. Of course, they're never going to fall in love. (978-1-63555-989-7)

Song of Serenity by Brey Willows. Arguing with the Muse of music and justice is complicated, falling in love with her even more so. (978-1-63679-015-2)

The Christmas Proposal by Lisa Moreau. Stranded together in a Christmas village on a snowy mountain, Grace and Bridget face their past and question their dreams for the future. (978-1-63555-648-3)

The Infinite Summer by Morgan Lee Miller. While spending the summer with her dad in a small beach town, Remi Brenner falls for Harper Hebert and accidentally finds herself tangled up in an intense restaurant rivalry between her famous stepmom and her first love. (978-1-63555-969-9)

Wisdom by Jesse J. Thoma. When Sophia and Reggie are chosen for the governor's new community design team and tasked with tackling substance abuse and mental health issues, battle lines are drawn even as sparks fly. (978-1-63555-886-9)

A Convenient Arrangement by Aurora Rey and Jaime Clevenger. Cuffing season has come for lesbians, and for Jess Archer and Cody Dawson, their convenient arrangement becomes anything but. (978-1-63555-818-0)

An Alaskan Wedding by Nance Sparks. The last thing either Andrea or Riley expects is to bump into the one who broke her heart fifteen years ago, but when they meet at the welcome party, their feelings come rushing back. (978-1-63679-053-4)

Beulah Lodge by Cathy Dunnell. It's 1874, and newly engaged Ruth Mallowes is set on marriage and life as a missionary…until she falls in love with the housemaid at Beulah Lodge. (978-1-63679-007-7)

Gia's Gems by Toni Logan. When Lindsey Speyer discovers that popular travel columnist Gia Williams is a complete fake and threatens to expose her, blackmail has never been so sexy. (978-1-63555-917-0)

Holiday Wishes & Mistletoe Kisses by M. Ullrich. Four holidays, four couples, four chances to make their wishes come true. (978-1-63555-760-2)

Love By Proxy by Dena Blake. Tess has a secret crush on her best friend, Sophie, so the last thing she wants is to help Sophie fall in love with someone else, but how can she stand in the way of her happiness? (978-1-63555-973-6)

Loyalty, Love, & Vermouth by Eric Peterson. A comic valentine to a gay man's family of choice, including the ones with cold noses and four paws. (978-1-63555-997-2)

Marry Me by Melissa Brayden. Allison Hale attempts to plan the wedding of the century to a man who could save her family's business, if only she wasn't falling for her wedding planner, Megan Kinkaid. (978-1-63555-932-3)

Pathway to Love by Radclyffe. Courtney Valentine is looking for a woman exactly like Ben—smart, sexy, and not in the market for anything serious. All she has to do is convince Ben that sex-without-strings is the perfect pathway to pleasure. (978-1-63679-110-4)

Sweet Surprise by Jenny Frame. Flora and Mac never thought they'd ever see each other again, but when Mac opens up her barber shop right next to Flora's sweet shop, their connection comes roaring back. (978-1-63679-001-5)

The Edge of Yesterday by CJ Birch. Easton Gray is sent from the future to save humanity from technological disaster. When she's forced to target the woman she's falling in love with, can Easton do what's needed to save humanity? (978-1-63679-025-1)

The Scout and the Scoundrel by Barbara Ann Wright. With unexpected danger surrounding them, Zara and Roni are stuck between duty and survival, with little room for exploring their feelings, especially love. (978-1-63555-978-1)